Let Me Love You

LILY FOSTER

This is a work of fiction. Names, characters, places and incidents are either the product of the author's imagination or used fictitiously. Any resemblance to actual persons, living or dead, events, or locales is entirely coincidental.

Let Me Love You
Copyright © 2014 by Lily Foster

All rights reserved. No part of this book may be reproduced in any form or by any electronic or mechanical means, including information storage and retrieval systems, without written permission from the author, except for the use of brief quotations in a book review.

Cover by Cover Me Darling

First paperback edition September 2014
IBSN 9780990594123 (paperback)

Shorefront Books

Let Me Love You

Chapter One

RENE

Bleary-eyed, I instinctively reached out, patting around blindly for my phone to check the time: 2:30 a.m.

Here we go again.

Best case scenario, it would be a good twenty to thirty minutes before I could even attempt to get back to sleep, and I'm talking best case scenario.

The routine was now familiar: hunker down by the door with the girls, call for back-up as my roommate's ex screams profanities while pounding on the door hard enough to rattle its hinges, then wait it out until one of the guys or the campus police come to put an end to it.

"Please open the door, Darcy. Please, baby...I just need to talk to you." The pounding weakened to a thump. "Don't do this to me."

A blessed moment of silence.

Giving up easy tonight, Nick?

"I can hear you in there. Who is that, Beth? Open the fucking door, you twat."

Wishful thinking.

I shuffled out, joining Beth, Caitlin and Jenna by the front door.

Beth raised the volume of her voice to match his. "Did you just call me a twat, or were you under the impression that your mother is in here?"

"Shut up and open the door."

"The only thing I'm going to do is call the cops. Go. Away!"

I shot Beth a side-eye when Nick started up again, pounding on the door and kicking at the lock. She wouldn't admit it, but I knew she got off on riling him up.

"I swear, I'll break this fucking thing down!"

I wondered how on earth he hadn't broken his hand by now, then offered up a silent prayer that tonight would be the night he finally did.

I looked over to see Darcy standing in her doorway, mouthing the word "sorry" as tears streamed down her cheeks.

"Don't you dare apologize," I whispered. "It's all on him. Go back into your room and close the door. We've got this."

"You're nothing but a filthy slut, Darcy, you know that?" he slurred. "You're nothing special, just another cheatin' bitch. Wouldn't take you back if you begged."

It's the same old tired pattern every night. His sugary sweet bull-shit always turns vile and degrading.

I counted myself lucky when only ten minutes passed before Chris and Mac showed up to drag his sorry ass away.

This has gone from a one-off nuisance to beyond ridiculous. Darcy was in a constant state of anxiety, and we were all lacking a solid night's sleep running on three weeks now. Finals were coming up. This had to stop. Mostly I was concerned about Darcy. The girl was always looking over her shoulder now, jumpy and afraid. But I also one hundred percent depend on my scholarship, which depends on my grades. I needed to study and I needed rest. I couldn't take any more of this nightly drama.

. . .

"I know I keep apologizing, but I feel terrible that he's waking all of you up every night. Everyone on the damn floor must hate me by now."

"Shut your trap, pumpkin. This isn't your fault and you know it," Caitlin reassured her.

Jenna pulled Darcy in for a hug. "Dan told me he's paying Nick another visit today. Hopefully he'll talk some sense into him."

She nodded absently as her eyes searched the dining hall. "Tell Dan I said thanks."

It was the first time she'd met us for a meal in weeks. Now she only went to class, grabbed take-out and went home. I got angry every time I walked into our place and saw her studying as she picked at a sandwich, knowing it was Nick who had her running scared.

Before she got up to leave for class, she reminded us that her brother was going to be in town this weekend and had invited us all to lunch on Sunday.

When I suggested she tell him about Nick, Darcy shook her head and shot back, "Absolutely not. You don't know Caleb. I mean, he's great, but he's got a short fuse. If he finds out about this he'll be facing felony assault charges."

I poked her and laughed. "I'm at the point where I'd pay good money to watch someone assault Nick Brunner. But seriously, this is too much for you to handle on your own. I absolutely hate him for what he's putting you through."

"I'm sorry, Rene. I know this is hard on all of you, too. I just don't think...No," she resolved, shaking her head, "I definitely can't tell Caleb. Maybe I'll call the campus police today and tell them what's up. Maybe if they send someone to speak to Nick when he's sober then he'll ease off. I'll definitely do that today."

Yeah right, that'll work, being that the campus police were about as intimidating as a pack of butterflies.

Chapter Two

CALEB

I stretched, slow and lazy, smiling as I looked over to my left.

Lying next to me in bed was Cherry, a very beautiful redhead from work. Her name was Christine but she preferred Cherry. She worked with a bunch of obnoxious guys on a trading floor, so she had to be confident and ballsy to carry off a nickname like that. I liked her company and found myself hooking up with her every so often. She wanted it just like me: just sex, no drama. Take today for example. I was meeting up with Sean in an hour, and with Cherry I wouldn't feel bad about waking her up and sending her on her way.

The sun was rising, streaking patterns of bright light throughout my place. I still wasn't used to the remote control function that shaded over the floor-to-ceiling windows in my apartment, and since I liked getting up early anyway, I really couldn't be bothered.

I looked her over, still sleeping peacefully. Cherry was like the subject of a Titian painting come to life—long auburn hair against fair skin, creamy and soft. I rolled the sheet down slowly, admired the most perfect ass known to man, then gave her a spank.

"Morning, gorgeous."

She arched back into me, for what, another swat? When she didn't get one, she groaned, "Oh my God, what is it, like six-thirty? I've got to start making my way back home at night so you don't wake me up at the crack of dawn. Like most normal people, I like to sleep in on the weekends."

"Sorry, babe, I've gotta start my day."

She rolled over onto her side facing me, palms pressed together underneath her cheek. Cherry looked angelic there for a moment, and I laughed to myself thinking that she was anything but. I was considering texting Sean to cancel.

"What are your plans, Caleb?"

"I'm supposed to be meeting a friend for a run and then I'm heading up to Boston for the night. One of my college roommates is having a thing."

"Kind of *thing* you need a date for?"

And just like that, she killed my boner. "Nah, it's not that kind of night."

She stretched like a contented cat before making her way to the bathroom. She wasn't shy about prancing around naked and had no reason to be. When she came back out fully dressed, she smiled at me and grabbed her bag. "I'm outta here. See you Monday."

Cherry was either still good with our arrangement or she was a very talented actress.

Sean and I ran along the reservoir. Clear blue sky, the sun was shining, and Central Park was more crowded than usual with people biking, running or walking their dogs. Summer was within reach, right around the corner. I was up for a long one, but my friend looked like the run was kicking his ass.

"What's up, Sean? You hurting?"

"I feel like I'm sweating Jack and Cokes right now. You drank as much as I did last night. How are you ok?"

"Dunno, just feel fine."

"Did you leave with that girl from work again?" I nodded, an uneasy feeling settling over me. "Makes like three times in one month, right?"

"More like four or five. She's great, but it won't be happening again. She was dropping hints about coming to Boston with me tonight."

"Would that be so terrible? She's hot."

"Yeah, but she's not like that to me. We're not dating, and I don't want to string her along."

"Oh how I wish I could go back to those days. No strings attached, just sex."

"You're so full of shit, Sean. You love Maggie. You wouldn't hit a Penthouse Pet if she was right in front of you begging for it."

Sean laughed. "I know, but sometimes I like living vicariously through you."

Driving up north, I was thinking back to last night again, trying to view things through a different lens.

I definitely enjoyed myself with Cherry, and not just in the sack. She was fun to hang out with, she was smart and she made me laugh. Why then, did I want her to leave so badly this morning? I literally let out a sigh of relief when I heard the door shut behind her.

My relationships have always been on the casual side. I've dated, been exclusive with every woman who's been in my life no matter how long the arrangement lasted, but I've never been able to hang in for more than three or four months. Guess that's my limit. That's when they seem to want something more serious and I start itching to get out.

Taking in the scene as I turned into my friend's driveway was sobering, and it served as a stark reminder: *Right, I don't ever want to be a part of whatever this is.*

From the looks of it, my college roommate had officially been spayed or neutered—I no longer knew if Drew qualified as a male or female member of the species. He was pruning branches, and the massive hands that once earned him undefeated status in a seedy underground fight club were now so delicate they needed the protection of gardening gloves. Chloe, meanwhile, was pulling weeds out of the flower beds.

How fucking domestic.

"Wow, check out the two of you!"

Drew looked to the heavens, knowing he was about to catch shit as he tugged off his gloves. "Don't laugh, Caleb. This will be you one day soon, whether you like it or not."

Next I had to suffer through the grand tour. As they were yammering on about kitchen remodels, Drew took pity when he caught me downing my beer. "Chloe, stop. I think we're boring the shit out of him."

I opened my eyes wide. "No way! What were you saying? The advantages of granite countertops over marble? Totally engrossing... Go on, please."

Chloe pushed on my chest and laughed. "Shut up, Caleb. I know it's totally lame, but I find this stuff exciting lately...Mortgage rates, kitchen remodels, best school districts to live in. Am I getting old?"

I put my arms around her and pulled her in close. "No, you're perfect, totally age appropriate. I'm just an immature ass."

"Yeah, 'bout that," Drew said, frowning. "Chloe's making it her mission to hook you up with a bride, so I'm sorry in advance. She's got two single friends coming tonight and she talked you up big time."

"I did not!"

Drew looked to his woman, a smile playing on his lips. "Did too. I heard you on the phone with Lauren, and I'm sure you said the same to Emily." Looking to me, he said, "She gave them your stats... rugby player, finance guy, swanky loft apartment in Manhattan."

"Think they'd be down for a threesome?"

She flicked a bottle cap my way—always did have good aim for a girl. "Once a pig, always a pig."

The night was bearable. There were a lot of people there so I didn't feel like Chloe was setting me up on some lame blind date. I did wind up sharing a bed in the guestroom with one of the eligible bachelorettes, Emily. But when she pulled that tired old *I really like you* crap when I was kissing her and trying to get her out of her clothes, I decided it just wasn't worth it. *I really like you.* Please, she didn't know the first thing about me. So I bowed out gracefully, rolled over and got a good night's sleep instead. Emily pulled an early exit, thank the Lord, so there was no awkward scene to deal with the next morning. When I went down for coffee it was just me and Chloe.

"Good night?"

"Emily's a nice person, but there's nothing there for me, you know?"

"Sorry, Caleb. I know you're not hurting for female company, and I don't want you think I'm on a crusade to set you up with someone or get you to settle down. I think Drew's a little annoyed with me. He thinks you'll never come up here again after last night."

I couldn't help but laugh. "No chance." I did my best rendition of the Terminator to reassure her. "I'll be back."

"Good. Drew really misses you."

"Come down to New York this month. Or better, in July we'll head down to my parents' place at the beach."

"Sounds like a plan. How's Darcy doing? She's a sophomore now or a junior?"

"Sophomore. I'm heading over there to take Darcy and few of her roommates out to lunch before I head back."

"Ok, but you're not leaving before you help Drew move some furniture. I have to take advantage when I have two able-bodied guys in the house."

After moving a truckload's worth of furniture, I needed another shower before I made my way over to campus.

Taking in the lazy Sunday atmosphere at my alma mater, I was feeling nostalgic. College was a time of no responsibilities, late nights, starry-eyed girls and marathon Call of Duty games. But that train of thought quickly switched tracks as I recalled all the term papers, savage hangovers and cramming for tests. *No thank you*, I thought as I crossed the quad. *Been there, done that.*

Darcy and her friends were waiting on me at the only semi-upscale restaurant on campus, and I smiled once I caught sight of her. My little sister was like sunshine in a bottle. Coming up behind her, I leaned down and kissed her cheek.

"Caleb!"

She jumped up, leaned in and squeezed me tight. How could you not feel a sense of conviction that you'd surely lay your life down for a person who makes you feel like the sun and the moon, like you're good, important and worthwhile? Maybe the combination of fatigue and hunger was responsible for making me sappy and emotional, or maybe spending time around a happy couple like Chloe and Drew had triggered this mess. But for the first time in I don't know how long, I was thinking something might be missing from my life. Surprised at my own weakness, I shook off the sharp ache and squeezed my sister back.

"I feel like I haven't seen you in forever!" Little brat switched from overjoyed to miffed inside of a second. "And what took you so long? We're starving!"

"Sorry, ladies. I got roped into moving pretty much all of Drew's furniture. What's up, Jenna? Long time, no see."

"I'm good, how about you?"

"Excellent. A little tired from last night and very hungry, but I'm good."

Darcy finished the intros. "Caleb this is Caitlin, and this is Rene."

"Hi Caitlin, hey Rene. Good to meet you."

The one she introduced as Rene was, shit, just beautiful. Sounds corny, but she took my breath away for a second there before I recovered myself. Dark, silky brown hair, hazel eyes that were more greenish than brown, and skin the color of a perfectly cooked crust on a warm apple pie—ok, I was starving at that point. She was wearing a soft sweater that was shifting off her shoulder on one side to reveal a lacy pink bra strap, and the fabric of her top clung just enough to show off the sweet curve of her breasts. As Darcy was sitting there yapping about something I wasn't really catching, I found myself thinking about biting Rene right where that exposed strap was.

"Caleb? Jeez, are you even listening to me?"

"Sorry, I had a late night. I'll be more coherent after we eat."

The girls were fun. You could tell they were a tight group. I figured Caitlin for a spark plug—quick-witted and a little rough around the edges, despite her obvious wealth. I wasn't super observant, but things like her latest trip to the Seychelles and the name of the prep school she attended in Virginia didn't escape me. Jenna I already knew pretty well. She'd been spending weekends at our house since the beginning of their freshman year. She was Ethel to Darcy's Lucy. Now Rene, she was kind of quiet during lunch so I dubbed her the mysterious one. I laughed to myself, knowing full well I was tagging her as mysterious because I desperately, for some very messed up and inappropriate reasons, wanted to know more about her.

I excused myself towards the end of the meal and was surprised to see Rene waiting for me outside of the men's room when I came out.

"Are you all right?"

"Um, is there anyone else in there? I need to talk to you, but Darcy will kill me if she finds out."

I led her back inside, towering over her in the cramped space. Rene's breathing picked up when I locked us in, and the sight of her chest rising and falling had me forgetting the fact that something was obviously troubling her.

Nope, nope nope. This girl was young and she was my sister's friend. I had no business thinking about her this way, thinking about how shy and sweet she was, about how full her lips were, about how good her tight, round ass would feel in my hands. *What the fuck is the matter with you?*

I took a step back. "What's up?"

"Darcy's been having a hard time. She doesn't want you to know, but I think she's in over her head. Nick, the guy she broke up with last month, has been harassing her."

"How?"

"Um, well, he calls her all the time, screaming into the phone, he comes over drunk at night banging on our door, yelling at her. He says," she crossed her arms over her stomach, "some really awful things to her." She swallowed and then looked back to me, unsure and uneasy. This girl was battling a serious case of nerves. "Jenna's boyfriend and the other guys have tried to take care of it, but he keeps on coming back, *every* night. We had to call the campus police one night last week when he was trying to push past us into her bedroom."

"Where does he live?"

"You can't tell her I said anything. Darcy's trying to handle this on her own but it's too much. He's out of control."

I was trying to keep calm, but I could feel it edging in on me— the rage, the need to physically lash out. "Please just tell me where he lives. I won't let on that you told me anything. Trust me."

"Turner Hall...213."

Talking myself down, I handed her my phone. "Put your

number in there." Both hands braced on the sink basin now, I took a few breaths, calmed down enough to realize I was probably scaring the shit out of this girl. "Just want to be able to check in with you if I need to. And thanks for telling me, Rene. You did the right thing."

I sent her back and then splashed some cold water on my face so that I didn't look like a complete maniac when I returned to the table. Taking my seat, my eyes met Rene's for a split second before she looked away.

"All right, I've gotta head back to the city soon. Darcy, just hang back a minute so we can talk?"

We ordered some cappuccinos and a mediocre cannoli to share. I focused on controlling my temper as she rattled on about this and that, but it was hard to school my expression. Darcy was like the best part of me. The thought of some piece of shit hurting her or making her feel scared just ate me up.

"So, anything new and exciting with you?"

"Uh, hello, have you been listening to a word I said?" *No, little sis, not a word.* Darcy looked to the sky, shaking her head as if I spaced out like this all the time. "I met with my advisor the other day about studying abroad next semester. It's kind of late to be approved for it, but since my grades are strong they're going to let me go. Spain, Caleb! How great is that?"

"Wow. What brought this on?"

She was all enthusiasm and smiles, but I knew this girl too well, knew whatever she was about to say was no more than well-intentioned bullshit.

"My Spanish is pretty good now, but if I spend a semester in Spain I think I can become fluent. It'll look great on my med school applications."

"Any reason in particular you want to leave here?"

"No, it's just a good move for me. I'm excited about it, so don't rain on my parade. It's totally safe there. I'll be in a dorm. I know two other girls going, and we're planning to take side trips all over Europe together. It's going to be great."

"It sounds great, Darcy, really great."

She nodded, but here eyes were sad. She looked lost. "I've missed you. Talking to you on the phone and texting isn't the same as seeing you, Luke and Kate all the time. I've been a little homesick lately. I'm kind of glad summer break is almost here."

"You have to let me know if you need me, need my help or anything." She cocked her head to the side, curious, so I took on a more casual tone. "I mean, if you're homesick again or there's anything you need, don't hesitate. You know Luke and I would be up here in a wink, right?"

"Yeah, I know. I love you."

"Love you right back."

* * *

RENE

Darcy's brother was fifteen minutes late and I was secretly annoyed. I was really stingy with my free time, as I had so little of it.

The entire bread basket was already polished off when I looked up to see a freaking god-like creature walking towards our table. Of course this had to be Caleb. Darcy gave off that girl next door vibe, a natural beauty, so it made sense that her brother would be equally as attractive.

My quick assessment pegged him at around 6'3", broad shouldered, muscular but slim. He had sandy blond hair with a natural wave to it and really spectacular blue eyes. His look was effortless, but his haircuts probably cost three times what I paid for mine, and it was easy to see that his casual clothes were not inexpensive. Ok, I was no longer annoyed. It was impossible to be ticked off at someone who looked so good.

Hanging back, just listening and observing, I was taken by how relaxed and confident he was. Not cocky, just sure of himself in a very good way. And watching the back and forth between Caleb and Darcy hurt me in a way that was unexpected. Everything he did, from the way he hugged her tight to the way he looked on at her smiling every time she spoke, showed his love and concern for her. I was some mixed up combination of jealous and sad, and it wasn't easy to shake the feeling.

I wasn't foolish enough to think that all was storybook-perfect for Darcy. I knew that behind anything that looked perfect was a reality that told otherwise, but her life did seem idyllic compared to mine.

My breath hitched when Darcy introduced us and Caleb's eyes met mine. His gaze lingered, like he was drinking me in, and his attention made me feel exposed. I could feel my skin flush, and practically emptied my water glass in one go to get some much-needed relief. When I looked to him again, his smile was playful and knowing, but I couldn't smile in return, couldn't flirt or play along. I was too new to this game. Feeling ridiculous, I fixed my eyes on my lap.

After that shaky start, I gave myself a little pep talk and was able to relax enough to enjoy lunch. I liked being around him—probably too much for my own good. He was down to earth, funny to the point of being silly, and just easy going. I couldn't understand why Darcy wouldn't let Caleb help her out. I had no doubt that a guy like him could handle this situation with ease. So when Caleb excused himself, I made my move. He must have thought I was nuts practically pushing him back into the men's room, but I was suddenly panicky, worried that Darcy would find out what I was up to. As he pulled me into the bathroom and I heard the lock click into place behind me, I was questioning my sanity and my decision making skills. Darcy had plainly stated that involving Caleb would be disastrous, and now I'd gone and set it all into motion.

Once I opened my mouth I regretted butting my nose in where it didn't belong. Caleb seemed like he was doing everything in his power to keep himself from punching the wall. He looked set to kill. When he came back and joined us at the table he was calmer, but I noticed that his fists were still clenched tight and his hair and collar were a little damp. He must have literally felt the need to cool off.

Yep, this is exactly why they coined the phrase, "Mind your own business."

I left for work about an hour later and Caleb was on my mind the entire shift.

I worked at a high-end restaurant about twenty minutes from campus. The clientele and the management were demanding, but the tips were great, so I therefore depended on this job. When I forgot to drop salads twice before entrees arrived, my manager pulled me aside. Craig was hard on most of the wait staff, but I wasn't used to being reprimanded so his words stung. My co-workers playfully teased that he was easy on me because I was easy on the eyes, but I preferred to think it was because I was never late, I was dependable, and I worked my ass off.

I made sure to stay on my toes for the rest of my shift, but still ducked into the bathroom to check my phone a few times. I knew if anything major was going down, Caitlin would text.

Nothing.

No news was definitely good news.

Chapter Three

CALEB

I walked Darcy back to her place and then made my way over to Turner Hall. My goal was to scare the shit out of this kid while avoiding a run in with the police.

A fairly big dude wearing a shirt with the school's rugby logo opened the door. Darcy never mentioned Nick playing rugby, so this one probably wasn't him.

"Is Nick around?"

"Yeah, he's here." Taking me in, he asked, "Do I know you? You look really familiar."

"I don't think so." I put my hand out. "I'm Caleb Donovan, Darcy's brother."

He looked wary for a split second but then smiled when he shook my hand. "I'm Chris. Yeah, that's Nick's door right there. Go ahead in."

I walked into a room that stank of stale beer and a guy in need of a shower. Closing the door behind me, I had to step over dirty clothes, empty cans and a bong as I made my way towards the bed.

"Are you Nick?"

He took me in, eyes wide, but then quickly adopted a controlled, bored expression. His tone was full of false bravado when he raised himself up onto his elbows and replied, "Yeah, and?"

"I'm Darcy's brother."

Silence on his end.

"Darcy never brought you home to meet the family." Taking another look around the room, I shook my head in disgust. The liquor bottles lined up on a shelf above his desk were all nearly empty, and a pizza box with what looked like last night's dinner was discarded on the floor—this kid was a train wreck. "Guess there's no mystery as to why." Still not a peep out of him. I stepped closer to make sure I had his full attention. "I'll make this quick. If you look at my sister, talk to my sister, show up at her place, call her, text her, or attempt to interact with her in any way, I *will* find out and I'm going to beat you fucking senseless. Beat you 'til there's not a tooth in your fucking head. Do you understand, Nick?"

"Uh...Yes."

I was toying with the idea of landing one punch just to give him a preview of what he might be in for, but from the chickenshit look on his face, I didn't think it was necessary. And besides, I'd done a good job of reining in the angry young man I'd once been. This piece of garbage wasn't worth taking a big step backwards for.

When I stood fixed in place staring him down, he swallowed nervously and repeated, "Yes."

On my way out, Chris and I gave a quick nod to one another. I got the distinct impression he was glad I'd stopped by.

I thought about hanging back for a day or two just to make sure my message had gotten across, but I knew that wasn't realistic. I smiled to myself thinking that my way of checking up on the situation was programmed into my phone.

And yup, that girl was on my mind for a good portion of the drive home, which was ridiculous. Besides that bizarre exchange in the men's room, we hadn't said a word to one another during lunch. She was gorgeous, but lots of women are. No, there was something else. I liked how assertive she was, taking matters into her own hands even though you could see she was unsure of herself. Liked that she wasn't just concerned about my sister, but also did something about it. But the way her skin heated, and the way she looked away in embarrassment when I did nothing more than say hello to her? The idea that I could affect her so easily, that's what had me shaking my head and smiling. It's like I had the bad angel on one shoulder egging me on: *Oh yeah, Caleb, imagine what it would be like to kiss that creamy skin and love that sweet thing?* While the good angel was on the other shoulder laying into me: *You're a shit. She's too young for you. You'd corrupt her.*

The good angel was always right.

Knowing I had to address the Cherry situation put a damper on my Monday morning, but I still had pep in my step as I hopped out of the cab. Grabbed myself a green tea and ordered a caramel latte for her, hoping the sugary sweet concoction would soften the blow.

Have to say, I'm not one of those people who hate going to work. I love it. I work with some of the most amusing people on the planet. But it's a stressful environment that lends itself to some intense emotions, so people are always looking to let off steam, and that's done on a nearly nightly basis. Still only twenty-five, I can hang with the best of them, but I marvel at the fifty, even sixty year-old guys who still knock back drinks with us every night. Then again, they generally don't look like they're in the best of health. They're the ones chewing antacid pills nonstop while telling you about the giant re-finance they just did to remodel the kitchen at their sprawling Bedford home yet again, or their kid's plan to go on to law school after they just finished paying the backbreaking 75K-a-year tuition at Duke.

Can't say I wanted to walk in those footsteps. I lived nicely. I had a great apartment in Tribeca and I didn't sweat what I spent on dinners or traveling, but I was socking away a lot of my money so that I wasn't a slave to this business for life. My commissions were always healthy, so I had more than enough to live well while I planned for the years ahead.

I saw myself hitting forty on a beach somewhere, spending my days surfing while trading part-time. I didn't see the wife, kids and picket fence. I saw a beautiful woman, someone I could grow old with, or not. I wanted a companion and a lover, not an encumbrance who made demands or expected too much from me.

I ran into Cherry first thing. Bradley, the one absolute tool in the office, was hanging over her shoulder yapping like a Chihuahua. He was pretending to look at her computer screen while zeroing in on her cleavage. *Go for it*, I thought, fairly certain this was the only kind of action he ever got. He was the stupid, son of a bitch nephew of one of the managing partners. And that's without a doubt the only reason he had a job. Anyone else who couldn't pass the Series-3 would have been shown the door a long time ago. Changed my mind —dumbass didn't deserve to enjoy that view. And Cherry did look like she needed a rescue.

"Got a minute, Cherry? I need to see the buy order on that contract we were talking about."

She jumped up. "Sure!"

Bradley gave me a dirty look, to which I chuckled in reply, and then he skulked away.

Handing her the coffee, I gestured to her beautiful bosom. "Sorry, but I had to break that up. Looked like your boyfriend was getting off on ogling the goodies from his vantage point."

She cringed. "He's such a disgusting excuse for a man. He's always coming up with pointless questions just so he can hang around my desk." She held up her hand to silence me when I went to speak. "Save it if you're about to tell me that's some sort of twisted compliment." Her brow furrowed when she asked, "So, how was Boston?"

"Good. Saw my old roommate and his wife, then paid a visit to my little sis at school. How was your weekend?"

"You mean after you showed me the door?"

I threw my head back and let out a breath. "Cherry, I didn't think we were like that with each other."

She looked a little wounded for a second there but then shook her head. "We're not. Look, I enjoy the nights we spend together, I *really* enjoy them, but the next time we're on the verge of a late night romp, please do me a favor and don't let me go through with it, ok?"

"Whatever's best for you. I mean that."

"I'm just...I'm starting to like you too much and I know you're not *that* guy."

"I'm not, sweetheart. I'm sorry."

"You have nothing to be sorry about. You never lied to me or led me on. I'm a big girl, Caleb. I just need to put an end to it."

"Understood. Friends?"

She smiled but her eyes looked tired. "Absolutely."

I've had conversations like this one before, and every time the feeling is the same when it's over: pure, unadulterated relief.

RENE

The day after we had lunch with Caleb, I ran into Chris and couldn't help but fish around for information. Last night was quiet at our place, no late night visit from Nick, so something must have happened.

"How was your weekend?"

"It was good...Interesting."

"Interesting?"

"Yeah, we had a visitor yesterday."

"Chris, what's with the cryptic snippets of info?"

He laughed. "I should probably keep my trap shut, but it's just too good. I just might have to share."

I was trying to come off as indifferent, but all the back and forth was driving me mad. "Just spit it out," I demanded.

"All right, all right. Darcy's brother came to our place yesterday, barged into Nick's room and laid into him. Nick looked like he was in danger of shitting himself after the guy left. I wish you could have seen the look on his face, it was classic."

"Really?" I feigned surprise. "You're not Team Nick?"

"What? Fuck him." Poking me in the side, he added, "You know me better than that." Chris shook his head. "I'm tired of being woken up by you girls every night to fetch his stupid ass at some ungodly hour, and I can't stand what he's doing to Darcy. She's a nice girl. If I was her brother I would have slaughtered him."

"So, should I be expecting my usual, two in the morning wake-up call, or do you think he's done?"

"Can't be sure, but he did look pretty rattled. I'm betting he won't be bothering you girls, at least for the next few days."

"Excellent. I need my beauty sleep."

For that I got a hip check. "Now *that* is a lie. You just need your sleep."

* * *

CALEB

Ed could definitely still party like a rock star. My boss got his start on Wall Street in the late eighties, when it was like the Wild West, and the guy was still at it like nothing had changed. And because our team was the biggest producer at the firm, Ed was still afforded all the trappings, like the big corporate expense account that covered ridiculously lavish client dinners and whatever other shenanigans he was prone to get into. He's taken us axe throwing and drinking in ice caves, but old school strip clubs like this one on the Upper East Side were his jam.

I wanted no part of it, but Ed was all about being a team player, and since Rob and Finn were totally on board, I was stuck. Pulling up, there were no neon lights, no beefy bouncers, no obnoxious red velvet ropes that basically scream: *Welcome, all you Tony Soprano wannabes.* No, this place, with it's respectable looking doorman and hefty cover charge, wasn't some seedy rub and tug, but a strip club is a strip club. Not my thing. The dark, smoky rooms, loud thumping shit music, and the girls with their teased hair and fake tits—everything about that scene made my skin crawl.

Guess I've got Sarah to thank for that. My father's wife, the woman who mothered me through the toughest years of my life, is an angel here on Earth. Sarah's always been the type of woman to care for strays, feed the homeless and volunteer for any worthy cause. She made a casual comment once, reminding me that the girls who worked those clubs were someone's daughter, someone's sister, maybe even someone's mother. Were they hot? I guess, but I could never feel anything but sad watching them.

I cut out early and found myself calling Rene as I walked down Lexington Avenue while half-heartedly hailing a cab.

"Hello?"

"Hey, it's Caleb Donovan."

Her voice picked up. "Hi, Caleb."

Good sign, she sounded happy to hear from me. "I just wanted to check in with you. Has Nick been behaving?"

Rene had a light, breezy laugh and I liked it. A lot. "Not a peep out of him. Mission accomplished."

"Yeah, that was like our very own spy mission, Secret Agent Rene." She laughed that sweet laugh again. "Well, I'm glad Nick was so easily intimidated."

"So am I. Four nights in a row now...I don't want to jinx anything, but it's been so peaceful."

"I'm glad." I scrambled for something to say, for some reason to keep her on the line. "So, you must be starting finals this week. Are you ready?"

"I cannot wait for them to be over. I've been at the library until after midnight every night this week."

"Lots of papers due?"

"Of course."

"You'll have to come down to the beach this summer to unwind with Darcy."

"Yeah, I might. She was just talking about it."

"I really hope you can make it. Well, um, good luck on your finals. And Rene?"

"Yes?"

"Please call me if Nick pulls any shit, ok?"

"Definitely. Bye, Caleb."

Caleb. I got a warm, buzzed feeling every time she said my name. I wanted her to say my name again, to whisper it.

I kept on walking, lost in thought as I fantasized about Rene on the beach with me this summer.

RENE

I almost didn't answer my phone when I saw the unfamiliar number, but was so, so, *so* glad that I did. When he said, "Hey, it's Caleb," my heart began to race in a good way. And I'm sure I sounded a little too happy in my reply, but hell, I couldn't help it. The sound of his voice did make me happy. No, happy is a woefully inadequate way to describe the feeling. His voice made me ecstatic, joyful, elated...hopeful.

I think the reason he was having such a powerful effect on me, aside from the mouth-watering good looks, was because I'd never once experienced the whole knight in shining armor coming to save the damsel in distress-thing, and it was kind of intoxicating. He was like this all-powerful, fiercely protective man, and I didn't know a whole lot of those.

I never wasted time feeling sorry for myself, and I wasn't about to start now, but I found myself thinking that it would be really nice, just for once, to have someone like him watching out for me.

After he ended the call, I stared down at my phone, down at his name and number in my contacts. I caught myself falling down the rabbit hole, indulging in another ridiculous daydream, but quickly snapped myself out of that lust induced fog. He was sweet and kind on the phone, seemed like he was fishing for topics to keep me on the line, but I knew he was just being polite, just looking to thank me and nothing more. From what Darcy implied, her brother had more beautiful, willing women than he knew what to do with. There wasn't a snowball's chance in hell that an established, intelligent, successful hottie like Caleb Donovan was interested in me, a nineteen-year-old juggling school with two jobs, struggling every day just to keep my head above water.

Chapter Four

CALEB

From Memorial Day to Labor Day, one o'clock on Fridays is quitting time. Time to hit the beach.

I vaguely remember visiting the Hamptons once when I was a kid, when my mother was still alive. Don't remember much about that trip except my father grumbling about the traffic. Just wasn't his scene. So we had a house in a sleepy outer-borough beach community just a short thirty-minute ride from the city. It's the place I'd spent my summers working as a lifeguard, hanging out in the bars, and basically getting an education in life. The surfing was decent, as far as northeast surfing goes, and we had a house just a few off the beach.

I've been surfing these waves since I was in grade school, but my favorite thing to do at the beach was to wake up early on the weekends and walk the shore with my chocolate lab, Bosco. There's a whole doggy community. A few of us dog lovers would meet up, drink coffee and shoot the breeze while tossing tennis balls into the surf for the dogs to fetch. Bosco was holed up in my apartment during the week, his only outings on work days limited to quick strolls with his "professional" dog-walker, so this place was paradise. He had birds to chase, friends to play with, and endless stretches of sand to dig up.

When I got back from the beach that morning, Darcy was making a shopping list for a barbecue. I overheard her telling Sarah that Beth was now a vegetarian, so they had to remember to get soy dogs and seitan bacon. I was about to bust out my rendition of *Ain't Nothing Like the Real Thing* because I tasted that crap they tried to pass off as bacon and it was nasty, but there was now a more important matter at hand.

"Your roomies are heading down?"

"Not all of them, just Beth, Catlin and Jenna. It's hard to drag Rene away."

Aw, shit.

I played it off like I was merely curious. "Why's that?"

"Rene works all summer waitressing. She sublets an apartment by school and takes two summer classes because she's juggling a double major. She also interns at a local television station."

"What is she, some kind of masochist?"

Sarah and Darcy laughed, but then Darcy's smile faded. "Rene doesn't have anyone to lean on. She has a scholarship, but has to take care of everything else on her own. I mean everything, like *all* of her living expenses."

"Where's her family?"

"She never mentions her parents, and I know better than to ask. What little I've heard isn't great. I'm pretty sure her mother is out of the picture entirely, and her dad sounds like a drinker who is no help whatsoever. She has an uncle she's in contact with, but I can tell they aren't super close either. The person closest to her, besides Caitlin, was her high school English teacher, and she died a few years ago. I got the impression she was like a mentor to Rene."

"So she's out on her own, no real home?"

"Jeez, you're going to make me cry. She spends some holidays with Caitlin, but Rene is really proud and you have to watch it with her. She gets pissed if she thinks you pity her, or God forbid you attempt to pay her share for anything. I learned that the hard way." She paused and then added, "Like I said, I ask Rene and if she says no, I leave it alone. She has her reasons. Jenna's coming down again in two weeks with Dan. I'll ask Rene again and hopefully she'll come."

Shit, I felt terrible. The man in me wanted to provide for Rene and make it so that life wasn't so hard for her. The concept was foreign to me, and one that I really didn't understand being that I hardly knew the girl. I tried to shake off this sudden case of the blues, but couldn't.

"I really do admire her. Think about it, Caleb, she's fierce, being able to do all of that on her own at my age."

"I agree, she sounds pretty amazing."

* * *

RENE

Another hot, sweaty July in Boston.

Seasons changed but my routine stayed the same. My schedule hardly ever deviated. I took classes in the morning, went to my internship or the restaurant afterwards, and squeezed in a late-night run to clear my head whenever I could, year-round.

I was running along the Charles, laboring for breath, dreading another night in that cramped studio apartment on Sullivan Street. No air conditioning, no breeze, no way to cool off besides an ice-cold shower. Bet there was a beautiful breeze down at beach. I pictured Darcy and the other girls sipping on frozen drinks, laying out in the sun, talking about nonsense and laughing without a care in the world. Caleb also featured prominently in my daydream—of course he did. Shirtless, rippling muscles on full display, I bet he looked like a bronzed god in the summertime. Feeling sour, I reminded myself that it was no one's fault but my own that I was sticky and miserable and alone.

I wanted to take Darcy up on her invitation, but with the Boston Pops concert and the fireworks show on the Esplanade this week, I was needed at the studio. I had to score a solid recommendation from my station manager. Without it, I wouldn't have a prayer of snagging an internship next summer in New York, the most competitive television news market in the country. That's been my game plan from the beginning, to work in broadcast journalism in New York.

With that internship I could make connections and use them to apply for production assistant or copywriting jobs after graduation. The pay wouldn't be great, but I knew I could waitress or bartend to make ends meet those first few years.

So I'd just have to dream of the beach for now. Climbing up the stairs to my little hovel, my clothes clinging to my sweat-soaked skin, I figured it was just as well. I was getting hung up on a fantasy as it was, so seeing Caleb again wasn't a good idea. A little taste would be way worse than nothing at all, and I knew I'd be craving any little crumb I could get where he was concerned.

CALEB

I was downright cranky after I found out she wasn't coming, and it was time I got a grip. I was several years older than this girl, and the last thing she needed was a wolf devouring her and then moving on after he'd had his fill.

I always did want to move on. Even though Rene had me thinking about things I'd never even remotely entertained before, I'm sure it was just her innocence and need for protection bringing out the chivalrous side of me.

The feelings would pass.

They always did.

After spending no more than thirty minutes with Darcy's friends to be social, I left to meet up with Mick and Conner at our favorite dive bar. It was filled with lifeguards ranging in age from eighteen— the slick kids who could maneuver their way around the drinking age —to forty. The old timers worked as teachers or ski instructors during the winter and hung onto their beach jobs for the summer. Not a bad life.

One of my old flames was there with a few of her girlfriends. Nan cornered me the second I walked into the bar and offered herself up with no strings attached. She was engaged to her college sweetheart, but that commitment didn't stop her from whispering in my ear that I was the best she'd ever had, and didn't stop her from telling me that she needed one more time before she was "stuck" with the same guy for the rest of her life.

We wound up in her childhood bedroom, pink flowered bedspread and all, with her parents sleeping downstairs. Not exactly ideal.

Unsatisfying was the only way to describe it. I just didn't want this anymore. And I had this uncomfortable feeling I couldn't shake because while I was burying myself inside of Nan, I was envisioning this girl Rene in her place.

Not good.

Mick and I were on our surfboards the next morning, sitting, talking, and just letting the choice waves pass us by.

"Damn, I hope you didn't break up an engagement."

"Not a chance, but I feel sorry for that poor bastard if she's looking for outside action before she even makes it up the aisle."

"Maybe you were just her last hoorah. Go out with a bang as they say, right?"

I let out a cheerless laugh. "Glad I could be of service."

"What's up with you, Caleb? Do you like her or something?"

"Nan? No, just feeling a little weird about last night. I think I'm losing my desire to screw around."

Mick dipped a hand down and flicked some water my way. "Come again?"

"I don't know, just feeling restless lately and sick of the same old shit. Maybe I should look into getting myself an actual girlfriend."

"I get it. I'm definitely the front-runner for office manwhore this year. Not gonna say it totally sucks, but it is getting awkward."

"But a few weeks ago, when I was at Drew's house? I mean, Chloe is great, she's the total package, but I'm not ready for that life yet either. They're in suburban, minivan-driving nirvana. Boring as shit. It was weird to see Drew like that."

Mick put his palm to his forehead like he was having a vision. "You'll find your way. Someone is going to turn your head soon. I can foretell these things, feel it in my bones."

While I heard myself brushing him off, "All right, asshole," I was thinking that someone had most definitely turned my head already.

* * *

RENE

Sitting in class, I was daydreaming about my life, about my future. I was envisioning a luxury Manhattan apartment, me sitting opposite my agent in the midst of some heated contract negotiations. The network was playing hardball, but my agent assured me that I was worth more than what they were offering. I was lost in this ridiculous fantasy when I heard my phone ping with an incoming text from Darcy:

We missed u this wknd.

-Thx D, believe me, I missed u too.

What r u doing today?

-Class then restaurant. U?

Working 10-6 then dunno. Can u get away for a wknd soon? J and Dan r coming wknd of 7/16. Plz...don't want to b their 3rd wheel!

-Count me in. I deserve it!!!

Yay! U made my day!

Nervous and excited. Just the thought of being in the same state as Caleb had me coming undone. *Ugh, snap out of it, Rene. He's eye candy, he's nice, he's your friend's brother—that's all.* I would certainly look, but I'm sure I'd never have the opportunity to touch.

I was just longing for someone good. My last boyfriend? Ryder was a sad excuse for a boyfriend. Just another guy who made it his mission to change my status once he found out I was a virgin. I'm sure if he was decent for just a few more weeks he would have been successful, but he had an itch he just had to scratch. I walked in on him doing a girl from our sociology class and had to go the rest of the semester with those two sitting just a few rows in front of me. Good times.

Worker bee that I am, I let Craig know about my plans as soon as I got into work so he had time to cover my shifts.

"Where are you heading, Rene?"

"My roommate's beach house."

"Good. I'm glad you're getting out of town. Sometimes I think you work too hard, so don't feel uncomfortable about asking me for time off. You're my best worker. I don't mind doing you a favor here and there."

Aw, I always knew deep down he was a good guy. "Thanks, but I doubt I'll be looking for much in terms of time off."

The next day I took care of my station internship schedule. I was good to go. Now I just had two loooong weeks to wait.

I splurged on a new bikini, one I couldn't afford.

I need a new suit anyway. I'm not doing this for him.

* * *

CALEB

"Where have you been? I don't mind taking care of Bosco, but I'd like to see my brother at least half as often as I see his dog."

Sitting at my desk, I rubbed a hand over my face. "Sorry, I've just been busy."

"Too busy for surfing? Sure you don't need to see a doctor?"

"Wow, you're quite the little brat today. Doesn't suit you."

"Who pissed in your coffee this morning?"

My boss had actually shit in my coffee when he conned me into mentoring his nephew, Bradley. He was so nice about it that I felt obligated to say yes, even though I knew I wasn't patient enough to teach that prick how to tie his shoelaces, let alone teach him how to do his own job. That's why I was in such a craptastic mood, but there was no need to take it out on her.

"Just having a bad day…Work stuff, that's all. I'll be down this weekend at some point. Are Luke and Kate coming?"

"No, but some of my friends are. I hope that doesn't keep you away. Last time they were down we hardly saw you."

"Stop, I like your roommates. Same crew as last time?"

"No, this time it's Rene, Jenna, and her boyfriend, Dan. I think you've met him before."

Well, hell-oh.

I had to play this right. "You finally got Rene to ditch work and come down?"

She laughed. "Yep. I was planning to beg and plead, but it didn't come to that. I really don't want to be stuck with the two lovebirds alone, and she took pity on me. They'll be frolicking in the ocean and taking moonlit strolls along the shore, like, all weekend long."

"I'm glad she's getting a break. I felt terrible for that girl after what you told me."

"I know." Then Darcy said, "Please, Caleb, do *not* let on that you know anything about her. She'd be really embarrassed, not to mention furious with me."

"Don't worry, I won't. She's proud, I get it. So how's the beach treating you?"

"Good. I'll be ending work pretty early, like August tenth, so I'm trying to sock away as much money as possible."

"Why so early?"

"I want to take a week off before I leave. I need to get back into the city, do some shopping and packing, and then hopefully, *if* you have time, spend some quality days with the fam at the beach before I go. Orientation starts August twentieth."

"Yeah, that'll be here before you know it. Don't worry about saving up, Darcy. You *do* have a wealthy older brother, remember?"

"Yeah, but I don't want to hit Luke up for cash."

"You slay me, Sis."

"Love you."

"Love you right back."

Sarah let me know that Darcy's friends were arriving on Friday. Steer clear for the entire weekend—that would have been the smart thing to do and the decent thing to do as far as Rene was concerned.

My compromise was to head down on Saturday.

I took my time leaving the city—my last futile attempt to be good—and by the time I got to the house they were already down on the beach. I scoped out the waves from the upstairs deck, waxed up my board and headed out. Darcy was out on the paddle board, while Jenna and Dan stood ankle-deep in the water. Making my way down towards the shore, I finally spotted Rene. Her chair was tilted back and she was looking totally relaxed, soaking up the sun with her eyes closed and a contented smile playing on her lips. Unfortunately for me, I now had a clear visual of her body. Her legs were long and toned, like a runner's. My gaze traveled north then, taking in hips that curved into a slim little waist, and breasts that more than filled out her blue bikini.

Deep breath.

"Good to see you're finally getting a little rest and relaxation, Rene."

She opened her eyes and then shielded them from the sun with her hand to look up at me. "Hi, Caleb. I was wondering if you were going to make a cameo this weekend."

Damn, she was cute. "I couldn't stay away." I leaned my board against the cooler, took a seat in the sand next to her chair and handed her some sunblock. "Here, thought you could use this. Don't want that perfect skin of yours getting scorched. You look like you've never gotten sunburned once in your life."

"I didn't spend a lot of time at the beach growing up."

"Really? A Jersey girl and all?"

"I was more Jersey City than Jersey Shore."

"Right."

I looked straight ahead at the water as she rubbed sunscreen onto her arms and legs. When she moved onto her abdomen, I could feel my body reacting to her. I was fighting an internal battle, telling myself she was too young but at the same time finding it impossible to look away. The good guy in me was losing out when I heard myself ask if she wanted me to get her back with the sunblock. *Nice, you sound like a creepy pervert.* My need to put my hands on her was pathetic. Thankfully, Mick came bounding down the beach before she could answer and before I could embarrass myself any further.

"Where the hell have you been hiding?"

"Been staying in the city. Just, you know, busy." I looked to her.

"Rene, this is my good friend, Mick. Mick, this is Darcy's lovely roommate, Rene."

"Nice to meet you, Mick."

"Shit, is every girl at that school gorgeous? I totally went to the wrong university."

I shook my head at his absolute lack of tact. "Down boy."

Rene laughed and then put her tank top back on. She rose from her chair slowly, allowing me to get a good long look at her fantastic ass, and then went to meet Darcy at the shore as she was paddling back in.

Lowering himself next to me, Mick started to sing some old Zombies song from the sixties about a girl and her rich sugar daddy.

"An oldie but a goodie."

"Yes, and seems very apropos, don't you think, Caleb?"

"I don't follow."

He flicked a little sand in my direction. "You don't follow, my ass. That fine, young thing is just that...A fine, *young* thing."

"Your point?"

"No point. You just look a little smitten, that's all. Can't say I blame you. She has a great smile, great hair, great legs, great ass, great rack."

I couldn't help but laugh. "Ok, shut the fuck up. Let's get out there."

We spent the next two hours surfing. I was catching waves here and there, but spent more time than usual just sitting on my board letting perfectly good sets pass me by. I was glad to see Rene in the water with Jenna and Darcy. For someone who didn't spend much time at the beach growing up, Rene swam like a little dolphin. Found myself smiling whenever I heard her laughing with the girls, and I couldn't have looked away if I tried when she got out of the water. Not an exaggeration to say I was pretty much transfixed as she shook out her long hair with the sun glistening off her damp skin.

I stayed around after dinner longer than I did last time, but I did leave when Conner and Mick came by to collect me. Darcy asked me to come with them to McCabe's, a little beachfront bar, but I begged off. I really didn't trust myself around Rene.

The party at Conner's girl's bungalow was good, but I just wasn't into it. I got home on the early side, around one. Tried to sleep but couldn't—too restless. After staring at the ceiling for a while, I decided to head down to the beach.

I was making my way across the backyard when I heard her call out to me softly, "Is that you, Caleb?"

"Rene? What are you doing out here?"

"We came back early. Jenna and Dan had a few drinks too many."

"You're not sleepy either?"

She had one leg curled up underneath her and one long leg dangling over the side of the hammock. "I need less sleep than most humans."

"Ah."

She cocked her head to the side, and the movement sent her long hair tumbling over one shoulder. That alone made my pulse hammer. I liked the sound of her voice way too much when she asked, "Where are you off to?"

"A little night swimming. Ever tried it?"

Her eyes went wide. "Aren't you afraid some sea critter will sting you, or a serial killer will be lurking on the beach?"

"What? I'm starting to think you're a little nuts, Rene."

"Maybe I am."

"Come and try it. Tonight's perfect. No waves, calm like a bay, the moon dancing off the water…This is my favorite kind of night for a dip." She looked unsure, and I wasn't about to beg. "Suit yourself," I said as I started walking. "If you change your mind, I'll be down there. I'll scout the area for serial killers."

A moment passed before she called after me, "Wait."

Sweet Jesus.

"Let me get my suit on. I'll be two seconds."

As she made her way across the lawn, I teased, "Sure, although swimsuits aren't typically worn. Since it's your first time, though, I'll make an exception."

She threw her head back and let out a sound that was half laugh, half frustrated groan. "Two seconds."

She took five minutes, but I wasn't complaining.

"Wow, it's so beautiful down here at night."

The moon, the water—it was a sight. But the look on her face when she turned to me and smiled put Mother Nature to shame.

I nodded, absently scanned the shoreline to give myself a moment. "Yeah, I can't see myself ever wanting to live far away from the ocean."

We made our way into the water, warm and ink black. Once I was waist deep, I took off my shorts and rifled them back onto the shore.

"Uh, hello?"

"I told you, swimsuits aren't required or recommended for night swimming. Not for me, anyway." I couldn't help but laugh at her slightly horrified expression. "Clothes ruin the experience."

The look on her face changed. She was taking it as a dare, deciding whether or not she was up for the challenge. She moved a little further out so that she was chest-deep. Then, kill me now, sweet little Rene reached back and undid the ties on her top and shimmied out of her bottoms.

"I don't think I can reach the shore with these. I have a terrible throwing arm. Here."

She tossed me her suit and I rifled those pieces in, watching them land alongside mine before turning back to her. "I'm impressed. Now you're getting the full experience as it was meant to be had. You have to admit, it feels better when you're as the Lord made you, right?"

Her smile was shy. "Yeah, it does feel pretty great."

Treading water with just a few feet separating us, it took an iron will to keep myself from closing the distance. I was in desperate need of a distraction. "So, since we're letting it all hang out there, tell me about yourself."

Rene threw her head back and laughed. "I just want you to know this is the most bizarre getting to know you experience I've ever had."

"It's my absolute best so far. So spill it, tell me some secrets."

"There's not much to tell. I was born in New York but basically grew up in New Jersey. I'm an only child." Then she blurted out, "My parents were never parental or reliable, so I guess I've gotten used to taking care of myself. And that's about it."

She looked a little shell-shocked.

"That's about it, Rene? No it's not. I don't even know your last name."

It was good to see her relax again. I think she was relieved I wasn't looking to dig deeper or making a big deal out of what she'd just told me.

"Beaumont."

"Rene Beaumont. Your parents are French?"

She cocked her head to the side and shot me a rueful smile. "It kind of gives one the false impression of being inherently chic and elegant, n'est pas?"

"Well, they can't be all that bad. I mean, they did produce you."

"Why thank you, Caleb."

"What are their names?"

"Rene and Lisette."

"You were named after your father?"

"Yes, and the two bumbling fools used the masculine spelling for Rene...One e instead of two."

I laughed. "Did you ever ask them about it?"

"I asked my father, but he never really gave me a straight answer. He said it didn't matter because I was an American." She laughed along with me but was shaking her head. "For all I know, they were both high when they were filling out the paperwork at the hospital.

Maybe they thought they were bringing home a son." I didn't know what to say in response to that. She filled in the awkward silence. "Maybe that was TMI."

I smiled and splashed her gently, needing to ease her discomfort, to make it better. "You know, Beaumont, I still owe you."

"Owe me?"

"For telling me about that little shit. I keep wondering why Darcy didn't reach out to me herself. It eats me up."

"Darcy likes to handle things by herself. That's a good thing."

"You must have some mutual admiration society thing going on 'cause that's exactly what she says about you."

"What?"

"She admires you, you handle everything on your own, you're independent, kinda fierce, blah, blah, blah."

Rene laughed. "Yeah, well I don't exactly have a choice."

"Everyone needs a little help sometimes, right? Even you?"

Rene shrugged and deftly took the focus off of her. "I guess. And Darcy did need your help, otherwise I wouldn't have stuck my nose in her business. Nick didn't make a peep after you paid him a visit. She's lucky she has you and Luke looking out for her."

She ducked under the water for a minute, and when she came back up I was taken off guard again by how beautiful she was. I didn't register what she was saying at first.

"Earth to Caleb. It's your turn now. You have to tell me something about yourself."

"Let's see. You know all the basics from Darcy. Devastatingly handsome, intelligent—"

She splashed me full force. "You're awful!"

"Ok, ok. I work in the city as a commodities broker, I just bought my first place, I...I don't know, Rene, tell me specifically what you want to know."

"Hmm." She thought on it for a moment. "What were you like when you were younger?"

"Guess I was your typical middle child. Then I went through a really rough patch after my mother died."

"How old were you?"

"Seven. Wanted to fight anyone and everyone from the time I was seven until I was about fourteen or fifteen."

"That's hard to imagine."

"I wasn't like that at home, just had a short fuse at school, the park, the baseball field."

Her eyes were sympathetic. "You were angry."

"Angry, guilty, you name it."

"Guilty?"

I don't know why I felt like I could say it. I'd never spoken about it to anyone besides Luke and my father, but in that moment it was important. I wanted her to know me.

"Yeah, I was convinced my mother's accident was my fault because I acted all disappointed that we didn't have marshmallows for our hot chocolate that day. I knew that was the reason she went out to the store and...she never came back."

Maybe *that* was too much information. Rene stared out into the night sky, lost in thought.

"Stupid, huh?"

She was still looking away. "No, not stupid at all."

She dove under the water, oblivious to the fact that she was flashing a whole lot of skin in the process. And I think this talk, the way it had taken a turn for the deep and dark, was making me desperate for some kind of comfort. God, I wanted to smooth my hands over her skin, drag her in close to me, kiss her until she begged me.

Rene surfaced again, then looked right at me. "What made you stop? I mean, stop fighting."

It took me a second to recall what we were talking about, too lost in the thought of loving her body.

"I guess I just started to believe what Luke, my dad and Sarah were telling me. Luke would always say it could have been him asking Mom for something. Would I have blamed him if the shoe was on the other foot? I'd never. And part of it was just growing up. I understood that all the trouble I was getting into was hurting everyone around me. Being able to slam people while playing rugby helped too...Elegant violence."

I ducked under then, shaken up by saying all of that out loud. When I resurfaced I caught her shivering.

"You cold? Let's get out."

Eyes wide, she laughed and shook her head. "I'm not just walking out buck naked with you!"

"Don't get your knickers in a twist, Beaumont. I'll go out first and then I'll toss you your suit. I hope you can at least catch." As I made my way out, I teased, "I feel your eyes on my bum. I'm not a piece of meat."

"I am *not* looking, you idiot!"

I put on my wet shorts and then went to find her suit. "Uh, Houston, we have a problem."

"Don't even tell me you can't find it."

I couldn't help but laugh. "I have the bottom. Here, make sure you catch this. I do not see the top, though. Give me a second. Shit, it must have washed back in."

"Oh my Lord."

"It's ok, no big deal. I'll turn around and carry you piggyback to the house. No one will see a thing. *I* won't see a thing."

"What!?"

"Otherwise I can run up and get you a towel. I'll be back in less than five minutes."

From the sound of her voice I knew the thought of being out there alone terrified her. "No! Oh my God, Caleb, turn around."

When she jumped on my back, she smacked my shoulder hard to stop me from laughing. She was like carrying a feather.

"This is so embarrassing!"

"Maybe for you, but I'm kind of enjoying myself."

"I hate you."

"You keep telling yourself that, sweetheart."

I *was* enjoying myself, far too much. The feel of her skin slick from the ocean, her legs wrapped around my waist, and her bare breasts pressing into my back had me practically busting up through the waistband of the wet shorts clinging to my lower half. If her gaze happened to drift down in that general vicinity there'd be no way to hide it. But I didn't want to tease her anymore. I was afraid I might have upset Rene, and that didn't sit right with me.

"I'm gonna put you down here. There's a towel right behind you. I actually feel terrible about losing your top. I'm sorry."

Her warm breath hit my neck when she whispered, "It's ok, really."

She was killing me. Throat tight, I managed to ask, "You want to go into the shower house quick and I'll get you some dry clothes?"

"Thanks."

I ran in, threw on dry shorts, then grabbed one of my plain black t-shirts and a pair of boxers. Handing them to her over the shower house door, I said, "Here, the best I could do."

When she walked out dressed in my things, she looked so damn sweet that I felt guilty for wanting her the way I did. She fixed her eyes on the grass instead of meeting my gaze. *No,* I pled in silence, *please don't be afraid, please don't look away.*

I tipped her chin up and was happy to see her shy smile. "Hey, are you good?"

"I'm good. I think I'll head to bed now."

"Good night, Rene."

"You're staying out here?"

"Yeah, I like to sleep in the hammock sometimes. It's one of those nights."

As she walked back towards the house, she looked over her shoulder and whispered, "Good night, Caleb."

Swaying in the hammock, I stared up at the stars, lost in thought. Couldn't stop thinking about that girl, all alone and taking care of herself. I wanted to wrap her up in my arms and tell her not to worry, that I'd take care of her.

I wanted to take care of her.

* * *

RENE

I looked away, stared down into the depths of my coffee mug trying to hide my smile when Caleb opened the screen door and walked in with his dog. Bare-chested, and with his board shorts riding low on his hips, to call him breathtakingly gorgeous wouldn't do him justice. I could have fallen off my stool at the sight of him.

"Good morning, ladies."

I felt uneasy then. Sometimes the light of day could change things, change the way a person feels. He bared his soul to me last night. Would he feel uncomfortable around me today?

Darcy asked, "Windy down there?"

"No, it's beautiful."

She shot me a pleading look. "You have to stay. One more day, Rene, come on."

"I wish I could, but I have class tomorrow morning and then work." *I am dying to stay, dying to have another night swim with you, Caleb.* I looked to my lap, not wanting him to read what was surely written all over my face. "Jenna said we're leaving at around noon."

Caleb was crouched down, setting out water for the dog. "That's unfortunate."

"Tell me about it," Darcy added. She came up behind me and gave me a quick squeeze before heading back over to help Sarah. "This is probably goodbye until next semester."

I nodded, knowing it was. I couldn't take another weekend off this summer to come back, much as I'd love to. "I'm going to miss you." I said that out loud to Darcy, but I was already missing this boy I had no business missing.

When Sarah and Darcy were occupied making breakfast at the stove again, Caleb came up close behind and whispered my name in my ear. When I looked up, he winked at me and then dropped my bikini top into my lap. I had to remind myself to breathe.

He looked drop-dead sinful last night, same as he looked in all those crazy daydreams of mine. It was hard to focus when he looked at me and smiled, hard to fight off the awkward tongue-tied feeling I always seemed to have around him. And the way he spoke to me, the tenderness in his voice, making me laugh when he knew I was uncomfortable? It was all so, oh Lord, I don't even know. What I do know is that I wanted to close the distance between us and will him to wrap his arms around me. Out there in the ocean in the black of night, it's like I was drugged with desire for him.

My head told me I was being ridiculous, that someone like him probably laid that act on every girl he was intent on getting into the sack. But my heart was beating double time, certain that he really did feel something for me. The way he looked at me, it was like he was fighting this war of wanting me while trying to be good or something. I don't think I was imagining it.

And would he say all of those things, be so open with just anyone? It took a lot for me to tell my secrets, no matter how close a person was to me, and what Caleb shared with me last night was deeply personal.

I found myself wanting to console the angry, sad little kid he once was. And I knew the feeling. We were the same age, just seven, even though the circumstances surrounding my mother's death couldn't have been more different.

My mother's overdose, my father's inability to hold down a job and stay sober, the fear, the poverty—my early years read like the most depressing book ever written. If we spent all of last night out in that ocean together, I still wouldn't have shared any of that with Caleb. But then again, what was it about him? What made me share as much as I did about my parents? I was still just about the opposite of an open book, but Caleb made me feel safe. Without even really knowing him, I knew I could trust him.

Chapter Five

RENE

School, work, and then work some more.

The rest of the summer crawled along at a snail's pace. I worked my butt off, and Craig was good to me, scheduling me to work as many shifts as possible. I was always tired and always on the go, but glad for it. I was proud of the nice nest egg I'd accumulated, and working also served the purpose of occupying my mind. When I had time on my hands, it was ridiculous how often I found myself dreaming of Caleb.

So I was glad to haul my stuff back into the dorms that last weekend in August. I was the only one to arrive in a taxi, my three suitcases and a backpack carrying all of my worldly possessions. Girls like me travel light. It used to bother me, but at this point I was pretty good at shaking it off and moving forward. I hardly noticed the other kids, most flanked by two parents, the boxes, rugs and furniture practically spilling out of their gigantic SUVs.

"Need a hand?"

"Thanks, Ryder, but I've got it."

He held the door open for me, taking one of the rolling suitcases and sliding the backpack off my shoulder. "Not taking no for an answer."

Being that I was practically tripping over myself trying to wrangle three rolling suitcases at once, I let him help me. It was the very least the jerk could do. "Thanks."

But when he lingered inside our suite looking like he wanted to have a heart to heart, I cut him off. "All right, I've got it from here. Thanks for the help."

"Rene—"

"How's Devin?"

"Who?" I shot him a look, heavy on the eye roll. "That was a mistake. Dumbest mistake I ever made, and I've been kicking myself for it ever since."

"Is this my long overdue apology?"

He flashed me his signature smile, but it didn't work on me anymore. "I think I've apologized like six times now."

"I don't take you seriously when you're slurring." When he went to speak, I gestured for him to stop. "And it doesn't matter anymore. That was a long time ago."

He looked defeated, and I didn't want that. I didn't care enough about him to make him hurt. "Really, Ryder, it's water under the bridge. I'm fine."

"I am sorry, though…Just want to make sure you know that." When I nodded, he said, "And if you ever change your—"

"I won't."

"Fair enough," he said, backing up before turning to walk out the door.

I thought I was alone until Caitlin popped her head out of one of the bedrooms. "Back on campus for ten minutes and there's already drama!" She flopped onto the couch laughing. "I thought with Darcy gone this was going to be a boring semester."

"I don't plan on providing you with any more entertainment this year."

And I meant it. Junior year was make or break for me. I needed to kick ass in school to maintain my scholarship and work hard at the station to add to my resume.

With so many people taking vacation in August, the station manager recently started giving me the opportunity to write copy for the evening news when he was short-staffed. Hearing the anchors speak the words I'd personally written was such a rush. An internship in New York next summer was the goal, and now it felt like it was within reach.

"Wow, it looks so beautiful over there. Gotta love those European towns that look like they're stuck in a time warp. I love cobblestones, don't you?"

"I haven't gotten a chance to look through Darcy's pictures yet. She's sent over a hundred already."

Caitlin nodded her head. "Means she's homesick for us. I'm going to have to hold back from clocking Nick when I run into him."

"I think she made a wise decision. A change of scenery is good sometimes."

When Caitlin started talking about heading over to Spain to see her at some point, I tuned out. Someday I'll be able to take trips like that without thinking twice, but not now. My life wasn't like Caitlin's or the other girls'. A trip like that would cost me my expenses for the entire semester.

And talk of Darcy made me think of him.

No kisses, no words of devotion, no relationship to speak of, but thinking back to that night on the beach still hurt. It's like he's the only thing that makes sense, the only thing that's ever felt so completely good and right in my life. I had to put it behind me, try to forget, because thinking of him felt good and warm and painful all at once.

* * *

CALEB

There was no anticipation, no excitement. I went down to surf and hang out with friends, but the summer did nothing but drag on after that weekend.

I wouldn't be seeing Rene again unless I reached out to her, and in my heart I knew that wasn't a good idea. She was only nineteen. A year younger than my sister and the rest of the girls thanks to an accelerated program where Rene crammed three years of middle school into two. Darcy dropped that little nugget over dinner one night and I damn near choked. Six years older than her, five years—didn't really matter—but twenty did sound a hell of a lot better to me than any word ending with *teen*.

No, she didn't need me messing with her head. She should be enjoying college and dating guys she went to school with. College was in my rear view mirror. Our lives were different.

Work got busy in September, rugby season started back up, and my days were pretty full. I made my days full. I worked past my normal quitting time, went out more nights than was good for me, and hit the gym like I was on a mission.

I went to the beach one last time in mid-October to close up the house for my parents. I spent the day putting away the outdoor furniture, covering the grill and emptying the fridge. It was an Indian summer kind of day, warm with no wind. I walked down to the beach and sat on the shore while Bosco chased the seagulls. Stayed as the sunset gave way to a full moon. Couldn't help but think back to that night with Rene.

I snapped a picture, and against my better judgment, sent it to her.

A few minutes later she wrote back:

U going in?

I slumped back into the sand, frustrated. I wanted to put it out there, tell her I've been dreaming about being back in the ocean with her damn near every night.

Not without u.

I hit send, regretting it immediately. I shouldn't be doing this, leading her on. But I want, I want...

I'm not an emoji girl, no smiley faces, but want u to know I'm smiling right now.

My fingers were itching to write back something like: *I know you are, baby. Know you want me just as much as I want you.* And I did know, knew she'd give without me having to so much as even ask.

Bosco trotted over and nudged my face with his wet, sandy snout, giving me the wake-up call I sorely needed.

I had to end this ridiculous shit right now, put a stop to it.

Goodnight, Rene :)

Chapter Six

RENE

He's the only person I'd risk sneaking a look at my phone for during class. And my Media Law professor was a total hardass, so texting back while sitting in the second row tells you just how far gone I was for this boy.

That's some cushy job. Hope I get paid to spend my day on the phone sending memes when I graduate.

I nearly busted out laughing when I got another ridiculous one a second later.

I'm in class, ur gonna get me in trouble.

He wrote back right away:

Sorry, sweetness. TTYL.

Caleb changed the rules that night. Once he sent that picture of the ocean, he changed everything.

And that's how we began.

At first it was just texting back and forth, maybe once or twice a week. Most of it was funny flirty nonsense, but as time went on, the banter morphed into something more. One night he asked about my mother, and when I texted back that she died a long time ago, he called and we talked until two that next morning.

I never wanted to be that girl: the latch-key kid, dirt-poor, born to addicts, another motherless child.

My whole life was lived in secret. I spent years pretending to everyone on the outside that everything was fine. I made sure my clothes were clean, that our dilapidated house looked reasonably tidy, and that I had the bare necessities so that I didn't raise suspicions at school. I was always on edge, petrified of being taken away from my father. Not that he was responsible or even remotely attentive, it's just that he's all I knew. And growing up that way made me into a very guarded, secretive person who rarely accepted help, even when I desperately needed it.

Exposing my past was difficult, but as the words flowed it felt as if a giant weight had been lifted off my chest. Caleb listened without judgment whenever I was in the mood to share. And he made me weep when he told me what I already knew but needed to hear: that I wasn't anything like my parents, that I was just a kid and had no control over what had happened back then, and that what I'd done for myself, *by* myself, was amazing. I thought he was amazing too. He was the most kind and caring man I'd ever known.

I knew I was heading for heartache as our texts and phone calls went from sporadic to regular and then daily, but I pushed that fear down. I needed what he was giving me.

Over the course of those long phone calls we became close. Talking into that receiver with his reassuring voice on the other end, I could say out loud everything I'd always kept hidden away. Well, almost everything. Caleb saw me as a friend and nothing more. I'd never let on that I was falling for him, hard.

Merry almost Xmas. What r u doing for holidays?
-Caitlin's. I hate when people ask...makes me feel like a sad little orphan!!!
Three exclamation points...is that equal to one smiley face?
-Ha!
U could come here.
-Wouldn't it b weird with Darcy?
Parents are spending holiday in Spain w/her. And weird? Oh wait...if we were together would u keep me as ur dirty little secret?
-Me? Yeah right. What is it u sang to me the other night...
Hey 19? You'd b keeping me as ur secret.
Never. When r u gonna b 20 anyway?
-Soon.
Wow, u really don't like to part with the personal info.
-Ouch.
Sorry...
-Have a Merry Christmas, Caleb.
U too

Two days later a package arrived for me. It was a beautiful black leather satchel from Hermes that must have cost a fortune. The note read:

For you, Rene
Merry Christmas,
Caleb

He knew I was hoping to land some interviews for the upcoming summer internships. Guess he thought I'd need a power bag.

He answered on the first ring. "Do you like it?"

"I love it, but—"

He cut me off, "But nothing. Stop talking. I saw it and I wanted to get it for you. It'll look great when you go on your interviews. I know you don't like people doing things for you, but just please accept this. Don't make it all complicated and awkward."

I couldn't help but laugh. "Okay. Thank you, Caleb. It really is beautiful."

When I was out the next day shopping for little gifts for my roommates, I saw a bright green scarf with little bottles of chocolate milk on it. It looked Christmas-y and crazy, and reminded me of Caleb's dog, Bosco. Waiting in line at the post office, I sent up a silent prayer that he'd get my little joke and not open the box and be like: *What the hell?*

Instead I got a picture of Bosco with a close up on his leash, matching color and pattern, and my phone rang a few seconds later.

"That's a bizarre coincidence."

He laughed. "Right? I just got this leash for him last week. And you didn't have to get me anything, but thank you, I love it."

The words, they went unsaid but were always on the tip of my tongue: *And I love you, Caleb.*

Chapter Seven

RENE

The call I was waiting on came at the end of January. Just getting a shot at an interview was a huge big deal, but this was with one of the biggest networks. I remember laughing when I hit send on that particular email, telling myself I was sending my resume out into the great abyss, not wanting to get my hopes up.

Flight booked for next Friday? Check. I was flying down, and even decided to splurge on a cab to the network offices so that I wouldn't be frazzled about directions or worried about being late. I could struggle with the subway map on my way back to the airport. I also splurged on a beautiful garnet red dress that looked professional but age appropriate, and a pair of good heels. I had a beautiful bag, thanks to Caleb, and I'd borrow jewelry and a coat from Caitlin's overflowing closet.

I wanted to tell Caleb but decided against it. He was becoming a major distraction, found myself thinking about him nearly every free moment I had. And this? This was everything I'd worked for. I needed to be on my A-game.

Stepping out of the cab in front of the network was surreal. I thought I might be overwhelmed or intimidated, but instead I felt energized, like I belonged. Didn't even fret about the others sitting in the reception area, didn't feel the need to compare myself to them. And being peppered with questions for close to an hour in that panel interview didn't rattle me in the least. I gave myself a mental high-five as I rode back down in the elevator. I demonstrated knowledge, had some solid field-specific experiences that I shared with them, and was able to answer every question that came my way. They wanted more contact information and specifics about my school schedule before they let me go, and I read that as a good sign.

I hesitated for only a split second before reaching for my phone. I knew I rocked that interview, and wanted to share my excitement with the person who was quickly becoming, at the very least, one of my very closest friends.

R u around? I'm in the city.

My phone pinged two seconds later.

NYC?

Try to think of something witty, Rene.

Does Boston qualify as the city?

I got a crying laughing emoji with:

Ha, definitely not. Where r u?

I knew exactly where I was, but still looked up at the street signs to make certain. Nervous much?

Columbus and 66th

Another emoji, this one a surprised face. Never should have told him I hated emojis. Then he wrote:

Whoa, that's big time.

I was smiling, but wanted to scold myself for being so needy, for wanting his approval.

Hope so.

I got nothing for a full thirty seconds, but then:

U like Italian?

He could have asked if I liked chili spiced crickets and I would have happily replied:

Yes and I'm starving.

In more ways than you know, Caleb.

Jump in a cab. Tell driver you're going downtown...corner of 6th ave and Franklin street.

Don't worry about it, this is why you have a credit card. That's what I was telling myself, sweating as the cab sped down West Street, the meter ratcheting up higher and higher every few seconds. I looked away when it hit twenty-two dollars, telling myself I could cram in one extra shift at the restaurant this week if someone needed off.

But all that stress melted away when I spotted him on the corner. Even with that silly green scarf looped around his neck, he looked like he owned this city. The man definitely did a suit proud. Before today, I'd only seen him in jeans, board shorts and, *ahem*, bare-assed.

Of course I snuck a peek that night on the beach.

Caleb opened my door and reached over to pay the cabbie before I could even get my wallet out. When I protested, he waved me off and took my hand to help me out of the car.

Looking me up and down, he shook his head and smiled when he said, "How could anyone in their right mind *not* hire you?"

I was getting used to it, the way he liked to tease, his comments both playful and suggestive. But I still felt a bit young and naïve around him. I wasn't sure I could handle someone like Caleb.

"Hi." It was all I could manage in my current state of fangirl. He leaned in to kiss my cheek, and that alone made me lightheaded. *Get a grip, Beaumont.* "Sorry to be so last minute."

"Yeah, why didn't you tell me you were coming?"

"I don't know. I guess I just wanted to stay focused on what I was here for."

He raised his eyebrows. "Are you saying that thinking of me distracts you from all sorts of important things? I like that."

"You have an over-abundance of confidence. It's irritating."

"Ha."

The hostess, who looked like she'd just walked off the runway herself, stared into Caleb's eyes like she was telepathically willing him to do her when he went up to give his name. And when she looked my way, her smile told me that being on this guy's arm automatically granted you approval from everyone. We were seated right away, even though there were a few groups waiting.

"Do you always get bumped to the front of the line?"

"Not if it's a man hosting, uh, unless he's gay, then it's a yes." I rolled my eyes and he poked me in the side. "I called ahead for a reservation, Beaumont."

Caleb didn't take anything too seriously, especially himself. That was just one in a very long list of things that made me crazy about him.

He was genuinely interested when he asked about my interview, and agreed that the way it ended seemed promising. We sat there for an hour, just drinking wine and talking before we even ordered. The conversation moved on to his job, and I found myself wanting to know everything about what he did. I mean, he could have been talking about his most recent dental appointment and I would have been hanging on his every word with rapt attention. I wanted to soak in anything and everything where he was concerned.

He waved me off when the food was set before us. "Enough shop talk. Let's get personal. Tell me about your old boyfriends."

I practically choked when I laughed. "How much wine have you had?"

"Not much. I'm just curious about you, Rene. I want to know how many hearts you've broken."

"Hate to disappoint, but I don't have a long and lengthy resume in that department like you do."

"Ouch."

"Sad but true. I was too concerned with making it through the day-to-day in high school to date anyone. Freshman year I dated a nice guy who had to leave after first semester when he lost his scholarship. Sophomore year I dated a football player who turned out to be a jerk." I shrugged my shoulders. "That's all, folks."

"How was he a jerk?"

"I didn't put out fast enough so he cheated on me."

He nodded. "Us guys are dicks."

"Can be."

His eyes widened. "Wait. So does that mean what I think it does?"

A big freaking grin spread across his face as mine turned purple.

"I'm not answering you."

He laughed, and I'm talking big, bellowing laughs. "Holy crap, Beaumont. I'm not making fun, I'm just surprised."

"Really? When someone laughs at me I tend to think I'm being made fun of. Do you know how awful it is? When a guy finds out, it's unbearable. He either thinks I'm like the Madonna, too pure to touch, or he's hell bent on changing my status. Wish I'd just gotten it over with in high school like everyone else."

"Not everyone got it over with in high school."

"Nice try, Casanova."

He straightened up. "Hey, I'm offended!"

Rolling my eyes, I challenged, "You were a virgin in college?"

"Damn straight I was...for the first week." He started to laugh when I gave his shin a gentle kick under the table, but then stopped and took my hands in his. "Yeah, crossing that bridge earlier probably would have made your life less complicated, but for what it's worth, I think it makes you special."

I couldn't meet his eyes. "Ohmigod, I feel like crawling under a rock right now."

He gently coaxed my chin up with one finger. "Hey, don't get all embarrassed on me. Now it's your turn. You can ask me anything you want to know. Fair is fair."

"I think the last shuttle leaves at eleven tonight. I don't think you have enough time to recount your dating history."

He gave me his best smug, conceited face. "You're probably right."

I threw my napkin at him. "Moron."

He covered his face defensively before he teased back, "Prude."

I couldn't help but smile. He was a friend, a true friend. But he was so much more than that. He was the man I wanted, and I wanted him to love me.

"I hate to break it to you, but it's already nine-thirty. If we hustle to the airport, you might make the last shuttle but you might not. I don't want to sound like a creep, but my apartment is just a few blocks from here. Stay with me tonight and you can head back tomorrow." He cocked his head to the side and shot me a teasing smile. "And before you think this is part of some nefarious plan to change your status, I have an extra room. You can stay in there if you're feeling Madonna-ish."

"Ok."

"Wow, I think you're getting easy in your old age. Thought I was going to have to plead with you for the next hour."

"Shut it before I change my mind."

Chapter Eight

CALEB

Never before in my life.

I've never felt this way, so hopped up on adrenaline and a mash of other hormones I attributed to happiness. The reaction I had whenever Rene was nearby was something entirely new to me. Felt it that night last summer, but taking her in as she stepped out of the cab today, I was overwhelmed for a moment there.

Jesus, that red dress.

She looked beautiful, polished and professional. Had an air of confidence about her, like she belonged. Not that it was missing before, but today when I took her in, dressed like she owned Manhattan, she captivated me.

And those three hours spent talking over dinner, with not so much as one awkward lull in the conversation, eased any concerns I still had where she was concerned.

I paused with my finger over the phone earlier, unsure if I should meet up with her, see her in person again. Our late night phone calls, the texts we shot back and forth everyday? They were perfect, meant more to me than I can put into words. I didn't want to jeopardize what we had.

Then I went and asked her to stay over. Swatted her hand away and told her I'd rather cut my dick off than have her pay for dinner—that's how impatient I was to get out of that restaurant. But I was nervous. That little nugget she let slip during dinner did make things a tad more complicated. I couldn't be her first, didn't deserve to be. But to finally have her here, so close to me and not touch her? I'd never wanted anyone more.

I opened another bottle of wine, talking myself down as I poured her a glass that had no more than two or three sips worth: *Not gonna happen, not gonna happen, not gonna happen.*

"Here you go, nineteen."

She cocked her head to the side as she took the glass. "You can't call me that anymore, Caleb."

"Really?"

"January tenth. I'm officially twenty."

"Why didn't you tell me? I didn't even get to wish you a happy birthday."

"I was afraid you'd shower me with another ridiculously extravagant gift."

"I would have and I still might."

"Don't! I'm warning you, it took a lot for me to accept that bag graciously." She kicked off her shoes and tucked her feet underneath her on the couch. "You can give me a birthday kiss, though. That, I will accept."

I let out a deep breath. "If I kiss you once I'll never want to stop."

She smiled at me, the sweetest, most trusting smile. I knew deep in my soul I'd never intentionally hurt her, but I didn't have a great track record. I was upfront, honest, and always treated women with respect, but I was typically the one who ended things. I reminded myself sadly that I was friends with very few of the women I'd been involved with, and a few straight-up despised me.

It was that same old push and pull—I wanted Rene but I knew having her would be no different than taking her, taking what I wanted. But who was I kidding? I was selfish when it came to her. If she was willing to give then I'd take and I'd take and I'd take.

Gently, I pulled her up to stand in front of me. My hands found both sides of her face and I kissed her. Her lips were soft and she tasted sweet, just like I'd imagined. I felt like I was holding onto a porcelain doll because God, the last thing I wanted to do was break her.

When I stopped a minute later and rested my forehead against hers, she murmured, "Please don't stop."

She laced her fingers through my hair and gently pulled my mouth back to hers. I let out a groan from the pleasure of feeling her body pressed up against mine, then felt her smile underneath my kiss.

Laying kisses along her neck, I whispered, "It's funny, huh, torturing me?"

"I don't want to torture you, Caleb, I just want you."

I pulled back and looked into her eyes. "I don't think I can be your first."

Annoyed and really cute, she practically stomped her foot when she said, "This is exactly what I mean! Do you understand how frustrating this is for me?"

I couldn't help but laugh a little. "It does make you...I don't know, Rene, like, am I worthy?"

She shrugged. "Okay, the next random guy who comes my way will just have to be the one I use to get it over with."

I gripped her arms. "No fucking way, Beaumont. You hear me?"

She smiled up at me, knowing she'd won. "Then please, Caleb."

Shit, this was torture. "I don't want you to wind up hating me."

"I doubt that could ever happen."

"I have a few exes who would tell you different."

"That's not hatred. That's longing, disappointment, just wanting more than you were willing to give them. Face it, you're a catch." She smiled. "You are, and it's not just the good looks and success. Well, the success part I'm not even certain about. You could be some well-dressed office gopher for all I know." When I laughed, her look turned tender, maybe a little sad. "It's just that you're a good man." She looked away, suddenly shy. "You're so good to me."

I shook my head. "You make me want to be a better man. I feel like I want certain things with you and I don't know what to make of it."

She put her hands on my shoulders, hopeful and expectant. *Forgive me*, I pled in silence, pulling her in and kissing her deep. I could feel nearly every inch of her pressed up against me, her soft and willing body a refuge for what's always been hard and isolated in me.

We stayed like that for the longest time, just kissing, and in that moment I decided kissing was wildly underrated. God, kissing Rene —I was drunk off the taste of her mouth and her skin. I nipped below her ear and trailed kisses along her neck, down along her collarbone and along the swell of her cleavage. Desire taking over, my hands skimmed up along her sides as my lips nudged their way down and into the neckline of her dress. I wanted her more than I wanted my next breath, but willed myself to stop when she let out a whimper. I reminded myself that I couldn't go too fast or too far, that I had to be ready to put on the brakes, even if it killed me. But what I saw in her eyes told me she wanted this just as much as I did.

"Can I take you to my room?"

She nodded, her eyes heady with lust. "Yes, Caleb."

My name on her lips made my chest feel light. I scooped her up, carried her upstairs, laid this treasure onto my bed and then stood above her, taking her in.

"God, you're so beautiful."

"You make me feel beautiful when you look at me."

She nodded when I gestured to the zipper along the side of her dress. "Stop me, I mean it. We don't have to do anything. If I just get to hold you tonight I'm more than good with that."

Rene blushed and looked away as she moved to slip out of her dress, and my fingers fumbled as I unbuttoned my shirt and undid my belt. Covering her body with mine, I kissed her sweet mouth again, and as I ran my hands over the curve of her hips, she let out a sigh that had me hardening to steel.

This was happening.

She was on my lap then, as naked as she was that night in the ocean, straddling me as I ran my hands over any part of her I could touch. And she was killing me, rocking her hips against my length, pushing me, but there was no way in hell I was rushing this.

It felt different this time, like I was committing myself to her through this act. I wanted her to know, but how could I say that out loud? All I did manage to say was that she was special to me, and that wasn't even the half of it. I'd shared more of myself with Rene over those late night phone calls than I had with anyone else. At some point she'd become everything to me.

Rolling on the condom, I gave one more check to make sure she was with me. "Are you sure? Tell me to stop now."

"I want it to be you. I'm sure."

Eased into her slowly, little by little, watching her head tilt back as she took me in. Bit my lip and shuddered, using every bit of restraint I had in me. "Tell me if I'm hurting you."

Rene shook her head from side to side as she gently nudged my ass with her feet. "No...I want all of you."

Her hips rocked against mine, fucking me so good, and I moved to match her. Her body felt incredible, being inside of her felt incredible. I was outside of myself, loving every fucking second of this, pushing into her again and again, unable to hold back anymore.

What had just happened to me?

* * *

RENE

I couldn't read his expression afterwards, just knew I was in a state of complete and utter bliss. He held me close but stayed quiet, his gaze fixed straight ahead. It felt peaceful at first, but after a minute the silence felt weird and anxiety crept in.

Please, please don't regret this.

"Caleb?"

He seemed to snap out of it then and looked to me with concern. "Are you all right? You feel ok?"

"I feel more than ok. I feel...That was just—"

I was so flustered that I had to look away. He took my chin and gently turned me back to face him. "Thank you for trusting me. That was so good. You were...perfect."

The way he looked at me? He made me feel like a woman, a beautiful woman. I had to stop myself from getting all emotional, but I really wanted to let go, to weep in his arms. I felt...loved.

"Come with me, sweet angel."

He led me into the bathroom and turned on the shower. Caleb washed me, and it was the most sensual experience of my life. He stood behind me and lathered my hair. I could feel his body pressing against my back as he ran the soap and a soft cloth down my arms, over my breasts, and then up the length of my legs. He took care as he ran the washcloth there, whispering in my ear, "I hope you're not sore later on."

I backed up just the slightest bit and felt him harden against me. I probably was going to be sore, but I didn't really care. I wanted him now, tomorrow, always.

He wrapped me in a fluffy towel before leading me back to bed. This was another first, sleeping naked with a man, but I wasn't self-conscious, didn't want to cover up and hide. I just wanted his body pressed up against mine with his arms around me, and that's exactly how I fell into the most restful sleep of my life.

. . .

Drowsy and dreamy, I smiled when I felt a hand moving across my abdomen and then lower. I scooted back, nudging my ass closer to Caleb, and he groaned with pleasure as his fingers circled me then entered. Against my lower back I could feel him, hard and insistent, and I wanted him.

"Damn, Rene." The words were hazy and muttered as I guided him into me. And when he began to move, thrusting into me over and over again, filling me, it didn't sting like it had before. It felt so good. He was awake now, digging his hands into my hips, pulling me closer, hitting me deeper. "Fucking love you," he murmured into my hair as he came.

Love you? Maybe he's not awake.

Those words, along with the sensation of his warm release trickling down my thigh stunned me. "I'm not on anything."

He pulled out like I'd just told him the building was on fire. "Shit, I'm sorry. That won't ever happen again."

I felt simple and childlike in that ruined moment, cursing myself. Every other woman who'd been in this bed before me no doubt came prepared and protected.

Caleb turned me so that I was facing him. He took me in with concern, but then smiled and laughed a split-second later, probably to counter the look on my face. "I've never done that, never had unprotected sex in my life. I was asleep at the beginning and thought I was having the best dream." When he succeeded in making me smile, he kept at it. "I had this brunette in my bed," he peppered me with kisses between words, "and she was so hot." He was moving down my body, placing kisses on my jaw, neck, breasts, and then my belly. "I couldn't keep my hands off her." When he came back up, he held my gaze for a long moment and then kissed my lips tenderly. "How am I going to let you leave me?"

I couldn't possibly be the one he wanted. My smile felt forced and weak when I said, "I'm sure you'll have someone else to entertain you soon enough."

Caleb pulled back, his expression pained. "Don't do that."

"What?"

"Don't go thinking you wanted this more than I did. You don't know how many times I've imagined us together. I can hardly believe that you're really here with me." I heard him open the nightstand drawer and rip open another condom. He moved his body over mine again, supporting his weight on his forearms when he asked, "Can I have you again?"

"I want you, so badly."

As he entered me, he whispered, "It's more than that. I need you, Rene."

"Can you take off tonight and stay with me until tomorrow?"

I threw my head back in frustration. "Can't, duty calls. Believe me, I'd love to stay."

Love to stay? Scratch that. What I wanted was a time machine. I wanted to fast-forward two years. I wanted to be rocking my new job, strutting down the streets of Manhattan, dressed to kill as I met my ridiculously gorgeous man for cocktails and dinner after work before falling into his bed like some cross between a supermodel and a power broker. Yup, yup, yup. All that and more, but I wasn't there yet. I had a plan and I had to keep plugging along. Part of that, unfortunately, was waitressing nearly every night so that I could sock away as much money as possible.

"It's one o'clock already. I have to go."

"I know. Just being selfish. I'd like to lie in bed with you for the next few hours and then take you out to a great dinner." Skimming a hand up my side and then cupping my breast, he whispered, "Some wine, a little tiramisu…Mmm, doesn't that sound nice?"

I hit him with a pillow. "Stop, you're torturing me!"

"I know you have to go, but I figured I'd give it a try. I won't tease you anymore. I've already called a car. It'll be here in half an hour."

"You didn't have to do that."

"You're going to have to get used to me doing things for you. I get you, Rene. I know you're used to doing everything on your own, and I respect you for it. But you have to let me take care of you, just a little bit."

"Take care of me?"

He shook his head. "That didn't come out right." After a quick pause he said, "Like today, Mick borrowed my car for the weekend. The thought of you on the subway heading back to the airport would drive me insane. So if I want to call you a car, you have to let me."

"Well," I teased, "I don't want to make you go insane."

He was grinning from ear to ear as he grabbed me and held me close. He nestled into me and whispered, "I want to remember how you smell, so goddamn sweet, and how you feel against me. These next two weeks are going to be hell."

"Two weeks?"

"I'll be in Boston in two weeks for a friend's wedding and I'm hoping you'll be my date." He gave me a pleading look that I'm sure no woman had the strength to deny. "Tell me you'll come with me." I was stunned, not to mention apprehensive, and I'm sure it showed on my face. "It won't be awful, I promise. My friends are great."

"No, it's not that. I'm just surprised. You want to be out there about everything, just like that?"

"I don't do secrets."

Ouch. I lived my whole life wrapped in secrets. He knew it and was giving me a subtle dig. I took a deep breath. "Is it okay with you if I'm not ready to be all out in the open with my friends? I don't want to yet."

He hugged me. "Yeah it is, no pressure. But will you take off from work and come with me?"

"Sure. A Valentine's Day wedding?"

"Not too original, huh?"

"I think it's romantic. Who's getting married?"

"My friend Mark. I don't know the girl. A lot of my friends from college will be there, and I want you to meet them. They'll be shocked I'm bringing a date."

"Why, you usually go stag so you can troll for desperate females?"

He laughed and pinched my hip. "Something like that."

I'm sure my fellow passengers thought I was seriously deranged on the plane ride home. My cheeks just about ached from the smile stretched clear across my face.

I felt as if my heart would overflow, as if bright, vivid colors were bursting inside of me. I felt alive.

Love was amazing.

I was in love with Caleb. I knew it before last night, but I was overwhelmed by the realization of it now. I loved him for all the nights we talked on the phone, talking me through things that were so hard to share. I loved him for the way he looked at me, like I was precious and worthy of his care and affection. I loved every side of him—angry boy, capable man, caring lover. I knew what I felt was love.

My head shook from side to side with that silly smile firmly affixed as his sleepy words replayed in my mind.

Fucking love you.

I most certainly fucking love you, too, I thought on a laugh.

Yes, the middle-aged couple seated next to me thought I was certifiable by the time we touched down at Logan.

Caitlin was going to be the one person I trusted with this. She'd been blowing up my phone ever since I'd texted last night to let her know I was staying in New York. I called her as soon as I landed.

"Hey, I just got off the plane. I'll be there in an hour."

"I'm not waiting an hour. Who were you with? I was going crazy last night and I had to cover for you with the girls."

"Thanks, Caitlin. And I'm sorry, I didn't want to worry you. I was fine. I was with, uh, Caleb Donovan."

"Holy shit! How did that happen?"

"I'll fill you in on everything as soon as I get home."

"No!"

"I'm hanging up now."

Caitlin was on my bed waiting when I walked in, and I told her almost everything. It was unlike me to have held out on her for this long.

She was, from the first day I met her freshman year, a kindred spirit. Our lives and our circumstances could not have been more disparate, but she and I just clicked. Within a few weeks she knew some specifics—enough to know I'd led a ridiculously appalling life —and she didn't think any less of me. In turn, she let me in on the joys and pitfalls of abundant wealth. The one thing we had in common was surviving as children of addicts. For all of the homes, trips, clothes, cars and whatever else she had at her disposal, Caitlin had suffered in her own way, just like me. We had similar battle scars and would laugh when we spied the other one cleaning obsessively or planning out minute details—feeble attempts to keep order and to keep up appearances. She was the sister I never had growing up, but so wished for.

The other girls knew the basics. Knew that I didn't have family to speak of and had no one to depend on, but that's all. I preferred it that way. I didn't want to revisit those days, and I definitely didn't want anyone's pity.

"Wow. I totally thought he was great when I met him, but he sounds like a prince. You deserve him, so don't fuck it up."

"Thanks for the vote of confidence."

Caitlin rolled her eyes. "C'mon, we both know how you are. I just meant to say don't push him away. Let yourself enjoy it."

"I will, I promise. Oh, do you mind if I go shopping in your closet? I need a dress. He's taking me to a friend's wedding."

"He's already looking to introduce you to his friends? Ohmigod, it sounds like he wants something serious, bitch!"

"I can't think like that. He's just so good, so perfect. I can't...I can't fall for him and then get hurt. God, I can already imagine just how badly it's going to hurt."

"You've already fallen for him, and he's probably thinking the same exact thing about you. You're gorgeous, smart, and an all-around badass. *You* are the one who's a catch here."

"Thanks for the pep talk. I just don't want to set myself up for a big let down. And Caitlin, for now this is just between you and me, all right?"

"I won't say a word. Yeah, the whole Darcy thing could be weird."

Could be weird? I was thinking it could be disastrous.

Chapter Nine

RENE

Valentino, Gaultier or Balenciaga? Decisions, decisions.

I went with a scarlet red beaded dress from Caitlin's closet—never worn, no surprise. Then I splurged on a beautiful pair of strappy heels that made my legs look a mile long.

Seeing him again, it's all I could think about.

I was on edge, nervous that it was nothing more than a dream, or that I'd imagined it all to mean more than it was. But then he'd call, and every conversation was easy and effortless, as if I'd known him forever. And before hanging up, he always said the same thing: *I can't wait to see you.*

I was in heaven.

* * *

CALEB

Pulling into the campus lot, I had to admit I was relieved she wasn't telling her friends about us. I was even thankful for my sister's last minute decision to spend the entire year abroad.

Just being on a college campus at my age? I mean, there was no way I was going to be visiting Rene here, going to keg parties or crashing in her dorm.

But all that internal chatter stopped once I spotted her walking towards my car, her eyes bright and smiling. I jumped out to get her door and take her bag, then couldn't help but grab her in my arms and lift her up to kiss her. "I've missed you."

My girl wasn't timid. On a breathy exhale, she said, "I've been thinking about you every minute. Do we have some time before the wedding? I really want to be with you."

So I happily spent the next two hours loving Rene, and she looked dreamy curled up in the sheets after.

"You look happy."

She flashed me a wicked grin. "Guess I didn't know what I'd been missing out on all this time."

I laughed but it faded quickly. "It doesn't feel like this with everyone. Let's just say, wedding or no wedding, I was driving up this weekend. I felt like I had to see you or I'd die."

"Are you telling me I've already had the best, so there's no need to sample what else is out there?"

I slapped her backside, making her laugh and yelp at the same time. "Yes, sweet Rene, that's exactly what I'm saying."

Heads definitely turned when we walked into the room. "Men notice you, you know that?"

She gave me a gentle hip check. "And women notice you, but you're already well aware of that, aren't you?"

Rene had an easy way about her. I was afraid she'd be uncomfortable but it was the opposite—the girl owned every room she entered. It was a relief to see her among my friends. The guys obviously thought she was great, but I also saw her laughing with Chloe and a few of the other girls, right there in the mix. She belonged here, with me.

"She's terrific, and I get the feeling this isn't a passing thing."

"I'm kind of crazy about her, Chloe."

"Where did you meet?"

"Don't judge me."

"Never."

"She's a friend of Darcy's"

"Oh."

"Yeah, she just turned twenty. Be honest, tell me if you think that's awful."

"No. I mean, you'll be twenty-six this summer? Six years, but it's not like she's sixteen and you're twenty-two. That would be creepy."

I nearly coughed up my beer. "You think?"

"You know what I mean. Seriously, all that matters is that you make one another happy. You seem happy, Caleb."

"I am."

* * *

RENE

"That girl looks like she's twelve."

Giggling, the other one said, "Come on, she looks like she's at least eighteen."

I decided to stay in the stall for a bit. Odds were good that I was the subject of this conversation.

"I feel like telling the bartender to card her. Typical Caleb."

Chloe must have come out of another stall. "Now now, Dani, be nice."

"Who is she, Chloe?"

"Caleb's girlfriend. I think she's great. She's smart, she's nice, and it looks like she makes him really happy."

I knew there was a reason I'd clicked with that girl immediately.

"Right. More like she's his little fuck buddy of the month. She just hasn't caught onto his act yet. Marty told me she's a junior in college. Is that true?"

"I don't know."

"He's going younger and younger. He just wants someone who won't place any demands on him."

"Well, he seems really into her."

"Puh-lease. If I wanted to, I could lure him into the coat check room for a quickie right now. Caleb only cares about himself."

Chloe shot back, "I guess I just don't get it, Danielle. What's he ever done to you? You two didn't end on a bad note. Why so bitter?"

"Bitter? I could care less."

I waited until they all left before I came out. When I did, I saw Caleb standing with two very pretty girls flanking him, both of them flirting heavily. Caleb spotted me then gave me a pointed look that told me he was looking for a save. Reaching his hand out to mine, he gestured with his head to each one of them. "Rene, this is Danielle and Melody. We went to school together."

"Nice to meet you."

Her smile was more like a sneer. "Great dress, Rene. So what do you do for a living?"

I felt like telling this witch it was no wonder Caleb dumped her.

"I'm still in school and I work part-time at WGB-TV."

She slapped Caleb's forearm. "Still in school?" Eyes wide, she looked to him and teased, "You're robbing the cradle nowadays?"

Both girls laughed, discounting me as if I wasn't even there. They were just rude, plain and simple.

"What can I tell you, love knows no age. Later, ladies," he said, walking off with me. "Ready for that dance, baby?"

"Absolutely."

Those two stupid cows had their eyes on us the entire time we danced. And they got an eyeful because dancing with Caleb was like sex with Caleb—he held you close and made your body feel incredible. I could tell that one, Danielle, was green with jealousy.

"So, Danielle...I'm guessing she's one of your angry exes?"

He laughed as he pressed in closer, staring down at my cleavage with the eyes of a hungry wolf. "I wouldn't call her an ex. They have to get past one month to be considered an ex." He leaned in even closer so that his lips grazed my ear. "She doesn't like you. She's like the wicked witch and you're young, sexy Snow White."

"And you're the handsome prince."

"*Your* handsome prince."

I sulked walking the short distance from Caleb's car to my dorm the next morning. Couldn't help but feel like Cinderella doing the walk of shame—glass slipper lost, flat hair, no makeup, dress hanging over my arm. If I had a carriage, it would be no more than a ratty old pumpkin now.

Guess you could say I was throwing myself a pity party.

Beth, Jenna and Caitlin were flopped on the couches. Despite being bummed about my dream weekend coming to an end, I must have still looked like I was in fairytale land, the memories of last night with Caleb still fresh in my head.

Jenna crossed her arms like a federal prosecutor. "All right, Rene. Where were you and who were you with? You look like the happiest girl on the planet."

Nope, nope, nope.

I could just picture Jenna jumping up off the couch and bolting upstairs—she'd be on the phone with Darcy in a hot minute. But I had to tell them something. I wasn't going to lie, but I wasn't going to come clean either.

"I was on a date. And I…I really like him. He doesn't go to school with us. He's older than me, and I, um, don't want to talk about it yet."

Caitlin spoke up first so they'd back off. "No pressure. We're just glad you're finally having some fun." And then a topic change—the girl was a master. "Please tell me you're off tonight. Dan and the guys are having a party."

"Sunday night party?"

Jenna shrugged. "Why not?"

"Sure. I'm working, but I'll be done by ten. I'll be there, just late."

I'd definitely lucked out in the friends department. I'm sure Beth and Jenna were curious, but they wouldn't push me. They knew I was a private person and they didn't hound me for details like most other girls would have. Even though it was the last place I wanted to be, I'd have to make a cameo at Dan's party tonight just to make an effort for the girls.

I was wiped out by ten o'clock, as I'd hardly slept the night before with Caleb, and the restaurant was fairly busy tonight. It was ten-thirty before I made it back to campus, and the party was in full swing.

I got a text from Caleb as I was walking in. When I told him where I was, he wrote:

Crap, now I have to think about some horny college guys ogling you.

-Yes, I hope ur jealous.

Don't do that to me. I might just have to drive back up there, throw u over my shoulder and spank u.

-Ooh la la.

Getting in my car.

-Haha. G'night. Miss u already.

Miss u too. Have fun.

A shadow fell over me. "Who's Caleb?"

It was Chris looking over my shoulder. "Holy crap! Since when are you so nosy?"

He laughed and put his hands up in defense. "Sorry, I just saw the name flash on your screen. I wasn't trying to be nosy."

I looked around to make sure no one else had heard, then looked back at Chris, at his hurt expression. Chris was like a brother to me. I wanted to tell him—wanted to shout it out at the top of my lungs I was so damn happy—but I couldn't. Not yet.

"Sorry I barked at you. He's a really nice guy but I want to keep this to myself. The girls don't even know about him."

"So he doesn't go here?"

"No."

"Promise he's a good guy?"

"Yes, a really good guy."

He kissed my forehead. "Good. You deserve it, Rene."

Chris didn't know everything about me, but he knew enough and he was perceptive. Freshman year he'd made a half-hearted play for me after Caitlin left him in the dust, but we both knew that wasn't happening. I knew he still had a thing for her. Why Caitlin didn't go for him, I couldn't figure. Chris was handsome, athletic, smart, and an all-around awesome person. Caitlin had a relaxed philosophy about sex, and she liked to sample the goods. She didn't seem interested in the committed, all-in kind of relationship that Chris would want and expect. They were friends, but you could sometimes cut the tension between them with a knife.

I'm glad I went to the party even though I had Caleb on the brain. Hanging out with the girls was always fun, and Dan's friends were some of my closest friends too. I snuck out with Beth at around midnight, going back to eat ice cream on the couch and stay up talking.

Beth had the bright idea to call Darcy, now that it was early morning in Spain. I felt dishonest, especially when Beth drunkenly told Darcy I was seeing a "mystery man."

"It's not as dramatic as Beth makes it sound. Just a nice guy. He's a little older and it's very, very new. That's why I'm not spilling."

She laughed and then said something in Spanish. When I asked for a translation, she said, "I said good for you, you sexy senorita. I hope he has a giant cock!"

I thought I was going to choke. Darcy and Beth were both cracking up as I sat there, speechless. Oh, if you could only speak the truth. I'd come back with something like: *Yes, he sure does, your brother has a giant one.* Yeah, this could get very weird.

In an effort to change the subject, I told Darcy about the somewhat odd, clingy little freshman who seemed to be following Nick around like a puppy at the party all night. She was relieved. "Good. I'm glad he's hopelessly devoted to someone else."

When Darcy asked about my interview, I felt awkward and suffocated again. After I told her the interview had gone as well as it possibly could have, she said, "I know you're going to get it, Rene. I just wish I could be in New York with you this summer. Hey, I'll make sure my brother Caleb shows you around and looks out for you."

"No!" I probably yelled that a little too emphatically. "I mean, I haven't even gotten an offer yet, Darcy. And Jesus, I'm from Jersey, it's not like I don't know my way around New York City!"

"Calm down, girl. Fine, heaven forbid I do anything for you. But you *are* going to get the job. I have absolutely no doubt about it."

She was so freaking sweet and supportive. Must be a family trait.

"Thanks. I miss you, you know."

"I miss you too. I miss all of you so much. Next year is going to be awesome."

Next year.

I hope you're still talking to me next year when you find out I'm sleeping with your brother.

I hope I'm still sleeping with your brother next year.

Good grief, I needed sleep.

Chapter Ten

CALEB

Couldn't go an entire day without speaking to Rene. This, all of it, was a totally new experience for me. My head was definitely in it at work, but she was on my mind, a lot. I wanted to hop in my car and head up there that next weekend, but Rene was scheduled to work and I had to respect that. Told her two weeks was my limit, though.

So when Mick asked me to take a quick flight down to Rincon for the weekend, I jumped at it. I love New York but it sucks in February. We flew down Thursday night and were on the beach by daybreak Friday morning. There were few things I enjoyed more than sitting on my board in the warm surf, but while taking in my surroundings on that particular day, Rene was foremost on my mind. I couldn't wait to sneak her down here for a weekend.

"Why are you sitting there looking like you just hit the lottery or something?"

"No reason, Mick, just happy."

"Happy to be seeing Elena? Damn, I knew I was going to be flying solo this weekend."

"No, there will be no more hooking up with Elena."

"Really? What's up?"

"Remember that girl Rene I introduced you to this summer on the beach?"

He smirked when he asked, "Darcy's little friend?"

"Don't be a dick, she's twenty."

Mick laughed. "I'm just fucking with you. So how long has this been going on?"

"Couple of weeks. I really like her. She's different."

"Happy for you. Does Darcy know?"

"No. I introduced her to a bunch of people at Mark's wedding last week, but she doesn't feel comfortable with Darcy or her other roommates knowing anything yet. Since Darcy isn't around, I don't think it's a big deal."

Mick nodded. "Gotcha. Darcy would be ok with it, though."

"I know she would. The only thing is that Rene *is* still in college. Our lives are more than a little different, you know?"

"Absolutely. But I remember you saying something about her working a lot, right? Doesn't sound like she's a party-girl type. Sounds like she's a bit more grown up than most girls her age."

"She definitely is. I just don't want her to miss out on anything because she's with me."

"Don't worry so much. Just enjoy things while they last."

"Yeah, enjoy it while it lasts," I repeated.

But I wanted way more than that.

Mick and I had a few beers at the beachside bar close to our rental. I knew I'd probably run into Elena there, as her parents owned the place, and I was hoping to see her so that I could set things straight. The last two times I'd been with Elena she wasn't pushing, but she made comments here and there about how bored she was living on the island year-round, how she was more of a big city person, New

York was where all the opportunities were in her field. Elena was fishing, and she wasn't about to hook me.

I saw her mother first. I waved, and as usual, she scowled back at me. The woman did not like me. I was Elena's piece on the side. Elena had a serious boyfriend in San Juan, successful by her parents' standards. Her mother knew she ran off with me whenever I was in town, and was worried her daughter was in danger of blowing a perfectly good marriage prospect.

Twenty minutes later Elena sauntered in. Her accent and her badass attitude drew me in when we first met, and she was the personification of hot—a sensual beauty with flawless skin, light eyes and a mischievous smile. But smiling to myself as I watched her now, I realized she just didn't do it for me anymore.

Elena was scanning the crowd like a predator as she made her way out onto the deck, hips swaying, her long hair worn up to expose her neck—the way she knew I liked it best.

When she spotted me she came over and sat down close, her thigh touching mine. "Why didn't you tell me you were coming, papacito? I wish I'd known." She pouted her lips and knocked her knee against mine, hard. "I'm leaving in the morning."

"Where you heading?"

She rolled her eyes. "Diego's family is having a party. I have to be in San Juan tomorrow."

"Maybe he'll propose."

She cocked her head to the side and narrowed her eyes. "Would that make you happy or sad?"

"Elena, what makes you happy is all that matters. I'm with someone else now, too. It's just better if we don't see each other anymore."

She shrugged. "You're seeing someone, I'm seeing someone. That's never stopped us from fucking before. What's different?"

"She's different."

"Oh."

Elena had a hard edge. There was no telling me she was happy for me, no wishing me well. No, she looked like a venomous snake in position to strike. As she got up to leave, she turned and said, "Don't be bringing your little mamabicho around here, ok?"

Mick's Spanish was better than mine, so he and several other patrons were now having a good laugh at my expense. After she left, I looked that one up on my phone and had to laugh myself. No, I definitely wouldn't be bringing Rene here.

* * *

RENE

"What do you mean I can't come up? I don't care if I just get to see you in between shifts. I told you two weeks was my limit."

Can your heart actually take flight? I'd never known this kind of happiness.

He *had* to see me.

He *needed* me.

"I'm coming to you, Caleb. The network called and I'm going in for a second interview! I'm up for one of the few paid summer internship positions. The person I spoke to said I had more experience than most of the other candidates. They're considering me for a spot doing, you know, nothing glamorous, just production assistant-type work on the morning news hour with Glenn Bennett. It's a political current events show that airs at nine every morning."

"I know the show. I don't watch it but I've seen the promos. That's so great, Rene! I knew you'd made a good impression on them."

"I'm a nervous wreck. I have to meet with Bennett on Monday at eleven after he finishes taping. I was thinking of coming down on Saturday if that works for you. If not, don't worry, I can fly down early Monday morning."

"You're absolutely staying with me. So I get you all day Saturday *and* Sunday?"

He wants me.

I had to collect my spinning thoughts before I answered, "Yes, we've got all weekend together, but Sunday night I have to get a good night's sleep. No keeping me up, ok?"

"No problem. I'll have had my fill of you by then."

"If I was there I'd smack you!"

"If you were here I'd spank you."

Caleb was at the airport waiting for me. I could so get used to this. He smiled when he spotted me, grabbed my bag and then used his free arm to pull me in for a tight hug. He looked and smelled like heaven.

He did his version of taking care of me that weekend, and I let him without making a fuss. We had dinner Saturday night in a cozy little tapas place near his apartment, and then Sunday we walked around Soho, had a late breakfast and then shopped a little.

I picked up a dress that I thought would be better than the one I'd packed for my interview. For a split second Caleb looked as if he was going to try and pay for it, but then slipped his wallet back into his pocket without saying a word. I was glad for it. I certainly wasn't looking to have our first fight and ruin the mood, and I knew his intentions were good, but I was no one's charity case.

Later that night I laid next to him, naked but warm against him as he slept. I was envisioning how good my life could be with Caleb. He knew I needed my independence but made me feel good when he took care of me. He knew nearly everything about my past but didn't make me feel ashamed or less-than. He knew my bad habits, my tendency to pull away and shut people out, and wouldn't let me get away with it.

That next morning he kissed me before he left for his office at half-past six. It was a familiar kiss, sweet more than passionate. I didn't want to make too much of it, but it was meaningful to me. It was a kiss that said we were something more.

I lazed in bed for a short while and looked around his room, taking in the artwork on the walls, the order he kept in his large walk-in closet, the trinkets he kept on his nightstand. He wasn't a smoker, but there was a matchbook from that restaurant we went to. Why did he still have it? Did he look at it and remember me, remember that first night together in his bed? Stretching my body over his side of the bed, wrapping myself in his scent, I smiled thinking of him, and imagined the life we could have together.

Downstairs on the kitchen island there was a blueberry muffin on a plate with a glass of what looked like fresh-squeezed orange juice next to it. Propped against the glass was a note that read:

Good morning, sweet Rene.
I watched you sleep for a few minutes after my alarm woke me this morning. You looked so beautiful. I had to force myself to get up and go to work. Always so hard to leave you.
I'd wish you good luck, but you don't need it. You're going to get that job today, I'm sure of it. Call me when you're done.
-Caleb

I had to remind myself of what Caitlin said about just letting myself enjoy this. It was ingrained in me to expect nothing. Expect nothing and you'll never be let down. He was just *so* good that it was hard not to worry that it would all slip from my grasp. And I already knew that losing Caleb would shatter me.

• • •

Walking into the network headquarters again, I was nervous but excited. The studio buzzed with energy. Everyone looked dynamic, as if they were involved in something important.

A man I immediately recognized as Glenn Bennett strode over and took my hand. He was in his late forties, I guessed, and was fit, well dressed, and had the whitest teeth I'd ever seen.

"You're Rene Beaumont? You're even lovelier than Chad described. I'm Glenn, let me take your coat and we'll talk in my office."

I was a little taken aback by the *lovely* comment, but I blew it off. Thereafter, the interview was more like a friendly chat where he asked me a lot of questions about myself. I kept my early background vague, steering the conversation towards what I was studying at school and what I was currently working on at the station. He made me feel at ease when he spoke in depth about his program and what his goals were for the upcoming year. When he looked over my resume again, he commented on my working knowledge of French, seemingly impressed, then said, *"Tu as de très beaux yeux."*

Ugh, did he really just tell me I had beautiful eyes? I didn't reply, and I'm sure my discomfort was obvious. Bennett laughed it off and said, "My apologies, I only know pathetic pick-up lines in French."

For some reason I laughed along with him, even as my heart sank. I prayed this wasn't a preview to working with a perv. I wanted this job. If I got it, I'd find a way to handle him just like I've handled every grabby customer at the restaurants I've worked in and handled the one or two seedy creeps my father allowed into our home when I was a child. Life had toughened me up at a young age. It would take more than some guy on a power trip to deter me.

As I rose to leave, he confirmed my misgivings when he held both of my hands in his and then rubbed his thumb in circles over the back of one of my hands. It was too intimate a gesture. I shifted and broke his hold casually, told him how much I enjoyed meeting him, and how I looked forward to hearing more about the position. His assistant walked me out and told me I would hear by the end of the month if I got the job.

I was thankful for the cold air that hit my face as I shuffled through the building's revolving door and met the pedestrian traffic on Columbus Avenue. I walked a few blocks before hailing a cab and making my way back to Caleb's. His doorman ushered me in as he informed me that a car would be here soon, "as per Mr. Donovan's instructions." No protest from yours truly today, the poster child for female empowerment. No, today I was glad for it. I practically sank into the rich leather seat, disheartened as I stared out the window on the ride back to the airport. I promised Caleb I'd call, but I needed some time to wrap my head around this.

* * *

CALEB

"Hey."

Finally. I'd been looking at the clock nonstop since noon. I had a lot riding on this interview too—wanted my woman here with me in New York this summer—so I was anxious to know how it went.

I walked out into the hallway. "How did it go?"

"It went well."

"What's wrong?"

"Why would you ask that?"

"Can just tell by your voice. What happened?"

"Nothing really. He just...He was friendly, charismatic. I just didn't like that he made reference to my looks *twice*, and then kind of held my hand and rubbed it in a weird way as I was leaving."

"Motherfucker."

"Please don't get angry, or else I'll feel like I can't discuss stuff like this with you."

I was steaming but she was right. "I'm listening."

"Anyway, I know I just have to be careful and clear with him. I've been in situations like this before and I can handle it. It just blows if this is the way it's going to be. But I'm overreacting and getting ahead of myself. I mean, I haven't even been offered the position."

I *knew* she was going to get an offer. "Trust your gut, Rene. I'm sure you're not overreacting."

"His assistant told me that I'll hear by the end of the month. This nonsense aside, it does sound like an unbelievable opportunity." I could just picture her shrugging and smiling. "I know I'll be able to handle it."

"I have no doubt you can handle it, you just shouldn't have to. Some guys are assholes."

"I can't imagine or assume it's going to be like that."

"Did he do anything else that made you uncomfortable?"

"No, that's it."

I let out a long breath. I felt so frustrated for her. "I know working there is a huge big deal and all, but I don't like this."

"Like I said, Caleb, I can't get all twisted about it since I haven't even been offered the position, and nothing really offensive has gone down. Listen, I shouldn't have burdened you with this."

"No, I'm grateful that you told me. I want you to let me in. Please, even if it's telling me something tough, ok?"

She had to go then, her plane was boarding.

I made up my mind that if Rene got the job, I'd somehow convince her to stay at my place for the summer. I'd make sure that douchebag Bennett knew who I was when I showed up on set, make sure he knew Rene had someone looking out for her.

Chapter Eleven

RENE

Looking back on it now, I could laugh.

I spent the plane ride home and all of that night strategizing about this big problem that didn't even exist yet. I was all pep talks and girl power, plotting out the tactics I'd use to make myself invaluable to the network while presenting myself as a badass professional. No one, not even a megalomaniac like Bennett, would dare to mess with me.

Walking to class that next morning, I was feeling better, more confident. I smiled when I read the text reminding me of my appointment at the student clinic later that afternoon. Caleb, dreamy Caleb. *Focus on the positive, Rene.* After the weekend we just spent together, seeing Caleb again as soon as possible was number one on my list of good things to come.

A few hours later I was having a flashback to those months when I lived with my uncle and his wife. When my aunt yelled at my younger cousins, she'd always end her tirades with the same stupid line: *Stop crying, or I'll give you something to cry about.*

Handling Bennett, getting that job? Please. Now I had real problems. Now I had something to cry about.

"You wrote down here that your last period was four weeks ago with a question mark." The nurse practitioner tapped her pen against the clipboard. "You don't keep a record?"

"No." My answer came out sounding like a question.

"Have you had unprotected sex?"

I stuttered, sounding stupid to my own ears when I responded, "Wuh—wuh-once."

"I'm not going to tell you that once is all it takes. I'm sure you already know that." She was matter of fact, shaking her head when she said, "Honey, I can't write you that prescription. I think you're pregnant."

She kept talking, but everything was blocked out by the whoosh-whoosh sound of my pulse hammering. "What?"

Scribbling notes into my file and reaching for a notepad, she said, "I'm certain of it. If it was just the urine test, I'd say let's repeat the test in a week, but the routine blood I drew for an STD screen confirms it. You're pregnant."

I walked home in a daze. The prescription for vitamins of whatever shit she was talking about was balled up in one sweat-soaked fist. I dropped it in a garbage can a few feet from my dorm.

Those nightly phone calls I once lived for? Now the ringtone I programmed just for him was the sound I dreaded most. *Here Comes the Sun*. Caleb sang it to me that first time we woke up in his bed together. I couldn't bear the memory of it now. The way he ran his hands over my body, the way he kissed me, the way he looked at me. The opening bars of that song, so hopeful and pure, now I closed my eyes in an effort to block it all out.

I would turn off the ringer, text back after midnight telling him I was studying late, and sign off wishing him goodnight. Sometimes the phone would ring a moment later, but I'd ignore the call. To make up for it, I'd call back during his workday as I was rushing to class or mid-shift at the restaurant. Kept the calls short without any real time to talk.

With every passing day it got harder to pull it off. He wanted to whisk me off to Puerto Rico next weekend. I kept hedging, making up excuses, and he was getting antsy.

Pregnant.

Was my lot in life really this bad? From my vantage point, everyone else seemed to sail through life, but me? Never. The universe was always looking to kick me in the ass.

Back and forth, back and forth. The need to break down and tell him everything had the words pushing past my lips during my weaker moments. I wanted more than anything for him to tell me everything was going to be all right, but at the same time, I despised myself for being so needy.

Caleb had changed me. This man, this relationship, this happiness—it made me carefree, reckless and stupid.

A baby.

I can't have a baby.

I woke up in the middle of the night crying, even though I recall feeling content and happy in my dream. I was with Caleb on a beach. I was snuggling a baby close to my chest, our baby. We were laughing about something as he came up behind me and wrapped his arms around both me and the child.

I sat up in bed, turned on my small reading light and scribbled out a list.

Go through with it:
- He would take care of us
- I think I would make a good mother
-I love him
-I don't want to have an abortion
Don't:
- There's no way he wants a baby now

- He'd only stay out of a sense of duty
- It won't work out between us
- He'll wind up resenting me
- Everyone will think I trapped him
- I won't be able to finish school
- I'll have to depend on him for money

Those last few items on the list burned like acid and stopped me in my tracks. I was on autopilot.

The next morning I called a clinic. Within five minutes, I had an exam scheduled and an appointment for the procedure set for the following week.

So easy.

Too easy.

I knew the difference between right and wrong. I knew I should tell him, knew I should give him the opportunity to voice his opinion, but I shut all that down.

For most of my life I've been a solo act. Life was just easier when I kept things to myself and handled my problems on my own.

Chapter Twelve

RENE

Looking around and taking inventory, I determined I was the oldest person in the waiting room. The overhead fluorescent lighting and chipped blue industrial paint reminded me of the free clinic I went to as a child. Only the posters covering the walls of this dismal space were different.

A Healthy Pregnancy Begins with a Healthy You
Keep Choice Legal
Free Mammograms Here
Teen Clinic Tuesdays

Skimming over a poster listing the signs and symptoms of chlamydia: funky vaginal discharge and pain upon urination, sparked the thought: *Oh, how I wish I was here for that.*

The girl sitting across from me looked to be no more than fifteen. She was alone, clutching a backpack to her chest. Did she skip school today to come here? A young couple seated a few chairs down looked to be around seventeen, I guessed, the dirt on the cuffs of their ill-fitting winter coats branding them as poor. They didn't hold hands or speak to one another. Two broken souls with no trace of the smiles I'm sure they once shared.

What stories were they dreaming up about me? I took care dressing today, which seemed important at the time but now left me feeling so utterly pathetic. What was I trying to achieve with my smart business casual look? Tears threatened and I fought to hold them in. I was too old, too accomplished, and smart enough to know better. I was different from everyone else here, wasn't I? *No, you stupid girl, you're just like them.* I was alone and without resources. I was just as poor as they were.

"I'm terminating," I told the doctor in a clipped voice, cutting him off when he started rattling off my options.

He didn't look surprised.

After the exam I had to sit there and have a mandatory counseling session. I sat like a stone, nodding when I knew it was expected of me but hardly listening. I just wanted my prescription for something I had to take the morning of the procedure and then to get the hell out of there.

The train rattled along the tracks as I looked out the window. Taking in the barren branches, the snowbanks stained with car exhaust and the bleak late winter sky, I tried but failed to keep my thoughts from drifting into dangerous territory.

What would it be like to have Caleb's baby? I pictured a boy with curly hair and a sweet smile. His little fist curled around my finger when I held him, my baby's gaze locked on mine. My heart swelled with the feeling. I saw Caleb holding him then, looking down at his son with love in his eyes. And it was the only thing I knew to be true —Caleb would be a devoted father to his child no matter how he ended up feeling about me.

I didn't even realize I was crying until an older woman next to me put her hand on my shoulder and asked if I was all right, startling me. I assured her I was fine, but the caring tone of her voice made me want to sob, to set the river of tears flowing and to let my shoulders rise and fall with pent up sorrow. But I didn't do that. No, I did what I do best. I shut it all down, iced the feelings over, set the dial back to autopilot.

I could do this.

I had to.

The waiting over the next week proved difficult. I was so nauseous that I called in sick to work on Saturday and skipped classes Monday. The smell of coffee in the morning made me retch, and that damn coffee maker in our suite was set on a timer. After the second morning of waking up to that smell and running to the bathroom to puke, I unplugged the thing.

Caitlin looked positively homicidal when she woke up on day three to an idle machine. I tried to play it off but she wasn't buying it.

"Really? We share a room, Rene. You think I don't notice that you're practically green with nausea, and that the bathroom always smells of disinfectant?" When I didn't answer, she came over and sat next to me. "You think I haven't heard you crying every night this week?"

A mixture of sadness and relief washed over me. The tears came like the floodgates were finally let open.

"You're pregnant. You haven't told Caleb yet. What else do I need to know?"

"That's all," I managed to choke out.

"It's all right."

She held onto me, and after what was probably only five minutes but felt like a solid hour of crying, I told Caitlin everything.

"You need to tell him." When I immediately said no, she put her hand up to silence me. "It's not just because it's the right thing to do, it's because you need to stop doing everything alone. If I didn't just call you out, you wouldn't have even told *me*. You would have been living with another giant secret, another lie. Don't you see how bad this is for you? You're just piling one secret onto another. I know it won't be easy to tell him, but you need to do it. Doing the right thing? It's hard, I get it. But he's been so good to you. He's not going to be an ass about this, ok? You *have* to tell him."

* * *

CALEB

I knew what was wrong.

She was different. She was avoiding me like the plague, ducking my calls and anxious to cut our conversations short when I did manage to get in touch with her.

"Rene?"

"Um, hey, what's up? I'm at work so I only have a sec."

I was at work too and whispering into the phone. "That's bull-shit. You've been avoiding me. I have to ask you something. Are you —" Shit, I could barely voice my thoughts. "Are you pregnant?"

Click.

She fucking hung up on me.

The thought first crossed my mind a week ago after she made another lame excuse as to why she couldn't get away to see me. Nothing else made sense. I should have asked her then, but the idea of it made me so goddamn petrified that I just pushed the thought away each and every time it surfaced.

I was just about to hit redial when my phone rang. I answered as I made my way out to an empty corridor.

"I am."

Aw, hell...

Deep breath...

Be there for her, asshole.

"Everything's going to be all right, I promise. I'm coming up."

"You can't. Please don't."

"What do you mean? I need to see you."

"I can't, not right now."

A bad feeling settled in my gut. "What's happening here?" She was silent on her end as I began to piece it all together. "Were you even planning on telling me?" Choking up, I braced my hand against the wall for support. "Just lie to me, Rene. Lie to me and tell me that you were at least going to fill me in."

"I don't want you here. I won't be able to handle it if you're around."

"Handle it? What are you talking about? You got it all figured out already? It's your decision alone?"

She let out a sarcastic laugh. "We both know I'd be doing you a favor if I just took care of this without telling you."

"Is that what you think? That's who you think I am?" Again, she gave me nothing. "So what's the plan? What did *you* decide?"

Her words were controlled, icy. "I have an appointment Friday morning."

"I'll be there with you."

"No."

"I'm coming."

"I don't want you here."

Click.

Hung up on me again.

My thoughts began to race. It was Wednesday afternoon. I was going to do what? Head up there Friday morning to hold her hand? I was a coward. I was giving her shit for not telling me, for not letting me in on the decision, while a lot of what she said was true.

What *did* I want? Did I want a baby? I had to think about it, but came to the conclusion that yeah, someday I did want to be a father. With her, yes. Now? No. But I would. I would in a heartbeat if that's what she wanted.

I would.

I practically fell into my chair when I came back in. Cherry was there, placing a comforting hand on my shoulder.

"What's the matter? You look like shit."

I shook my head, needing a moment to collect myself. "I can't talk about it. I'm not coming in tomorrow or Friday. I have to take care of something."

"All right. If you need anything, I'm here."

"Thanks."

It was around noon on Thursday when I got to Boston. Rene stopped answering her phone right after we spoke the day before. For all I knew, she'd already blocked my number. Wouldn't put anything past her at this point.

I sat in the campus parking lot for fifteen minutes, praying to God I'd get lucky and catch sight of her, but that wasn't going to happen. Knocking on the door, I had no clue what I'd say if Jenna or one of the other girls answered. When Caitlin opened the door, her face fell, and her pitying look told me she knew. She quickly closed the door behind her, took my hand and led me out towards the lot. Neither one of us said a word until we were in my car.

"Rene didn't tell me you were coming. So you're picking her up?"

"From where?"

She turned pale. "She's there now, Caleb."

"She told me the appointment was tomorrow." I slammed my hands against the steering wheel and looked out the window away from her, ashamed. "When did she leave?"

"I was just about to leave to go get her. It's over with. She went early this morning, didn't wake me up to drive her like she was supposed to. She needs someone to accompany her home or they won't release her." She added bitterly, "I'm sure that's the only reason she told me."

"I'm getting her."

"Caleb?"

"Yeah?"

She reached down into her pocket. "I shouldn't give you this, but maybe you need to see it. I found it when I was straightening the room up just now." She grabbed a pen, her hand trembling as she wrote on the back of a folded up piece of paper. "You have to understand, she's been through a lot." Caitlin handed it to me, the dark circles under her eyes compelling me to feel a deep kinship with this girl I hardly knew. "I was so happy for her when she found you."

The address of the clinic and Caitlin's telephone number were scribbled on the back of the paper. I read it over, shaking my head as she got out of the car. It was as if she already knew that Rene wouldn't be taking my calls from now on. I was already shut out.

Instead of pocketing the paper, I unfolded it. Confused for a moment, I soon recognized it was a list of pros and cons written in Rene's precise script.

I think I would make a good mother? I knew without a doubt Rene would be a loving mother. And when I read that she loved me, I already knew it without her saying the words. I loved her so much. I felt like a piece of shit when I read that line about not wanting to have an abortion, so guilty. This was all on me.

The list of cons turned my stomach. I wanted to say no, no, no, checking each one off. I wouldn't be doing this out of duty, I wouldn't feel resentful, I wouldn't feel trapped. But in all honesty, I wasn't sure how I'd feel if she'd kept the baby.

My baby.

What a fucking mess.

Rene looked pale and wiped out when she came back into the waiting room. Looking around, her jaw tightened when she spotted me. She went to the reception desk and gestured to me, I guess to get the ok to leave, then walked right past me without making eye contact. I followed silently as we made our way to the car, her strides long and quick, leaving a distance of several feet between us. Rene got in, slammed the door shut and kept her gaze fixed straight ahead.

"Are you going to talk to me?"

She turned away from me, choking back tears when she said, "I don't know what to say to you, I'm sorry."

I reached over to hug her but she stiffened. Her eyes were fixed on the T-stop across the street. I feared she'd bolt out of the car if she saw the next train coming, so I backed off and spoke softly. "I'm the one who's sorry. I'm *so* sorry. But don't you think you owed it to me, at least the chance to be here with you? To talk about it face to face before you made the decision to do this?"

She moved as far away from me as she could, pressing herself against the passenger side door. When Rene looked back at me her eyes narrowed and she laughed. "You're being ridiculous, Caleb. I'm twenty. You and I don't even live in the same city. I need to finish school. I'm relieved, I'm *so* relieved. And you...You *know* this is what you wanted me to do."

"I never would have asked you to do this. I would have taken care of you."

She stifled a cry. "I know, but it would have been out of duty. That's not how I want it to be. I don't want to be your responsibility or some kind of burden. I only want to bring a baby into the world when it's out of love."

"I do love you, Rene."

She shook her head, attacking the few tears that spilled with rough swipes. "You're telling me that now? Do *not* tell me that now."

"You know I do."

"It doesn't matter. This is what I wanted, and whether you admit it or not, it's what you wanted too."

I knew she could put up walls, but I'd never seen this side of her. Shut down, ice cold—a complete one-eighty from the girl who'd been in my arms just a few weeks ago, so open and trusting. How could she turn her emotions on and off so easily, as if there was a switch? I was trying to be gentle and supportive, but I could feel the anger bubbling up inside.

"How the hell do you know what I want or what I feel?"

She practically spat the words back at me. "Who are you kidding? I'm just a girl who never even got to your commitment-phobic four month mark. I might not even be considered an ex, right? Wasn't much longer than a month."

I grabbed her shoulders, twisted her to face me and jerked her in close. "You think I've been with you a *month*? Are you fucking kidding me? How can you be so cold?" I was screaming at her, filled with rage. "I'm with you, and I've *been* with you since that night on the beach."

My hands were shaking when I let her go. I started the car and we drove back to campus in silence. My hands were still shaking when I pulled into the lot.

Rene looked at me like I was little more than a stranger. "I'm never going to be the girl you want me to be. It's better if we just end this." With that, she got out and walked away.

I started the engine and drove. I don't know how I made it back to New York in one piece. I sped down I-95 replaying everything she said and the way she'd said it—vacant and indifferent. My head felt like it was going to explode.

It's not like I didn't see this coming. It's not like I thought Rene would be able to turn around the next day and say, "Ok, that's behind us, back to normal now." But I did think—what? That she'd want me beside her? That she'd accept my comfort, accept my love?

No answer when I called Rene to check on her that night. I called her the next day, same thing. When she ignored my call again that next night, I broke down and called Caitlin.

"Hi, it's Caleb. She won't answer her phone."

"I'm not surprised. She's fine, I mean physically. Otherwise, she's kind of acting like a zombie. She's working tomorrow night."

"Is that allowed? I mean, is she physically able to work?"

"I asked her the same thing and she basically blew me off. She's acting strange, like she's totally fine, like it's no big deal. I know she's going to crash soon."

"I'm coming back up tomorrow but don't tell her. I'll meet her after her shift at the restaurant."

"I don't think that's a good idea. She'll be upset."

"Don't care. I have to see her. I'm not just walking away."

Well, upset was an understatement. When she saw me standing outside the restaurant, she lost it. Rene scanned the dark parking lot quickly to make sure no one could overhear, then laid into me.

She was trembling, her tone desperate. "What are you trying to do to me? Every time my phone rings and I see your name, I'm back to square one. Please, I'm begging you, I need you to go!" Her voice quieted then. "I can't be any clearer than that."

With that, a cab pulled up and she got in, quickly closing the door behind her. She didn't even look my way as the cab drove off.

Holy shit.

In shock, I think I stood there for a full five minutes before getting back into my car and making the four hour drive back home to my empty apartment.

Two days passed in silence before I got an email from her. I was hopeful when I saw her name in my inbox, but that feeling was short-lived.

I should have called you Saturday night. Leaving you there like that in the parking lot was harsh and it was hurtful—for that I'm sorry. But why did you come after I asked you not to? I meant it when I said that I can't handle seeing you. I know you want to talk, I know you deserve more than what I'm giving you, but I don't have anything to give right now.

I feel like I'm drowning. During the day, seeing people at work, class, the library—no one notices anything is different about me. I feel so awful inside, so terribly sad, that it's hard to believe it doesn't show. I feel so guilty over what I've done. More than anything, I wish I could go back, to be granted some magical kind of do-over, and that's just pathetic. Do I even deserve or have the right to feel remorseful? The "problem," the "situation" that I needed "resolved" in a quick and efficient

manner, I now see as a child. My first child, our child. Yes, I know—too little, too late.
I know your gut reaction will be to try and help me through this, but you can't. I know what's happened will always be between us, and I don't see us getting past this. For me, it would be easier to cut ties and put this behind me. I know that I'm the one losing out here. No one, no man has ever been as caring and good to me as you have, Caleb. I just know that right now, seeing you or talking to you is something I cannot do.
I hope you understand and can forgive me.
-Rene

Sad, so terribly sad—those were the best words to describe me too.

I sat at my desk reading and rereading her email. I was searching each sentence, looking for something, anything that would give me an opening, an indication that I still stood a chance. But I knew what type of person Rene was, knew she was strong-willed and obstinate. Once she made a decision she wasn't likely to waver.

Cherry came up to my desk and placed her hand on my shoulder once again. "Are you ready to talk about it?"

I reached up and placed my hand over hers, shaking my head. I did need to talk about this, so badly, but the only person I wanted to talk with had shut me out. As desperate as I felt in that moment, I would never betray Rene's trust in that way.

I left work early and went home. I turned on my computer and sat in front of the screen, reading her letter again.

* * *

RENE

I still can't believe I just jumped in the cab and took off like that. He drove all the way up here and I didn't even take a minute to talk to him. But I felt panicky when I saw him, as if I'd actually lose it and fall to the ground crying at the sight of him. I had to get out of there. It was like that fight or flight response, and I chose flight.

I always ran.

Caleb accused me of being cold that day at the clinic. And I think he's right, there is a part of me that's cold and dead inside. It's how I've survived, how I got by, but he would never understand. How could he? He's never walked so much as a foot, let alone a mile in my threadbare, worn out shoes.

I owed him more. At the very least, he deserved to know what was in my heart. And I needed him to know that I felt remorse, that I was sorry, that I wasn't a monster. So I pled my case through that email, then vowed it was the last time I'd ever allow myself to be weak.

I shook my head as I read his response, heartbroken but determined.

No, we could never go back.

I'm so glad you reached out to me. I've been going kind of crazy these past few days wondering how you are. I'm worried about you and I want to be with you, to take care of you. I'm miserable without you.
But you know that.
I feel like I've caused you so much pain. I'm the one who put you in a position where you had to make such an awful decision.
The blame is on me. I meant it when I said I would never have suggested you do it, but at the same time, you were right when you said that deep down, I didn't want a baby right now either. I feel like a real piece of shit admitting that.

Now it's done and I also feel terrible about it. I know it's something that will always be between us, but I do think it's something that we can help each other through.

Please let me love you, Rene. I need you. I need to hold you, be with you and have you in my life. There's never been anyone who makes me feel the way you do.

The saddest and most ironic part of this is that when we were together, it was the first time I could ever imagine wanting to marry someone, wanting to spend my life with one person, and wanting to have children of my own.

All I can do is tell you that I'm here waiting. If what you really want is for me to leave you alone, I'll do that, but I'll never stop wanting to be with you and I'll never stop loving you.

-Caleb

The days that followed seemed endless, and when I settled into bed, sleep rarely came. I was running on empty.

Two weeks later I had to return to the clinic for a follow-up appointment. I considered blowing it off, but managed to drag myself back there. I was basically a mess. I undressed, put on the paper robe and then started to sob. Being back in this place was torture.

A different doctor walked in, a young woman. She immediately dragged a stool over close to me, put her hand on my knee in a reassuring way and handed me a tissue.

"It's rough around this time. Your hormones are haywire and you're realizing the permanent nature of the decision you've made." I looked up at her and nodded. She understood. As she looked over my chart, she said, "Rene, I feel as if I'm looking at myself ten years ago. I sat in your place. I thought I couldn't fit a baby into my life then, I was in med school. I thought I was a modern woman making a choice, but afterward I felt the most crushing longing for that baby. I wished like a silly five-year-old that I could turn back time and do it all over again."

That's exactly how I felt.

"It gets better. Time fades the hurt. Back then I decided to honor that child by doing everything in my power to make sure that decision wasn't made in vain. I studied like a mad woman and graduated with honors."

"I didn't know how I would feel, that it would feel this bad. I feel like I'll never get over it."

As she gestured for me to hop up on the table and started the exam, she said, "You will. It will always be a part of who you are, but you'll be ok. It's so odd, isn't it? How many times, among friends and as groups of women, have you discussed abortion? What strong opinions we have when we know nothing. I find that now I don't judge so harshly, people who support either side of the issue." She gestured for me to sit up. "You're healing well. No sex for two more weeks."

"I don't care if I ever have sex again."

She smiled, her eyes gentle. "Like I said, I feel as if I'm talking to myself ten years ago. Here's my card. I'm at Mass General. I work here at the clinic twice a month pro bono. If you need to call, then do. The first month can be very hard. Take care of yourself, Rene."

The kindness of a stranger brought the tears on again. I'd wept more in the past month than I had in my entire life.

I read Caleb's email again when I got home. It was the last time he'd reached out. I wasn't surprised, I knew he would respect my wishes. If I said that contacting me would hurt me then he wouldn't do it. He wouldn't do anything to hurt me.

Shutting my laptop down, I resolved to do everything in my power to make sure this decision wasn't made in vain, just like the doctor.

Heard from the network the next day.

I got the job.

Plug along, that's what I do.

I was always a hard worker, but now I was like a robot—classes, work, study, sleep a couple of hours, repeat. My grades were perfection, I was getting rave reviews at the station, and I was working every available shift at the restaurant.

Caitlin was worried about me, but I think she also understood this was how I got through. And I *was* doing better, I was getting through.

I found two girls to share a summer sublet with in Manhattan. I knew if the circumstances were different, I'd be tap dancing with excitement about this summer, but achieving what I'd worked so hard for now felt bittersweet. I would be there, in the same city as Caleb, but I could never be with him.

He did reach out a few times. The notes were less personal, just checking in to see if I was all right. I always answered back but kept it simple: *I'm doing well, thank you.*

Being on formal terms with Caleb was just about the saddest thing ever.

I would always write more, but I'd go back and erase it before pressing send. I had so much to say to him. I missed him terribly, not just as the man I loved, but as the close friend he'd become.

I couldn't have it both ways.

I knew that.

Chapter Thirteen

CALEB

Second time this month I woke up with a black eye.

When I dragged my ass downstairs to get some water, Mick was parked on my couch, looking pissed off and weary.

"You almost got arrested last night, shithead, you know that?"

"I think you're exaggerating."

"Really? If that dishwasher didn't let me sneak you through the club's service entrance, you'd be in central booking right now. That guy didn't know what hit him. What the hell is going on with you? You were a total asshole last night, just itching for a fight."

My body felt sore and my head was thumping. "Mick, please stop yapping for a minute."

"Luke's on his way over."

"What the fuck did you do that for?"

"Because I'm in over my head. I don't even know how to talk to you anymore. Something bad is gonna happen if you don't get your shit together."

With that, Luke let himself into my apartment. "Looking good, brother."

"Thanks, *brother*. Can we reschedule this intervention for tomorrow? My head is pounding."

Mick jumped up like the couch was on fire. "I'm outta here. Talk to you tomorrow, Caleb. Later, Luke."

"You looked fine when I left last night. What happened?"

Luke was still playing rugby but didn't stay long at the after-parties. I knew Luke and Kate were trying to have a baby. He was maturing and happy about it, while I was regressing back to my fourteen-year old self: the boy who wanted to slug anyone who looked at him funny. I was unhappy, plain and simple.

I raked my hands over my aching head. "I'm messing everything up."

"I can see that. What's up, though?"

"I was seeing this girl. She was special." I shook my head. "I love her."

"Things ended?"

"I got her pregnant."

"Shit, Caleb."

"She ended the pregnancy. She won't see me anymore and I can't get over her."

"What did you want?"

"I don't know."

"Don't be too hard on yourself. It takes two, you know?"

"No, this was entirely on me."

He shook his head. "I'm not buying that."

"But it's true. Obviously you weren't there, so take my word for it. She's young. I was...I was her first."

"Explain this to me." His look was a mix of doubt and confusion. "What do you mean?"

"It's Darcy's roommate, Rene."

"What?"

"Yeah, I know, I'm a shit. And Darcy doesn't know anything."

He stood and walked over to the window, shaking his head, lost in thought. "Is she ok?"

"I don't know. And it's not what you're thinking, Luke. She wasn't a hook-up. Rene and I were friends for a long time before anything happened. But it's all a mess now. She asked me not to contact her anymore and for the most part, I haven't. It's fucking killing me."

"Her first time? Shit, that's rough."

"I know."

Luke came back and sat across from me. "You've got to tone it down. You can't think straight if you're drinking heavy and you're out every night."

I gestured to my eye. "Does Dad know?"

"Dad and Sarah are worried. I think you need to be spending more time with us. It'll keep you grounded. Kate and I are going over to see Darcy the second week of August. We're meeting her in Greece and you're coming. It'll be good for you."

"I'll see."

"I'm buying your ticket, you're coming."

I leaned back and looked to the ceiling, too tired to argue about it. "What would you do...about Rene?"

"It's hard for me to say. I don't know what your relationship was like. But I'm sure she's a bit messed up right now. If she asked you to stay away then you have to do that for her. Doesn't mean the situation won't change. I wouldn't necessarily give up, but I'd give her space for now."

"She's working in the city this summer, interning for one of the big morning news shows."

"Ball is in her court. If she wants to see you she will, and if she doesn't, Manhattan is a big island."

Luke went into the kitchen to start some coffee. "Get in the shower. We're going to Mom and Dad's for lunch." He cut me off before I could stage a protest. "Before you say no, I was at their house when Mick called." Gesturing to his own eye, he added, "They know, so just go face the music, all right?"

Trudging back up the stairs, I muttered, "Can't wait."

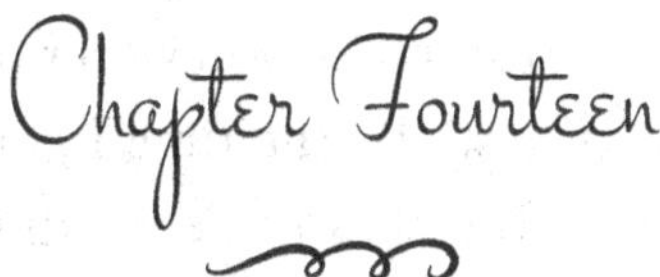

Chapter Fourteen

RENE

I was worried about running into Caleb until I checked out my new digs. My tiny one-bedroom in a fourth floor walk-up in Chinatown was not exactly choice real estate.

I dropped my bag to cover my nose and mouth with one hand while I waited for one of my new roommates to answer the buzzer. The trash bags piled three deep along the side of the building smelled of rotten fish, and even without that assault on the senses, the air felt heavy and polluted.

An unfamiliar voice barked, "Who is it?" And when I announced myself, she said, "Ugh, I'll be right down. The fucking buzzer doesn't work."

Talk about a warm welcome.

My new bestie took her sweet time getting downstairs. Holding the door open as I dragged my one giant suitcase inside, a smile played on her lips when she said, "If you think it smells bad now, just wait until July."

I hadn't realized I still had my free hand covering my face. "It's not *that* bad."

She smirked and took my backpack from off my shoulder when it began to slide down my arm. "My sister said you were nice." She turned back as she began her climb up the stairs. "I'm Penny. I work twelve-hour shifts at the hospital, so you won't be seeing much of me this summer. Same with Ivy." By the time I got to the second floor landing I was pulling for breath, but Penny didn't break her stride, just spoke louder. "You pay your rent to Ivy by the first, so that's like Monday. No television so no cable bill. And Ivy's uncle owns this shithole, so he doesn't charge us extra for the air conditioning. He's a prince."

Air conditioning, that's good.

In an effort to be social, I managed to wheeze out a few words when I finally made it to the top. "At least I'll be in good shape by the end of the summer."

She laughed. "What's your name again?"

"Rene."

She handed me a set of keys that looked fresh from the locksmith. "You're a glass half-full kind of girl, Rene, aren't you?" And with that, she grabbed a bottle of water from the fridge, saluted me and left.

Taking in the bare walls, the mattresses on the floor, and the food marked with bold, angry handwriting in the refrigerator, I gave myself a pep talk. Told myself I was lucky to have a place that was affordable, and lucky to have roommates who weren't identity thieves or serial killers. And I wasn't certain about that. God knows what would happen if I made coffee with a splash of *HANDS OFF! IVY'S* soy milk.

You're not here to make friends.

The reminder was meant to shore up that hopeful part of me, the one that was always looking for something, for some sort of connection. Forget kindred spirits, this summer wasn't about that.

I did a dry run on the subway the next morning and clocked in at forty-two minutes one way—so much for being close to work. Afterwards I set out to find a second job and got lucky at a pub on Prince Street that was willing to give me three shifts: Saturday afternoons, Tuesday and Sunday nights. Not ideal, but it would bring in the extra cash I sorely needed.

Monday morning I walked into the studio practically bursting with excitement. Bennett's assistant greeted me and paired me up with the other intern on the show, Matt Quivers. She led the two of us on a whirlwind tour of the set with endless introductions. I smiled and shook hands, struggling to commit every new face and name to memory.

Matt came off as somewhat entitled, a little arrogant maybe. *First impressions can be misleading*, I reminded myself, *don't rush to judgement*. But as Bennett made his way over, he tested that theory.

Flashing those bright white teeth, he was silky smooth, ignoring Matt entirely as he took my hands and crooned, "Rene, *so* happy to have you on board. Come with me." As an afterthought, he gestured back towards Matt and snapped, "You too."

Bennett took us back to his dressing room with his assistant walking two paces behind, teetering on heels I would never be able to walk in. He was all sweeping gestures and declarations: *This is where the magic happens!* while his assistant gave us the skinny in hushed tones: *You are to report here at seven a.m. sharp and don't be late. Mr. Bennett doesn't tolerate tardiness.*

I was relieved to see the room buzzing with wardrobe and make-up people. The thought of being alone with this guy, let alone in a room where he dressed, had me on edge. Sitting in his chair, white tissues tucked into the collar of his dress shirt to avoid stains from the make-up and hair spray, Bennett flashed us another winning smile and instructed us hang back and observe today.

"But don't get too comfortable," he teased. "Tomorrow I'm going to start putting you through the wringer."

Ugh, he winked right at me as he said it. Yep, my first impression of this dude had been spot on.

I sent up a silent prayer that my new coworker hadn't noticed, but I had no such luck.

As Matt and I grabbed a spot off to the side of the cameras to watch the show, he asked, "Do you *know* him or are you normally the teacher's pet?"

I fixed him with a look. "Watch it."

He put his hands up defensively, sporting a cocky smirk. "Take it easy. Jeez, you're touchy. Come on, you have to admit that was more than a little odd."

Dismissing him, I said, "I'm here to work hard, just like you."

Oh, this was starting out just peachy.

I was relieved to meet Caroline and Maureen, two staffers I'd be working closely alongside, and was even happier still when I found out that Matt was being directly supervised by someone else.

The job wasn't glamorous. I ran for coffee a lot, and one of my regular responsibilities was stocking the green room with snacks in the morning. I treated every menial task as if it was important, treated every day like it was a job interview. Making a good impression this summer could lead to a position next year, and I could see my future in this environment. I thrived off the excitement of the newsroom and the unpredictable nature of live television.

On one occasion, thankfully, I did get to jump in and help out during a minor crisis. Caroline and Maureen were sent to the airport to retrieve Paula Kent, the frontrunner for the upcoming Republican presidential primary. They were at the airport waiting when Ms. Kent strode into the studio with her people. Bennett freaked that no one was there to handle her, and it so happened that our senior producer was out sick that day. One of the assistants ushered her back into the green room where I was busy setting out the goodies, as usual. When I sensed the air of panic and found out that none of the usual people were there to prep the guest, I offered to start it off while we waited for the others to get back. Bennett's personal assistant shoved a list of questions at me and then I was off and running. Ms. Kent was a warm and friendly woman, so that helped. And I'd done this before, albeit on a much smaller scale. Prepping a community activist protesting proposed fare increases on Boston public transportation was not *quite* the same as sitting across from the person who could, in fact, be the next leader of the free world.

Maureen and Caroline were flat-out frazzled by the time they got back, but then we all wound up having a laugh about our crazy morning. Following them all out to the soundstage, I gave myself a mental pat on the back. I'd done pretty well under the circumstances and I knew it.

Bennett approached me personally after the show to tell me that Paula Kent, Caitlin and Maureen had all sung my praises. And it was nice to be approached by Bennett in a totally professional manner for once.

Matt was standing there listening in as it all went down, and from the corner of my eye I saw him snicker once Bennett's back was turned. What an ass.

I knew his deal. He was here because his uncle was some big shot at the network. No experience, no burning desire to be in broadcast journalism—he had a golden ticket handed to him while a hundred other kids would have killed for this opportunity. And he was a misogynist in training, irked that a woman was showing him up at work. Whatever, I was in a good place. I wasn't about to let him or anyone else kill my buzz.

I learned something new at work everyday, and was soaking it all up like a sponge. This career, this city—I was exactly where I was meant to be.

Yes, Bennett still oozed sleazy at times, but for the most part, I was able to ignore him. One day towards the end of the summer, though, he pushed it too far.

We were regrouping after the show and Bennett was in a snit.

The lead guest was a female attorney who specialized in labor contract negotiations. She came off as no-nonsense, intelligent and direct, and at one point during the interview she'd corrected Bennett on some statistics that were misleading. He didn't like being challenged, and one of the research assistants bore the brunt of it as soon as the cameras stopped rolling. After ripping the poor guy a new one for his "shit fact checking skills" for a solid ten minutes, he settled into a chair in the conference room shaking his head, and we were a captive audience.

He looked to Maureen. "She doesn't come on my show again, got that?" As she scribbled the note in her book, he looked around the table. To another staffer he said, "And the next time I have to *ask* for water during a break, you're going back to sorting the goddamn mail, understand?" Mind you, this was a grown man with a degree in journalism from Northwestern.

"Jeez, everything about that broad." He actually shuddered. "Unrefined, a mouth straight out of the gutter, and that short, butch hair." Speaking to no one in particular, his eyes landed and stayed on me. "Curves, long hair, natural beauty...I like my women feminine."

He'd just laugh it off and say the comment was harmless, even though it certainly was not. I wanted to scream, to slap him for every off-color comment and for his slimy delivery, but I didn't have the position or confidence to address him directly. My actions would have to speak louder than words.

I jumped out of my seat and grabbed my bag. "I apologize, but I forgot I have an appointment. I'll be back for the staff meeting after lunch."

I made a bee-line for the upscale salon I passed every day walking from the subway to the studio. *Short, butch hair...What the hell does that even mean?*

When I approached the desk, the receptionist asked my name in a clipped tone. When I explained that I didn't have an appointment but was hoping one of the stylists could squeeze me in, she all but laughed in my face. "We are not a walk-in salon. If you like, I'll make an appointment for you now, but it will be at least two weeks before I can fit you in with one of our *junior* stylists."

Just as I was about to walk out with my tail between my legs, a very attractive man with a smooth French accent said, "Wait. I have some time free. I'll see you."

"Marcel? *You're* taking her?" Obviously this was no junior stylist.

He dismissed the receptionist with a flick of his wrist. "Come with me. Your hair is beautiful as it is. What exactly do you want me to do?"

"Cut it all off."

He took me in with wide eyes and then laughed. "I knew you would entertain me today, ma petite!"

After studying me from several different angles, he nodded. "I will only do this because you have the face for it. But now I must know…Did you just rob a bank?"

He gave me my first good laugh of the day. "Nothing like that, more like a depraved boss who's spent a good part of the summer leering at me. He just commented that he loved my long hair. I have a staff meeting in an hour and I'd really love to get my message across."

"I love it! But I must warn you, ma chère, you will still be very beautiful with the short hair."

I knew within five minutes that I'd made a new friend. As Marcel lopped off—gulp—numerous inches, we talked and laughed as if I'd known him forever. I told him all about Bennett without naming names, and he filled me in on some of the juiciest network gossip, as he styled many of the high profile talents' hair.

As I admired my very different look in the mirror, Marcel walked over and air-kissed none other than Meredith Carey on both cheeks. She was the lead anchor of the morning news program that led into our show. I admired her, and was impressed with how everyone, including Bennett, treated her with the respect.

Marcel introduced me as a summer intern working at the

network. She greeted me kindly and then commented, "I *have* seen you in the studio. I hope Glenn is behaving himself."

I smiled and nodded, hoping my expression didn't look forced. After telling her what a pleasure it was to have met her, I shot Marcel a desperate look and said, "S'il vous plaît, Marcel, ne dites pas mes secrets!"

She laughed out loud. "Marcel, she should know you're terrible at keeping secrets!"

He crooned, "I knew there was a reason I loved her just like I love you, Meredith. Belle, et elle parle français!"

Marcel called after me in French, telling me to come in for a trim before I returned to Boston.

The receptionist was now overly friendly. She gushed over my new look and then said, "No charge today, Rene. It's Marcel's gift to you."

Again, the kindness of strangers never ceased to amaze me. I took the salon's business card so I could write him a personal thank you note, blowing him a kiss as I walked out the door.

I raced in and plopped down into the one open chair after everyone else was seated for the staff meeting. Bennett's mouth fell open and Maureen stifled a giggle as the others sat there wide-eyed.

"Well, Miss Beaumont, that's a different look."

"Yep, just time for a change."

I wasn't sure, but from the corner of my eye I spied Matt smiling at me with what seemed like admiration. Maybe he wasn't so terrible after all.

The summer was winding down.

Caitlin finally made it in for a visit, and after spending two nights crashing on the mattress with me in my fleabag of an apartment, I know she was more than ready to head to her aunt's place in the Hamptons. We were taking off right after I finished work Friday afternoon with Caroline and Maureen tagging along. Monday would mark the beginning of my last week at the network before heading back to school, and I was going to miss my new friends.

Naturally, Caitlin's aunt had a gorgeous place just a short distance from the beach in East Hampton. Friday night was spent on the deck with lots of wine and great snacks prepped by a bona-fide personal chef. Then on Saturday afternoon her aunt's driver dropped us at a surfer bar right on the beach in Montauk. Talk about a convention of beautiful people.

I was just happy to cut loose. I'd spent every weekend this summer working the service bar at a small place in the East Village. The tips were mediocre at best—summer was not high season in Manhattan—but you wouldn't hear me complaining. Bennett's nonsense aside, I wouldn't trade the experience I had this summer for the world.

* * *

CALEB

Was time healing this wound? Somewhat, I guess. I still missed her and prayed she would change her mind, but I was slowly coming out of my funk.

Five long months have passed since I last saw Rene, but who's counting? And she was here in the city—my city—all summer. I texted to congratulate her when I heard she got the internship, but all I got in return was a curt *Thank you*. When Darcy forwarded Rene's contact info and asked if I'd take her out and show her around town, I deleted the message. No, that wouldn't be happening.

I tried to put her out of my head, but found myself searching for Rene on every street corner, every subway platform, just everywhere. Luke's words played over in my head: *Ball is in her court... Manhattan is a big island.*

I even tuned into the Glenn Bennett Hour a few times on my computer while I was at work. It's not like I was going to see her on camera or anything, I just did it because I knew she was there. And now that I knew about Bennett, I couldn't help but interpret everything the guy said as slimy and disingenuous. I prayed that she wasn't fighting him off or having to put up with his sexist crap the entire summer.

Misery loves company, and I was feeling pretty miserable. I was desperate for any and all kinds of distraction. I went up to the Cape with friends twice, played in a few rugby tournaments and made it out to our beach house to surf whenever I was free.

Rene made it crystal clear that we were done, so I wasn't guilt ridden over hooking up with a girl during one of those Cape weekends. And I made an effort to be attracted to Lauren, I really did. Even saw her a second time to force myself to give it a chance. It just wasn't good timing and I told her so.

I just didn't want any other woman the way I wanted Rene.

Those last two weeks of August were spent in Greece with Darcy, my cousin Erin, Luke and Kate. I hate to admit when my older brother is right, but being with family did ground me. We had a lot of laughs, just like when we were kids living at home together.

Mick texted one night as we were sitting at a beachside bar having drinks in Santorini, one of the most beautiful spots on the planet.

I'm at Surf Cove in Montauk. You'll never believe who's here.

I wrote back:

Yawn. Who?

Mick sent back a picture with the caption:

Still yawning?

Rene.

The picture looked as if it was taken from across the bar. She looked different, but yet still the same. The long hair was gone, now fashioned into a sexy, shaggy pixie cut. Zooming in, her eyes looked bright and playful, her head tilted back as she laughed. She was with friends and having fun. One of the girls had her back turned but looked like Caitlin.

Rene.

She looked great.

She looked happy.

Although I would always want only the best for Rene, her ability to maintain this distance with so little show of emotion had started to wear on me a long time ago.

Maybe I'd built up this idea of *us* into something more than it was. Maybe I'd always been in deeper than her. I was Rene's first. Maybe that's what made me special to her at the time.

For me it would be easier to cut ties and put this behind me. That fucking letter, every word she wrote still burned. Maybe cutting ties was easy for her, but I still couldn't put it behind me.

I stared at her picture, a part of me hating her for being happy, but underneath the anger was a deep, enduring sorrow. Seeing her brought me back to that awful day all over again, sitting in my car just watching, powerless as she walked away. That dull, aching pain settled right back into my chest.

Now having a drink with them. Got caught taking pics and had to assure them I'm not a perv.

A minute later:

Rene says hi.

A minute later:

Me thinks I like Caitlin. You there?

I shouldn't respond. Let *her* know what it feels to reach out and get nothing back for once. But who was I kidding? I was so damn weak when it came to her.

Tell Rene I like the haircut. Tell Caitlin to stay away...U are a perv. Bye Mick.

I stared at my thumb as I pressed down hard to power off. No more. I couldn't take any more.

"Who are you texting?"

"Mick." I took a long pull on my beer before adding, "He ran into a few of your roommates in Montauk."

"That's crazy!" Darcy chirped. "He must have run into Caitlin and Rene, they were staying at Caitlin's aunt's place in the Hamptons this weekend."

I shrugged. "Yeah, I guess."

"Beth stayed with Rene last month in the city. She said her sublet was an absolute dump but they had a lot of fun. She said Rene's having a fantastic experience at the network."

"That's good to hear."

"I know. I'll be pumped if she lands a job in New York after graduation."

"If that's what she wants."

"Yeah, that's her goal and she'll do it. I never doubt that girl."

Luke and Kate sat quietly, taking it all in. When Darcy and Erin got up to get another round, Kate asked, "Are you going to tell Darcy about you and Rene before she goes back to school?"

"I don't see any reason to tell her. I know Rene won't be advertising it to anyone. It's in the past, right? Doesn't really matter anymore."

With that, I got up and walked along the beach back to our rental. It still hurt, so fucking badly. What I wouldn't give to be at that bar in Montauk right now, just to have the chance to see her in person.

Hours later, the sun was getting ready to rise but I was still staring at the ceiling, unable to sleep. I powered up my phone because I was weak. I needed another picture, another update, anything.

I got nothing.

* * *

RENE

Caitlin tossed a coaster clear across the bar and yelled, "Excuse me, is there some reason you're taking pictures of us girls?"

The guy started cracking up laughing and put his hands up in surrender as he made his way over. Like everyone else in this place, he was one of the beautiful people. Board shorts, no shirt, chiseled torso, and a face that belonged in a magazine.

Caitlin was keeping up the snarky act but she was smiling. "Since we're the shortest women in the bar, it's clear you're not scouting for a modeling agency, so that means you're probably just some smarmy dude."

His eyes opened wide as he broke into another fit of laughter. "Smarmy? That's my new favorite word!"

Caitlin was now overtly flirting with the guy. Head cocked to the side, hand on her hip, she was even sticking her ample chest out a little farther. "So, I'm still waiting for an explanation."

"Sorry I creeped you out, ladies, but I'm not a stranger. Rene, don't you remember me? Mick?" He added, "I'm a friend of Caleb's."

"I didn't recognize you, Mick! Your hair is longer."

"And yours is shorter!"

I introduced Caroline, Maureen and Caitlin to Mick. What had it been, three minutes? Mick and Caitlin already looked as if they wanted to tear one another's clothes off.

Caitlin kept her head, though, and asked what she knew I so desperately wanted to hear. "How's Caleb doing? What's he been up to lately?"

He looked directly at me when he answered, "He's good, better now. I don't know what you did to him, Rene, but he was all sorts of messed up for a long while."

I got the impression when I first met Mick that he had no filter. He came off as easy going and lighthearted, but he was direct—whatever was on his mind came right on out of his mouth. And today his words landed like a sharp blow. The thought of Caleb hurting? Never in a million years would I set out to hurt him.

"Shit, I'm sorry, Rene. Like I said, he's doing great now. He's in Greece with Luke, Kate and Darcy. Can I tell him you say hello?"

I shook it off and composed myself. "Definitely."

Mick went back to chatting up the girls, but I could barely follow along. I was back there, to that day and the awful weeks that followed.

I woke up each morning and plastered on a happy face, but inside I was wracked with guilt and a suffocating sense of grief. Every mother pushing a stroller, every father holding their toddler's hand, every pregnant woman, every "right to life" bumper sticker—things I scarcely noticed before were now a constant in my life, mocking me, reminding me what a mess I'd made of my life.

Back then I believed I'd never get over it, but time does heal even the deepest of wounds. I still felt the heartache and I knew I'd never forget, but I had moved on. The happy days now outnumbered the unhappy, and I had a positive outlook on my future. But I missed him. I'd never stop missing Caleb.

Mick tapped my shoulder and smiled. "He said to tell you he likes the new 'do."

I smiled back but my eyes felt heavy and sad. When the DJ started up again, Maureen and Caroline dragged me out to dance. I forced myself to snap out of my funk. Looking backwards never did me any good, and I didn't want to drag down everyone's mood tonight. I didn't really snap out of anything, but I danced and drank, smiled and laughed. I always could put on a convincing performance.

The three of us headed back to the house much later without Caitlin—surprise, surprise. Maybe I should take a page out of her book moving forward. Caitlin didn't just look happy and carefree, she was. She wasn't lost in her own head, questioning every move she made like I did.

Sitting around the fire pit, Maureen mixed up a batch of margaritas and poured us one last drink for the night. She sat on the edge of Caroline's chaise and fixed her eyes on me. "What was that all about? When Mick mentioned that guy...What was his name?"

"Caleb? He's a great guy. It just didn't work out."

Caroline was looking to make me laugh when she asked, "Does Caleb look like Mick? I think I could endure a lot of crap for someone that delicious."

"Believe it or not, Caleb's better looking."

Maureen's eyes went wide. "Seriously?"

I couldn't help but giggle. "Yes. Don't say it...I'm a total idiot."

They went back to discussing their own relationship troubles, and I was relieved to have the focus off me. I liked and respected these women, and was so grateful for their support and friendship. Both took me under their wing from day one when they saw what Bennett was trying to pull, and they guided me through it. Maureen and Caroline were kindred spirits, the closest of friends, but still, I wasn't divulging anything more. Caleb and my memories of him were private. They were mine, they were all I had left. I could never talk about him in a casual way. I'd never dishonor what we once were.

I gave up after tossing and turning for a few hours, wrapping myself in a blanket to catch the sunrise.

The house we were staying in was straight out of *Town and Country*, and the garden was nothing short of breathtaking. The lap pool was bordered in flagstone, with a lush green carpet of grass covering the rest of the property leading to high privacy hedges. Shrubs bursting with blue hydrangeas were packed in clusters, and purple wisteria draped from the eaves of the main house, servants' quarters and pool house.

I made myself a coffee and settled into a lounge chair on the patio. As the sky turned from dark purple to pink and pale orange, my thoughts drifted to Caleb, wondering what he was doing at that exact moment. It was midday in Greece. The longest plane ride I'd ever taken was from JFK to Logan, but I had a good imagination. I conjured up an image of Caleb standing on the shores of the deep blue Mediterranean, with sun-bleached villas draped in bougainvillea in the background. I was tempted to text him just so he knew I was thinking about him, but like so many other times, I didn't.

A short while later, a very scruffy looking Mick came meandering out onto the patio. "Well, hello. I'll be your best friend if you show me where the coffee is."

"Sit down. I'm getting myself another cup, I'll make you some."

"Gracias."

He looked at me like I'd given him a cup of solid gold when I handed him the steaming mug.

I teased, "So, you and Caitlin have fun last night?"

"Lots." He rubbed one hand over his face and laughed. "I'm glad I ran into you girls, but I lost my friends at some point last night. I don't even know where I'm staying. Hopefully one of these drunken slobs answers my call." He went to scroll through his phone and then chuckled. "Caleb is asking how my night went. He wouldn't give a crap how it went if I wasn't with you."

I lowered my head and drew in a shaky breath.

"Hey, I don't know what happened between you two, he doesn't talk about it. I just...I never saw him care about a girl the way he cares about you. When you guys broke up he was like, I don't know, devastated. He was back to his bar brawling ways. It got a little scary there for a while."

"I feel terrible hearing that."

"I'm not saying it to make you feel terrible. I just want you to know you mean a lot to him." He slapped his thigh then. "And that's enough of that. Hey, Caitlin told me why you cut your hair. I fucking love that story!"

I told him about the rest of my summer, and Mick told me about his job. He mentioned the plans he had with Caleb to start their own investment group someday in the future, and was surprised that I already knew about it.

"He always talked about how bright you are. A tech genius, those were his exact words."

"I don't know about that," he hedged, obviously pleased, "but it's true that we make a good team. He'll be the face out front, making the contacts and selling us, and I'll be the wizard behind the curtain, running the show."

Like Caleb, Mick was a really nice guy and easy to talk to. We sat talking about anything and everything for a good solid hour before Caitlin, Caroline and Maureen joined us.

I have to say, I think Caitlin was a little smitten. It's the first time I ever saw her act kind of shy around a guy. And he was cute, grabbing her hand and kissing it when she sat at the foot of his lounger. Interesting.

We wound up driving Mick to his friend's house before we headed back into the city. It was Caitlin's last night, so I treated to a small neighborhood dive that had become my absolute favorite. Translation: cheap and tasty.

"So, do you like him?"

"Don't look at me like that! Yes, Mick's gorgeous, he's funny, he's phenomenal in the sack—"

"Caitlin!"

"What? He is. But face it, I'll probably never see him again. I'm not getting all swoony over this, but it *was* nice." After a minute, she asked, "Did you two talk about Caleb this morning?"

"A little. Made me feel awful."

"Yeah, I know. He told me Caleb was a hot mess for a long time. Like he was out of control, almost got himself arrested. He said he's calmed down some, but he still isn't himself. Sounds like he still really loves you." She added, "I didn't share anything about you, Rene. I know you wouldn't have wanted that."

"I love him, I always will, but we're over and done with. There's no getting over what I did."

I snapped the elastic hairband on my wrist, closing my eyes against the sting. It was something I'd taken to doing whenever I needed a mental kick in the ass. Nope, I was done putting this all entirely on me. I made the decision, and I made many missteps along the way, but like the saying goes: *It takes two.*

I chose my words with more care. "I love him, but what happened was huge, and it's always going to sit there between us." Through hurt laughter I said, "And he's not too broken up. When Mick saw how upset I was, he reassured me by saying something like, 'Caleb's not a total basket case. I mean, he's been seeing other people, just not people he's into.'"

Caitlin winced and then laughed. "Man, Mick's adorable but he's a dumbass."

I couldn't help but laugh a little too, because Mick was an adorable dumbass, but it still felt like a brick was lodged in my chest. "Seriously, I can't blame Caleb. He *should* be dating. He's reached out to me a million times and I give him nothing in return."

"I still say to give it time, Rene."

"Too much time has passed."

* * *

CALEB

"So you're interested in how my night went all of a sudden?"

"Don't make me beg, Mick."

He laughed. "All right, all right. My night was fantastic. That one, Caitlin, is a hottie. I mean, she's something else. I wound up crashing with them."

I cringed. "Jesus, you hooked up with Caitlin?"

"Yeah, so what?"

Talk about muddying the waters. "I don't know, man, forget it."

"Don't worry, I'm not going to start dating her or anything. To be honest, she kind of gave me the brush off. I was a little insulted. She didn't even want my number when I offered it up."

"Aw, poor Mick."

"So what do you want to know about Rene? I know that's the only reason you're calling me right now."

"How is she?"

"I don't know. Good, I guess. She looked like she was having a great time until I came along and mentioned you. Then she looked like she'd been kicked in the gut. Kind of how you look most of the time. My opinion is that she's definitely still into you. And I can see why you're into her. She's a really nice person, easy to talk to, whatever. And she's hot. That little cropped kinda hairdo usually doesn't do it for me, but she rocks it. You there, Caleb?"

"Yeah, I'm here."

"So, she and I talked for a while the next morning. I mentioned that you seemed to be doing better and were seeing other people and—"

"What the fuck did you say that for?"

"Gimme a break, Caleb. I was still a little drunk from the night before."

"Fuck."

"She just seemed really torn up when I let it slip that you had a hard time dealing with the split. I wanted to reassure her, let her know you weren't still a total basket case."

"Jesus, I'm glad I never actually confide in you. What are you, a goddamn washwoman? Did Caitlin tell you anything about Rene? I bet *she* didn't spout like a geyser."

"No, she didn't say anything except that she thinks you two are meant for one another."

"Whatever."

"Listen, she didn't bawl when I told her you were seeing other people, but I wouldn't say she looked relieved either. Maybe it's good she knows...Inspire her to make a move."

"You don't know her."

"I'm sorry if you think I messed anything up, Caleb. Wasn't my intention."

"I know."

"Am I still picking you up at the airport tomorrow?"

"Yeah, a ride is the least you could do to make this up to me."

He laughed. "You still love me, admit it. Text me the flight info and I'll see you tomorrow."

Holy crap. Seeing other people? Why would he tell her that? God, I wanted so badly to talk to her. Wanted to tell her that I was so goddamn lonely, and that those few hook-ups were nothing, they were impersonal and empty and meaningless.

I wanted her to know I was still waiting, just waiting, for her.

* * *

RENE

Crab cakes, lobster rolls and champagne—the station was going all out for us lowly interns. After three months of working ten to twelve-hour days together, some of these people truly felt like family. Taking it all in, I hoped and prayed this was not goodbye.

As the party was winding down, one of the few people I was not keen on seeing came over and handed me a piece of cake.

"A peace offering." I took the plate from him, surprised because his signature smug attitude was missing. In fact, my fellow intern Matt looked downright contrite. "Uh, I'm thinking maybe I was kind of a dick when we first met. I made some assumptions, and to be honest, I think I acted like a jerk because you're a little intimidating. I'm sorry."

I smiled as I savored a bite of that red velvet cake. It tasted like satisfaction. "If we're being honest here, you were an absolute tool, but I appreciate the apology. So what's next for you? Are you looking to come back next year?"

"Nah, I don't think this is for me. Before I blew out my knee, I was on my way to playing baseball beyond college. That's not going to happen now, but I think teaching and coaching, maybe high school…That's what I'm meant to do."

"I think that's great, Matt."

"So, I know you would never date a coworker, but since we are officially on the cusp of no longer working together, do you want to grab dinner one night soon before we head back to school?"

My initial reaction was to turn him down, but knowing that Caleb was seeing other people made me reconsider. Yeah, thanks for that, Mick. That was a jagged little pill to swallow.

"All right, but just as friends?"

He looked a little disappointed but agreed. "Friends…Yeah, I could do that."

Meredith Carey made her way over as she was putting on her jacket, and Matt gave me a smile and a thumbs up as he backed away.

"Rene, I wanted to catch you before I left. I inquired about you and got some *very* positive feedback. You have a strong background, and from what I've heard, you were able to handle some very tricky situations with grace and fortitude. If you're interested, I want you to know there's a job waiting for you after graduation." She gestured to the woman next to her. "This is my personal assistant, Barbara Kern. If the answer is yes, I'll expect you to forward an updated copy of your resume to Ms. Kern by early March."

As Ms. Kern handed me her card, I said, "I can tell you right now that I want the job. It would be an honor to work with you, Ms. Carey."

She smiled warmly. "I'm pleased to hear that. You *do* know where the next winter Olympics are being held, don't you, Rene?"

"Chamonix?"

"Oui. Possibilites interessantes, no?"

I smiled broadly and nodded. Yes, exciting opportunities for sure.

Scarcely a minute after she left, Bennett slithered over. "I see you know my good friend, Meredith. I hope she wasn't trying to lure one of my best interns away. I'm counting on you to be on my team next year."

You know how they say to never burn your bridges? Although I would like to have personally detonated explosives underneath this bridge, I had to keep my head and be diplomatic. "I'm grateful for every opportunity I've been given at the station."

Thankfully, he didn't press the issue.

"So, give it to me straight, Miss Beaumont. Summarize the highs and lows of working with the great Glenn Bennett."

I couldn't help but smile. For as much of a jerk as he could be, I did learn from watching him. "Well, you're very knowledgeable about your guests and all related issues. Also, you're a master at improvisation. You don't get flustered easily, even when things aren't going smoothly behind the scenes. I learned a great deal from you in that respect."

"And now for the lows, Miss Beaumont?"

I took a deep breath. "When you're a superior and you refer to a woman's looks in the workplace, it's dead wrong and you *know* that."

"Fair enough. If you butchering your beautiful hair didn't get the message across, that certainly did."

As he turned to leave, he winked cheekily and said, "You know you have a job with me next year if you want it, but please, grow your hair back before next summer for Christ's sake."

Nice try, Bennett. Never gonna happen.

* * *

CALEB

The day after I got back from Greece I did something stupid and desperate. I rode the train uptown after work, hoping to see her while simultaneously praying that I wouldn't.

The area near Columbus Circle was packed on any given night. I didn't know her hours, didn't know what building she worked out of, so the chances of seeing her were one in a million, if that. But as crappy luck would have it, I spotted her walking across West Sixty-fifth with some guy.

I stopped a good fifteen feet away from them, looking on like some creepy stalker. Rene was all smiles as her man held the door open for her. *That your handsome prince now, baby?* And my hands curled into fists when he left his hand to linger on the small of her back. *Get your hands off of her.* But I kept my distance, kept quiet as he guided her inside the restaurant and out of my sight.

Out of sight out of mind? Nah, unfortunately it didn't work like that for me.

Why did I do it? Was I looking to torture myself? I turned, walked down the street in the opposite direction and made my way back down the subway stairs. The jarring screech of the trains and the hot whoosh of foul-smelling air that hit me as I made my descent were just fucking perfect. *Step right up, all you heartbroken losers. Welcome to the depths of hell.*

Riding back downtown wedged between a young woman juggling three kids and some hipster in need of a bath, I made a decision. Rene was happy, she'd moved on, and it was time for me to do the same.

I wasn't looking for a wife, just wanted to go back to the way my life was before I'd met Rene. I was happy back then, wasn't I? *Happy enough*, I told myself, *and that will have to do.*

Chapter Fifteen

RENE

I arrived a day before everyone else.

Standing in the center of my small room, I took in my surroundings. I'd go by the market on my way home from work tonight to get a cheap palm plant, and I'd hang the set of string lights and the one tapestry I carried around from place to place—a few things to make it look homey.

I moved around like a fugitive on the FBI's most wanted list, and I wasn't a nester, but I wanted to make up for the fact that I didn't have a lot of nicknacks or family photos to fill my room.

This was it, the last place I'd call home before leaving school and setting out on my own.

I was working shifts at the restaurant, but decided to give myself two weeks before I was due to report back to the television station. I wanted to experience my senior year, not just plow through every day working like a dog with my head down like I usually did. I knew there would be a lot of parties kicking off the semester, and I wanted

145

to be there whooping it up with everyone else. I was graduating and I already had a kick-ass job lined up. I deserved to celebrate.

Counting out the bills jammed into my apron at the end of my shift that night, I was grateful to be back, to be making the amount of tips I did at the restaurant. Even though my internship was paid, it was nominal. I had to dip into my savings big time to pull off paying rent and to give myself a clothing allowance this past summer. I desperately needed to start socking money away again. But I didn't feel pressure, didn't feel any anxiety. Drifting off to sleep, I simply told myself: *You got this.*

"She's like, in a coma."

"Let's leave her alone." I could make out Beth's voice. "She never sleeps in."

"Forget that." Now it was Caitlin's voice I was hearing in my dream. *What is she doing here at the network?* "I'm dragging her ass to the party." *Huh?* "Wake up, honey pie, it's officially senior year!"

Yeah, what I recalled as being a super good dream was cut short by Caitlin and Beth jumping on my bed. I was so happy to see them that I didn't even get mad about being woken up. Whether these girls knew it or not, they were my family, they were my home.

A few minutes later, Jenna dropped her bags at the door and clapped her hands, rallying us to get our asses in gear. It wasn't even noon yet, but the guys were already getting kegs set up by the field, and by the time we made it down, a crowd of about twenty friends were already there.

Nick was on the field, kicking a soccer ball around with Tom and Mac. Meanwhile, Jenna was texting Darcy, pressuring her come to the field as soon as she got dropped off. Today would be interesting. I said a silent prayer for Nick to behave, for both Darcy's sake and for mine. If Nick started acting up, would I have to call *him* to intervene? That would be awkward as hell.

Caleb, Caleb, Caleb.

I couldn't stop thinking about him. I was back to square one. I was sick at just the thought of him holding hands, kissing or—please God no—falling in love with someone else. But he was moving on and I had to accept it. I'd assumed as much even before Mick told me that Caleb was *doing great* and *hooking up with other girls*, but it hurt like hell to hear it confirmed. I'm sure he wasn't stuck in the past the way I was. To Caleb I was probably no more than a distant memory —a memory that was laced with pain, no less.

I had no desire to move on. I had no desire to date. That dinner with Matt was nothing, and I knew as much before I agreed to go out with him. And guys approached me at the field party, mostly to comment on the hair but some to flirt. I just wasn't looking for anything beyond friendship with any one of them.

Being at this party with Darcy and Nick took me back in time. I watched him as he chugged a beer and then tossed the empty to the ground, while the insults and threats he used to scream from outside our door replayed in my mind. I remembered being in that bathroom with Caleb, fearing his reaction but admiring the determination I saw in his expression. He rode right in and saved the day. I let out a breathy exhale the way I always did whenever Caleb came to mind.

Snapping myself back to the present, I reminded myself that a repeat of that day would be my worst nightmare. So I kept watch, took note as Nick stole glances at Darcy occasionally, but he stayed away from her. As long as he stayed away, it was all good.

Caitlin handed me a beer and whispered, "I wonder if Caleb ever mentioned anything to Darcy."

"I'd say no, definitely not."

"How do you think she'd react?"

"I don't know. Darcy's pretty easy going, but with the way things have turned out, I think she'd be pretty upset with me. No one wants to see someone they love hurting, you know?"

She nodded. "I wonder what our boy Mick is up to."

"Probably fantasizing about you."

"Ha! I'd say he doesn't even remember my name. Anyway, I'm thinking that Tom Farrell is looking especially tasty. He's just my type."

"You mean the easy, no strings attached type?"

"Yup."

"Well, I'd look elsewhere. He's been gazing lovingly at our girl Darcy all afternoon."

"Lord have mercy. Can you even imagine what's gonna go down if those two hook up?"

"Tough on Nick, she deserves to be happy."

The school year was in full swing before I knew it, and for once, I was enjoying a lighter course load. I was still waitressing and doing two afternoons at the station, but compared to years past, this was a cake-walk. I had more time to just hang out and relax with the girls, and I was grateful for it.

The free time gave me a chance to up my exercise routine, to get to know my roommates on a deeper level, and believe it or not, to go to Mass.

I wasn't particularly religious. I think I was baptized, but I wasn't taught prayers as a child and my parents certainly didn't institute any Sunday morning routine, or a routine on any day of the week for that matter. Jenna's spot on the student choir was the initial draw for Church on Sunday mornings, but then I came to enjoy it.

I had only one friend on my street growing up, and she moved away when I was around nine or ten. Her family had a routine, and I envied her for it. I'd watch in wonder as every member of the family loaded into the minivan dressed in their very best on Sunday morn-ings. An hour or two later they'd return, a big bakery box in her mother's hand, her father juggling a few grocery bags. I couldn't even remember her last name as I sat there in the pew thinking of her one morning, but I thanked her. I thanked her for the jelly doughnut she stashed away and brought in to share with me Mondays during lunch period, and thanked her for her friendship.

I didn't believe in the fiery pits of hell or the judgement of an angry God, so Church was a peaceful retreat for me. I'd stop at the offertory candles on my way out, sometimes lighting one for the decisions I've made in this life, sometimes for special people like Caleb and Miss Parsons, and occasionally I'd light one for my own mother, a woman I hardly knew.

Sometimes I'd tag along when Darcy went running after Mass. She took it easy on me, cutting her distance and speed when I joined her. She would talk the entire time we ran, understanding I was quiet and just listening because my stamina wasn't equal to hers.

She was in the early stages of a relationship with Tom Farrell and I was totally happy for her. After everything she'd endured with Nick, I was so glad she was seeing someone like Tom. Yes, he had a reputation in the past for hooking up with way too many girls, but he seemed reformed and it was obvious that he was totally into Darcy. As I labored for breath, she would go on and on and on about him. It was cute.

Sometimes the one-sided conversation veered in the direction of Darcy's family, and when it did, I kept as quiet as a mouse. It left me feeling like an absolute fraud, let alone a sad excuse for a friend. And it just hurt like hell every time Caleb's name came up.

Darcy asked me about my summer in New York one morning. I could scarcely breathe, let alone articulate a complete sentence. "Great," was all I could manage in reply. But she was used to being a one-woman show on our runs, so as per usual, she went off on a tangent.

"My parents told me they barely saw Caleb this summer. I worry about him. He didn't seem like himself when we were in Greece. Kate said that Caleb was seeing someone special last year, but it didn't work out and he's been down ever since. I know he's seeing someone from work now, but I don't think it's any kind of true love. I'm pretty sure he's also hooking up with some chick in Puerto Rico. He just goes from one woman to another. It's not good for him."

I nearly tripped over a crack in the sidewalk, so I stopped, bending over at the waist to catch my breath. She slowed and circled back, jogging in place as she waited for me. She let the topic drop, thank the Lord, because I was just about dying inside.

"What about you? You're not still into Ryder, are you? I hope you're not hung up on that loser 'cause there are so many quality guys who are dying to go out with you. Chris worships the ground you walk on. Mac mentioned that your new look was hot. Come on, what are you waiting for?"

I cried in the shower when we got back home. I hid out in there for so long that I'm sure I resembled a prune by the time I dragged myself out of the bathroom and flopped onto my bed.

And sure enough, a few days later Caitlin informed me that Darcy was fixing to make me her matchmaking project. The following Saturday, Darcy decreed a mandatory girls' night out because the boyfriends weren't going to be around.

Save me, please, I prayed to no one in particular.

I felt like a pageant contestant. I had one doing my make-up, one doing my hair, and one arranging my outfit. I was hating every minute of it, but even I had to admire the finished product when I looked in the mirror. And while Caleb was still foremost in my heart, hearing the details of his very active love life yet again left me feel nothing short of foolish.

How did I feel Sunday morning waking up snug in Tanner Westerly's arms? His arms felt good around me, truly, but it was still no use. I was lonely. I was lonely for Caleb but he was no longer mine.

Move on, Rene. He certainly has.

Tanner was a nice guy, a good person. He was easy to talk to, funny and considerate. He didn't try to push me into doing anything but kiss, and I appreciated that. And his kiss wasn't awful, it was nice. But liking his kiss made me feel good and bad at the same time.

Darcy was already awake and looking up at me expectantly when I walked in early the next morning. I schooled my expression, exchanging my pinched brow and downcast eyes for a bright smile. And it's not that I was unhappy, I was just lost.

* * *

CALEB

Cherry here and there. Elena the last two times I was down in Rincon. Lauren when I ventured up to Drew and Chloe's latest crappy dinner party. Yes, my life was back to the way it was before Rene: no attachments, no commitments.

I was fucking miserable.

Hooking up with Cherry was totally selfish on my part. I justified it by telling myself that she was the one who suggested it. She'd just broken it off with her latest boyfriend and said it would be a harmless way for us both to move on. That was horseshit. She was into me but I was not into her. She was beautiful, smart and full of life. She just wasn't Rene. But I didn't end it. I even changed our arrangement out of loneliness. We grabbed dinner together after work occasionally, we caught a concert here and there, and she came to watch a few of my rugby games. I was pretty certain she was exclusive with me, but I was not abiding by the same set of rules. I was always respectful of her wishes. I was always kind to her. Truly, though, I didn't have her best interests at heart. I was using her.

The only way I heard anything about Rene was through Darcy. But when Darcy was home for the long Thanksgiving weekend, she mostly gushed over her new boyfriend, Tom. I had to admit, I did like the guy. I liked him for Darcy. And he was a good addition to our team. Darcy's scouting report was on target, the boy could play rugby.

During dinner, I casually threw out questions with the aim of getting some intel on Rene. But when I asked Darcy what her roommates were up to during the break, I learned more than I wanted to know. First I had to listen to her yammer on about Beth and Jenna. Then I heard all about Caitlin's trip to see her crazy aunt in Dallas. Finally she got around to Rene, and yup, I heard all about Rene and her *great* new boyfriend, Tanner. And it *must* be serious if she's spending the *whole* weekend with his family, right?

That, as they say, was that.

The rest of the weekend was a blur. I swilled red wine like it was water from that point on, and by the time the desert dishes were being cleared, I sounded loud and obnoxious to my own ears. I met a group of my high school buddies at a bar on Bleeker Street the next day, and proceeded to drink more than my fair share. Thankfully, I passed out early so I wasn't a total disaster for the tournament Saturday morning. I did try to behave myself Saturday night at the rugby party for Darcy's sake—as her big brother I had no business acting like a complete ass in front of her new boyfriend—but that plan flew right out the window once I spotted a cute girl with short brown hair. She didn't even look like Rene, but I was a hot mess. After a few shots, I took my pent up desire out on Cherry. I'm thinking the level of physical affection between the two of us at the rugby party was borderline obscene. I'm pretty sure at one point I was mauling her in a corner.

I was in free fall again.

RENE

"I can't go home with you. Thank you for asking, but I'm going to stay here and work."

"Caitlin's going to be with her aunt, Darcy is staying with Tom part of the weekend, Dan is going to Jenna's, and Beth has her flight booked already. I won't be able to enjoy myself knowing you're here all alone. I'm begging you."

I didn't want to go home with Tanner, and I didn't want his damn pity. Maybe he really wanted me there with him, or maybe he just felt bad that I had nowhere else to go. Either way, he made me feel pathetic and a part of me hated him for it. And going home with him was just plain wrong. That's something you do when you want to be with the other person, when you want the relationship to move on up to the next level. Spending a holiday with Tanner? Meeting his big, happy family? It made me queasy.

"Caitlin, I don't want to do this."

"I know why you don't want to go, I get it. But are you going to reach out to Caleb?" I shook my head. "Then give this a chance, ok? Tanner is crazy about you. Let yourself enjoy it. It doesn't mean you're marrying him."

I caved under the pressure and went, and it started out fine.

His parents were sweet and his sisters were welcoming. Tanner is the youngest of four, the only son, the family prince. Two of his sisters are married and out of the house, but one is only fifteen months older than Tanner. I shared a room with Anne for the weekend, and we got to talking at night before nodding off. She was working on her master's degree in social work, and told me all about the internship she was doing at the local hospital. She was very nice, and it was easy to see she that was close to Tanner. She'd ask questions, fishing around to see how serious we were. I kept things vague because, well, just because I always did. I really didn't mind her line of questioning, though. She was just being protective, and I always liked the idea of brothers and sisters who looked out for one another.

Thanksgiving Day I met various aunts and uncles, and no less than a dozen cousins. It was all very nice, very Norman Rockwell-esque.

And then it wasn't.

Tanner whispered, "That's Miranda's baby," all secretive, right before he introduced me to a girl who looked to be no more than seventeen or eighteen with a baby perched on her lap. The familiar pang of sadness came and then ebbed slowly. But I must have kept sneaking glances at mother and child because Tanner's mom approached, gesturing in their direction.

"You look like you love babies, dear. My niece, Miranda, although I feel she is far too young, well, I think she made a brave decision to keep her child. So many girls today are reckless and then say, 'I'll just get an abortion.' They act like it's nothing. Real courage, that's what motherhood takes."

"Yes ma'am."

I said it to be fresh, but she took it as if I was being agreeable and respectful, which was absolutely for the best. I wasn't up for debating the issue with anyone, let alone Tanner's mom. And deep down I totally agreed with her. Motherhood took courage, and I was sorely lacking in that department.

It wasn't Tanner spouting this, it was his mom, but it did make me feel disconnected and at odds with him. Can't really explain why. Maybe it was the realization that if his mother knew everything there was to know about me, she wouldn't approve, wouldn't think I was worthy of her son. I don't know. And what if Tanner knew? Maybe he wouldn't want me anymore. What exactly was the plan here? If I stayed with him, would I hide this part of myself away, keep my secret, lie to him forever?

I had to fight my impulse to run. And I would have gladly traveled the seventy-five miles back to campus on foot, but no, I still had two more days of family fun to endure.

"Caitlin, I don't care if you're going to see your aunt's dead armadillo for Christmas break, you can't make me go back there."

She laughed. "You're such a turd, Rene. Was it really that bad?"

"No, it wasn't. He's great, his family is great. You *know* what's wrong. I just don't want to get any closer to him and I don't want to get close to his family. I do like him, but I'm pretty sure I'll never love him."

"Are you going to break up with him?"

"No...I mean yes. I don't know."

"Did you really mean it when you said you'd come anywhere with me for Christmas break?"

"Anywhere. I don't want anyone thinking of me as poor little Rene." I put on an exaggerated, super sad face. "No family, nowhere to go."

"Good, remember you said that."

I was suddenly wary. "Why?"

She lunged and pressed me into the couch with both hands planted on my shoulders. "Because my mother's newest boyfriend is taking us to Paris. December eighteenth through the twenty-eighth, so clear your calendar. There is no airfare because he has a private plane, and there is no hotel because he has a huge apartment right in the heart of the city. So you see, you have nothing to object to. You'll be accepting what in terms of charity? A croissant here, a dish of coq au vin there, a café au lait?"

I was giggling uncontrollably by then. "Okay, I'm in! Did I ever tell you that you are the best friend ever?"

"I'm doing this for purely selfish reasons. I'm going to make you translate for me so I can pick up hot French guys."

Darcy came in with Tom as we were plotting the details of our trip. Those two were so in love, you could feel the good vibes emanating from them. I wasn't jealous, but witnessing their happiness hurt. *I used to be like that.*

They plopped down on the couch across from us and told us all about their weekend. I was only half-listening while they were going on about a big Thanksgiving Eve party at Tom's friend's house, but my ears perked up when Darcy turned the conversation to her family. Kate was apparently showing now, and Darcy's family was really excited for the baby. I wondered how Caleb felt hearing about the baby all the time. I'm sure he was totally happy for his brother. I knew Luke and Kate had been trying for a baby for a long time. But I would think it had to be a regular reminder of us, of what happened.

Darcy was laughing then, telling us Luke and Caleb finally agreed to let her stay at the rugby tournament party because she had Tom as an escort. She added, "As if Caleb would have noticed anyway. He had his tongue so far down that girl Cherry's throat, I thought he was checking her tonsils."

Caitlin always knew how to ask something or fish around on my behalf. "What kind of name is Cherry?"

"It's short for something, I forgot what. I saw her with Caleb at a rugby game when I was down in October. He introduced her as a coworker. She seems nice enough, but," she shrugged, "I don't know. At least he didn't seem as down and moody as he was in Greece."

Rene, you're going to Paris.

You have a great job lined up.

You have a boyfriend.

I was trying to list the many things I had to be grateful for, because hearing about Caleb with some girl named Cherry made me want to simultaneously bawl and claw his eyes out.

Darcy broke into my thoughts. "So, Rene, how was it? You haven't said a word."

I'm sure I sounded thoroughly underwhelmed when I answered, "It was nice."

I excused myself and went to the gym. I needed a swim. You can't cry while you swim—messes up your breathing. So after my swim I needed a shower. I had a good cry in there.

We were coming up to the last big party weekend before people had to hunker down for finals. I've never been a big drinker. I've always had to get up early in the morning, so no time for hangovers, and having two substance abusers for parents made me averse to it. I never wanted to be sloppy or out of control the way I remembered my parents.

That Friday night was the exception to my rule. Beth pushed some shots before we made our way to Tanner's place, and by the time we arrived the place was packed with bodies. When I went for my third beer within the first hour, Tanner gently took my wrist to stop me. "Babe, what are you doing? Are you ok? You never drink this fast."

I yanked my wrist back. "I'm fine." I was drunk and angry, but then felt guilty because Tanner had never been anything but good to me. "I'm sorry. I think I need to go home."

"I'll take you."

"No, it's your party so please stay. I'm beat. I'm going right to bed."

Caitlin came over to us then, said something reassuring to Tanner, waved her newest fling off and then whisked me out the door. "Come on, let's go back."

Caitlin knew the reason behind my breakdown and held me as I cried.

"I'm good now. Go back to the party."

"Don't be silly, I'll stay with you."

"Really, I'm fine. I can barely keep my eyes open. I just want to go to sleep."

But I wasn't the least bit tired.

Once Caitlin left, I stomped up the stairs, grabbed my phone, and then I did the stupidest thing ever.

* * *

CALEB

Someone was sounding the calvary, and frankly it was a welcome distraction. Cherry had dragged me to some depressing performance art show down in the Bowery, and now more than one hour in, I was in need of a good laugh.

She elbowed me. "Caleb!"

Oh, it was my phone.

Oh, my phone...Shit!

Been a long ass time since I heard that ringtone.

I slipped my phone out of my pocket, holding it down and to the side so that the screen wasn't visible. The ringer was off, but then I remembered enabling the emergency bypass function so that, you know, Rene could get in touch with me even if my phone was silenced. That's how fucked up I was in the days and weeks after we broke up. Kept believing she'd reach out to me, come to her senses, come back.

I turned to Cherry and whispered, "I have to take this," and then proceeded to squeeze past several pissed off theater lovers on my way out of the aisle.

So how is it? Cherry on top, just like a sundae?

I felt hopeful for a moment there, but after digesting her bitchy text I was fucking outraged, indignant—cue some more synonyms for really fucking mad.

I went to type something back, but then thought: *No, you're not getting off so easy, sweetheart.*

Stepping outside, I dialed her number and was shocked when she picked up. Picked up on the first ring, no less. But the ballsy chick who typed that message was now MIA. Rene sounded timid and shaky when she answered, "Um, uh, hi."

"Well, well, well. What's it been, Rene, eight months, nine months? Sorry, but after that long you don't get to act like a jealous girlfriend when you find out I'm fucking someone else."

"Fucking someone? Sounds so romantic."

"There's nothing romantic about it, sweetheart. Cherry is someone I fuck. What about Gunner?"

"Tanner."

"Whatever. Do you love him, or are you just fucking him?"

She gasped. "Caleb....it's...it's not like that."

"How is it, then?" Radio silence. "You know what, forget I asked because I don't care anymore. Later."

I wanted to hurt her back, I really did, but hanging up on her left me feeling nothing but mean and hollow and shitty.

Mission accomplished, asshole.

What the hell was she thinking? Had she been drinking? That wasn't like her, but it also wasn't like her to show her cards like that. She was obviously jealous, and how was I supposed to feel about that?

Shaking my head as I made my way back inside the theater, I had to admit that the Cherry on top line was pretty good. But thanks to that text, I'd be ending my night as soon as the curtain dropped on this god awful show.

There would be no Cherry on top tonight.

I was already up at six the next morning when I heard that goddamn Sherwood Forest ringtone again. And I practically sprained an ankle hopping over the back of the couch to grab the phone, pathetic, lovesick loser that I am.

I had no business texting u last night. I'm so sorry.

I wrote right back:

It's ok. I'm sorry too. For everything.

My heart was pumping double-time.

U have nothing to be sorry for.

Shit. Although the pain in my chest felt crushing, I wanted to keep this dialogue going.

I really hope you're doing well. I'd ask what you're doing for Christmas but I know that pisses off your inner Orphan Annie.

She didn't write back for a few minutes. I figured she was probably staring at her phone wondering how deep she wanted to get with me, or she was spending Christmas with her new guy and didn't want to rub salt in my wounds.

I'm actually going to Paris with Caitlin. So excited. Merry Christmas Caleb.

Sweet relief.

I'm excited for you. Joyeux Noël.

* * *

RENE

I'm such a jerk, such a colossal idiot.

I held back from contacting him every time I had the urge to tell him I loved him or I missed him, but the first time I have an impulse to lash out? No second thoughts, I just fire away.

What he wrote this morning just about killed me. He was sorry for everything. Me too. I sat in bed, rereading his email from long ago. Did he still need me? I knew he wasn't just sitting around waiting for me anymore, but was there a chance that he still wanted me? Loved me as much as I still loved him?

I closed my laptop and put it under my bed when Tanner knocked and came into my room.

"Are you all right?"

"I'm fine. I'm sorry about last night. I'm not much of a drinker."

He laughed and shook his head. "No, you're not."

"It's like, only seven. Why are you up so early?"

"I wasn't into the party after you left. I snuck upstairs early. I was going to head over here last night but Caitlin convinced me not to."

"Sorry."

He waved me off. "Don't be. You think I care if I miss a party?"

With that he took off his sweatshirt and t-shirt, climbed into bed behind me and pulled me in close.

"I missed you last night. Are you sure everything is ok? Is there anything you want to talk about?"

Hmm, we could talk about the fact that I'm still in love with my ex-boyfriend, about the serious thought I'm giving to breaking up with you, or we could talk about my abortion. Pick a topic.

"Really, Tanner, I'm all right. I just want to fall back asleep and your arms feel nice around me."

"At your service."

He pulled me in even closer and kissed me just below my ear. Wearing nothing but panties and a tank top, I could feel his body through the thin sweats he wore, hard against me. And heaven help me, but I was achy with need. Turning around to face him, I kissed him as my hands moved down his abdomen and stroked him.

On an exhale, he said, "Damn, that feels good."

"Tanner?"

"Yeah?"

"Why don't you ever push to do more with me?"

He rolled me onto my back and gave himself a second to come back down to earth before looking me in the eye. "I don't know. With you I'm different. I've never been this careful with other girls, but I get the feeling you need to take things slow and I'm ok with that. For you, I'll wait."

I kissed him again and parted my legs as I pulled his hips closer. And I hated myself for it, knew I wasn't being fair. I wanted to go right to the brink, to ease this ache, even though I had no intention of doing the deed with Tanner. He would take it as a sign of commitment, as a declaration of my love. I was all about me, purely selfish as I rolled my hips and nudged his hand lower down my torso as I whispered in his ear, coaxing him to touch me.

Maybe this was my one last shot to see if this thing with Tanner was going anywhere, or maybe this intense need was brought on simply from hearing Caleb's voice last night. I just knew that I desperately needed to get off, to feel something.

I was on the verge of losing my mind. "Keep going, baby," I whispered. And closing my eyes tight, I pictured Caleb entering me, filling me, fucking me senseless. Those images—his muscles flexing, his face twisted in pleasure—that's what threw me over the edge.

"Do you want me, Rene?"

"God, ah, yes, Tanner."

I silently congratulated myself for moaning the right name as I came down from that blessedly good orgasm.

He rained soft kisses on my lips, the hollow of my neck and my breasts. As he took my hand and pumped it up and down along his shaft, he whispered, "Then it's ok, baby. I'll wait for you."

Curled up in bed with Tanner afterwards, his face happy and sated, I smiled even though my head ached and my stomach was in knots. I felt tormented—guilt, desire and love. Guilt for drawing Tanner in deeper, desire for both of them, and a desperate sense of love...for Caleb.

Chapter Sixteen

CALEB

Darcy called to ask if I was heading to Rincon after Christmas. When I said I didn't know, she told me she was going to ask her roommates to head down for a few days. She added, "It's totally cool if you're there, they all love you. I just want to know what kind of space issues I'm dealing with."

After hearing about Rene and her serious boyfriend over Thanksgiving dinner, the idea of being anywhere near the girl was unthinkable. I was incensed that entire weekend, consumed with thoughts of some other man holding her, touching her and loving her body. Sadness and rage are not the best feelings to combine for anyone, but yours truly is prone to erupt under those circumstances. So no, I had no intention of setting foot on the island.

During Christmas dinner when Darcy was talking about picking the girls up from the airport on New Year's Day, though, I have to admit I was tempted. That phone call and the texts that followed had stirred some hope in me. She might have a boyfriend, but she was thinking about me. Of that I was certain.

Maybe it was nothing more than a moment of weakness for Rene. Maybe hearing about me with Cherry made her jealous in that moment, and then the moment passed. But damn, I hoped she was jealous. Hoped she was burning up with jealousy just picturing me with another woman. Because me with anyone else but Rene? It was all wrong, not how it's supposed to be. I prayed that maybe enough time had finally passed. Maybe she was ready to let me back in again.

And the Cherry situation needed to be resolved. She popped over to my parents' house Christmas Eve without telling me first. I totally played it off like I was happy to see her, but it felt like an ambush. I'd never make her feel unwelcome, but I sensed she was looking to ingratiate herself with my family and that was not happening.

And her timing sucked.

We were always pretty wistful around Christmastime. It was a happy time, don't get me wrong, but we missed the presence of my mother every year she wasn't with us. We took some time every Christmas Eve to look through old photographs and to tell stories about her. It was important for Darcy most of all, as she had no real memories of our mother, but it was personal and meaningful for every one of us who loved her. It was our way of keeping her with us always.

Sarah was telling us about this one time when she and my mother were trying to arrange us for a Christmas photo. When they finally got me and Luke to stand still, Darcy spit up all over me and I started crying. Luke slipped in the puke puddle and fell, so he started crying. All the commotion made Darcy cry, and then the photo shoot was officially over.

Sarah had us all laughing, but Cherry wasn't in on the joke. This was too intimate a moment and she just didn't belong. The girl didn't know a whole lot about me. I certainly never once felt the urge to open up and tell her about my mother. She shifted closer to me on the couch, but I didn't take her hand or make any move to connect with her. I looked away instead, my chest aching as I remembered sharing everything about my mother, and so much more with Rene, long before I'd even kissed her.

Cherry stayed for two hours tops, but it felt like an eternity. I couldn't wait to put her in the cab.

"Your family is really great."

"Thanks, Cherry. They all seem to like you."

She looked unsure, like maybe she knew I was bullshitting her. "Caleb?"

"Yeah?"

She changed her mind, the question in her eyes left unspoken. Pasting on a pained smile, she shook her head and wished me a Merry Christmas before she leaned in to kiss me and then got into the car.

We were done. I was never going to let her in and she knew it. I stood on the sidewalk for a moment, watching as the tail lights grew smaller and then disappeared around the corner, hating myself for putting her in this situation again—for hurting her.

Coming in from the cold, my father caught my eye and motioned for me to carry the dessert dishes into the kitchen.

"She seems like a nice girl."

"Don't, Dad."

He joked, "She's not a nice girl?"

I smiled. "No, she's perfectly nice, just not meant for me."

"I definitely got that impression from you. I'm thinking she probably did too."

"This has been the most messed up year of my life. And I want to apologize for worrying you and Sarah. I'm making some changes, I'll do better this year."

He stopped loading the dishwasher and turned to me. "You're not messing up, Caleb. You have a lot to be proud of. We're so proud of you."

I couldn't accept those words. "Thanks, but we both know I've been going off the rails lately and making some bad decisions." He leaned back against the counter, listening, probably more than a little surprised that I was in the mood to share. "I'm seeing a woman I don't really care about, and she doesn't know that I'm seeing another girl on the side who's engaged, so yeah, my personal life is a mess. And at work," I shook my head, "I beat the shit out of the managing partner's nephew one night and didn't even get canned because financially, I've been having the best year of my life. Like I'm earning the most insane commissions ever. Everything just feels upside down to me."

"What are you going to do about this girl, Cherry?"

"I'll straighten things out with her, stop seeing her."

"She's not the one who had you tied up in knots this past year, is she?"

I laughed, shaking my head. "No." I looked out the window then, watched as the falling snow made the world look picture-perfect. "But I keep hoping that someday she'll be here with me on Christmas Eve."

"I hope so too, Caleb."

* * *

RENE

Beautiful doesn't adequately describe Paris.

There isn't a word in any language to do it justice. And to see Paris the way I was getting to experience it with Caitlin was like a fantasy come to life.

The boyfriend, Étienne, had a five bedroom apartment on Avenue Foch, one of the most exclusive streets in all of Paris. I had my own gigantic room with gilded trim on the walls, a four poster bed, and the lushest linens to ever touch my body. I felt like a princess for a minute there, but then quickly floated back down to earth once I started to unpack.

I transferred my jeans, tees and a few sweaters into an ornately carved armoire. I had one little black dress, a wrap to throw over my shoulders, and one pair of heels—nothing but the bare essentials, as usual. Thank goodness Caitlin packed enough clothing for an entire season, otherwise I would have worn that one black dress threadbare.

Every night started out with Caitlin's mom and Étienne. We would go to one of Paris's best hotel bars to have drinks, listen to jazz and to people watch. One night was Le Bar at the Four Seasons, the next was Bar 228, the next Le Bar du Plaza Athénée. And drinks were always followed by late, leisurely dinners. Some nights it was small bistro fare, while other nights he gave us the all-out experience of places like Alaine Ducasse. Those two were pretty intrepid, tagging along a few nights when Caitlin and I went out clubbing afterward.

During the day, Caitlin and I set out on foot and explored every inch of the city. I absolutely loved Paris, and speaking French gave me the feeling that I was, for better or worse, tied to this country in some way. It even made me feel a sense of gratitude towards my parents, flawed as they were.

On our last night in Paris, we ate at a cozy bistro that Étienne said was his favorite as a child. Thankfully it was affordable, and he was gracious enough to let me treat them as a thank you for the best vacation I'd ever had. I told Étienne he'd spoiled me for life, that it would be hard to ever top this trip. He replied, "Oh, ma belle amie, when you see Paris with your lover it will be even better."

I blushed when I thought of visiting Paris with who else? Caleb.

Landing on the twenty-eighth, I was squeezing in three days at the restaurant and then—so unlike me—we were heading down to Puerto Rico to stay with Darcy and her parents for a few days.

I could tell Tanner was a little miffed that I couldn't make it to him for a visit in between trips, but he knew I needed to work so he didn't push me. I did need to work, but it also served as a convenient excuse to avoid him. He was getting more serious while I was pulling away, and I felt more and more like a thief and a coward with each passing day that I allowed it to continue.

And while I was looking forward to my escape, I felt uneasy about staying with the Donovans. Being with Darcy at school was one thing, vacationing with her family in a place where they spent time with Caleb was another. Caitlin told me I was being crazy. I only agreed to go when I had it on good authority that Caleb wouldn't be there. It didn't feel one hundred percent right, but I told myself it was just four days and not to overthink it.

By the time we landed on New Year's Day, I was exhausted. Craig put me on double shifts at my request, capped off by an upscale private New Year's Eve party for two hundred guests. The tips were fantastic, but we worked from four that afternoon until four the next morning. I mean, we worked *hard*. It was almost five by the time I got back home, and by five-thirty I was on a train making my way to the airport. Caitlin claims I was drooling and snoring on the plane, and I'd say she was exaggerating but it was probably true.

The town they stayed in was just as Darcy had described it: paradise. It was low key and sleepy, nothing fancy. They always rented the same house from one of Dr. Donovan's colleagues. It was big for the area, sat right on the beach, and had a second story deck and large windows overlooking the ocean. There were hammocks in the trees, tropical flowers everywhere, and a pool surrounded by comfy loungers. The whole atmosphere just forced you to relax.

We were in our bikinis and out in the water with cold beers in hand by noon that first day. In Paris of all places, Caitlin and I shopped for new suits. Correction: she picked out multiple suits while I splurged on one very expensive white bikini. I was wistful as I packed my new bathing suit along with the blue one Caleb had rescued from the beach that night.

After we came out of the ocean, we lounged around the pool with Darcy's parents for hours. No family was perfect, I knew that, but seriously, they came pretty close. They laughed and joked together, asked questions and listened intently, they showed affection like it was the most easy and natural thing in the world. Happy but aching at the same time, I wanted what they had—parents like Darcy's and a partner who looked at me the way Mr. and Mrs. Donovan looked at one another. It hurt to think of it, to think of Caleb.

Focus on what's good in your life, my inner therapist/cheerleader nagged. And that first night, when we went to some mom-and-pop joint right on the beach, I focused on the best tostones I've ever tasted and the people surrounding me with laughter at the table. *Yes, this right here, be thankful for this.*

It was definitely a more mellow vacation, and for that I was thankful. We spent the next day paddle boarding, floating in the pool and laying out in the sun. Dr. Donovan tried to teach us to surf, but all of us except for Darcy were basically hopeless.

Dinner and drinks on the deck closed out day two of the trip. Heaven.

I woke to the smell of coffee and voices in the kitchen the next morning. Rolling over, I was shocked to see Caitlin's bed already made. I smiled as I stretched. *Who is this new Rene Beaumont, jetting off on vacations all the time and sleeping the day away?*

CALEB

I was feeling pretty confident until the plane touched down. Now I was seriously questioning myself, wondering if I'd made a big mistake.

Luke and Kate were the only ones who knew about Operation Get Rene Back.

"You think I shouldn't go, Luke?"

"No, I think you should. You've got to know once and for all, right? If it doesn't work out, though, it could be all sorts of awkward with everyone there in the house with you. That's my only concern. But if I were in your shoes, I'd go."

I gave Kate a kiss and a pat on her giant belly before I left for the airport. "Call me if there's any news, ok?"

"I'm not due for another four weeks, but we'll keep you in the loop, Uncle Caleb."

I pulled up to the house and took a deep breath as I cut the engine. I sat there for a moment, tried and failed to form some kind of plan, to think of something to say to her.

I had nothing.

Darcy was alone in the kitchen, and with my confidence now in the toilet, I was thankful I didn't have an audience.

I shushed Darcy when she called out my name and threw her arms around me. Damn, she was going to wake up the entire house. When she asked what had changed, why I was there, I started in with some bullshit about wanting to surf. I checked the conditions before I left and they weren't ideal, but I guessed from the way she was looking at me funny that there were no waves to speak of.

"Sure this trip isn't because you're missing a certain waitress?"

For a split second I thought she was referring to Rene, but then it dawned on me that Darcy had probably seen the way Elena all but preyed on me when we were in town. I looked around to make sure no one had heard, and my tone was full-on hostile when I shot back, "What the hell are you talking about?"

Now I had my sister shaken up and confused. Could I do anything right? I managed to smooth it over with Darcy and get the message across that my coming here had nothing to do with Elena. Fucking hell, that's all I needed Rene thinking.

I heard faucets going and muffled voices, then Jenna and Caitlin made their way out. Where was Rene? I was about two seconds away from losing my shit.

Jenna ran over and gave me a hug as Caitlin's eyes went super wide. She collected herself before saying, "Hey, Caleb, I thought you were swamped at work."

I think I managed to joke and banter back and forth with them in a reasonably sane manner, even though I wasn't fully paying attention and my heart was hammering in my chest.

Where is she?

And just when I was beginning to feel sick with the realization that I'd come all this way for nothing, Rene walked into the kitchen, frightened eyes fixed on me.

Everyone kept on talking, but I couldn't register the words, couldn't see anything but Rene. Bare feet, tanned legs, the curve of her waist, her chest rising and falling with ragged breaths—the body I'd once claimed as my own. Her lip trembled, and her eyes told me it was taking a herculean effort for her to remain composed.

Please don't be afraid.

I needed something, and when my eyes took in the pale blue ties peeking out from underneath her tank top, I took it as a sign and breathed a sigh of relief.

"How are you, Rene?"

"I didn't think you were coming."

Are you upset that I'm here?

Do you want me to leave?

Are you in love with that other guy?

Do you still love me?

My mind was racing with all the questions I needed answered.

My voice hitched when I said, "I wasn't planning on it, but I couldn't stay away."

Before it got even more awkward, I grabbed my stuff and said something about going surfing. I didn't want to surf, didn't want to do anything but grab hold of her and hang on for dear life, but that wouldn't be happening right now or maybe ever. I went downstairs, threw my things next to the couch and grabbed some board shorts out of my bag.

"Caleb?"

I turned to see my parents coming in from the deck and tried my best to sound casual. "It was so crappy and cold in New York that I decided last minute to shoot down. I'll just crash on the couch or in the hammock. How are the waves, Dad?"

"Not a wave in sight. Nada." He cocked his head to the side. "I'm surprised you didn't check the conditions before booking your flight."

"Definitely should have." I shrugged, keeping up the casual Caleb act. "Ah well, the sun's shining. That alone will make the trip worthwhile."

"Yesterday there was nothing but ankle busters, really small. I was trying to teach Darcy's friends the basics on an easy day. Either I'm an awful teacher or they don't possess any natural talent for surfing."

Mmm. I'd like to have Rene out in the water, steadying her on the board, holding onto her lower back before I helped push her off into the waves.

Maybe someday...

* * *

RENE

At the sound of his voice I stopped in my tracks. What the hell was he doing here? I stood in the hallway nearly paralyzed with fear, but I couldn't hide out all day. I had to face him.

Breathe, Rene.

I don't remember what I said or what he said, but he was looking straight at my chest when I saw that familiar smile play on his lips. The bikini, did he remember it? I felt myself flush crimson, finding it so hard to act natural. He looked a little flustered himself before grabbing his bag and leaving the kitchen.

Starting another pot of coffee, I snuck glances at my friends to see if our awkward exchange had registered with anyone. Besides Caitlin, who was sporting a huge grin, no one else seemed to have noticed.

I was nervous but hopeful at the same time. Why would he come here unless he wanted to see me?

As soon as I could get away unnoticed, I went to find him. I had to clear the air and see what his deal was. Was he still with Cherry? If so, why did he come?

He wasn't on the beach or by the pool.

Caitlin followed after me. "He just drove off a minute ago, said he needed wax or something."

"Why is he here?"

"You *know* why he's here."

"I don't know anything."

"Please, the way he looked at you? He wants you, Rene, and you better decide right now who it is that you want. If you push him away again it might be the final straw, you know? He's the one taking the big risk here, showing up knowing he might get his heart broken again."

Darcy and Sarah walked in just then and suggested we all go into town for lunch and some shopping. We didn't get back until nearly dinnertime. Dr. Donovan and Caleb were outside on the deck getting the grill ready. And, um, yeah, Caleb wasn't wearing a shirt.

When Dr. Donovan started taking requests for shrimp or steak, I heard Caleb start in, "Rene can't—" He was about to tell his dad that I couldn't eat shrimp, that I had a shellfish allergy, but stopped himself. "Rene, can't hear you. Did you say shrimp or steak?"

"Steak. Thanks, Caleb."

We sat out on the deck until late. Margaritas were flowing, but I was nursing the same one all night. I was too nervous and had too much on my mind. I needed to be clear-headed. I noticed that when Caleb walked by with the pitcher, he refilled everyone else but skipped over me.

Everyone was calling it a night, but Darcy didn't look like she was going down easy. The thought crossed my mind that she might have been waiting for us to leave so she could talk with Caleb alone, so I went back to our room but didn't go to sleep. After an hour I made my way back out into the darkened kitchen.

I had to know.

He wasn't on the couch or on the deck, but I wasn't really looking for him there. He was sitting in the sand facing the ocean, and I stopped cold when I got close.

I must have stood there for a full minute before he patted the sand next to him and said, "Come sit with me. I've been waiting for you." When I sat, he took my hand and kissed it. Without looking at me, he added, "I've been waiting so long for you."

I took a deep breath in an effort to calm myself, but it was no use. I began to cry when I asked, "Do you still love me?"

He looked over and smiled. "I loved you way before I even kissed you, Rene, and I've never stopped."

The tears really came then, but they were tears of relief. He said nothing, just wrapped an arm around my shoulder.

"I'm sorry I stayed away for so long. I'm used to handling things by myself and keeping people from getting too close. That's all I've ever known." He kept silent, but kissed my hand again, letting his lips linger on my skin. Another deep breath, because I was putting it all out there. "I love you, Caleb, and I need you. I don't want you to be with anyone else."

I lowered my head and braced for the worst.

He scooped me up in one quick motion and laid me down into the hammock before he climbed in and hovered over me. He shook his head as he whispered, "No one else for me, no one else for you." In between soft kisses, he whispered, "I love you, and you're mine."

The cloud of tension, sadness and anger I'd been living under for the past year finally lifted. I felt peaceful. "My God, I've missed you."

He pulled me in close, tucked my head under his chin and

wrapped his body around mine. "Just stay here with me. I've wanted to hold you again for so long. I can't let you go."

And I let it wash over me, let myself slip under and just live in this good moment. I didn't know where I was heading, didn't know if this was real or lasting, but I let myself enjoy the feel of his arms around me as I drifted off, fully content for the first time in a long while.

I woke to the sound of waves crashing, seagulls chatting and the feel of Caleb planting kisses on my face.

"Good morning, sweet angel."

I smiled up at him, so relieved, but no sooner was I reaching up to wipe at my tears. "Thank God. I was afraid I was just in the middle of some really awesome dream."

He traced his thumb over my cheek, smoothed away another tear. "You up for a swim?"

"Um, yeah? Now?"

"Yup, early morning swims are the best."

"I thought night swimming was the best."

He laughed. "Yes, naked night swimming with you *is* the best. I'm just saying that unless we jump in for a swim soon, I'm going to have to explain to my dad why I have one of my sister's roommates trapped in a hammock with me."

I struggled to get up, but was getting nowhere in that web of ropes. "Help me get out of this thing!"

"Easy, we have a few minutes. And Rene, I've been thinking...I'm all for full disclosure, but shocking the family and friends with this right now would leave us with a lot of explaining to do. I feel like our history is *our* history. We don't have to share anything with anyone."

I nodded. Then I peeled myself away from him, shimmied out of my shorts and made my way into the water. I looked back to see Caleb lifting his shirt over his head. So beautiful.

Right on schedule I heard Dr. Donovan call out, "Who's taking such an early swim? Is that you, Rene?"

"Yes, I couldn't sleep. Anyway, I love early morning swims."

Caleb stifled a chuckle.

"I'm surprised Caleb isn't out there with you. Oh, speak of the devil. Morning, Caleb."

"Good morning, Dad. Yeah, she just woke me up with all that splashing around."

"Sorry," I teased. "What are you doing sleeping out here anyway?"

"Are you kidding? I just had the absolute *best* sleep of my life out here. You should try it sometime."

Now I was holding back a laugh.

Dr. Donovan seemed none the wiser. "All right, I'm off. See you two later. Caleb, the waves are picking up a little. Maybe you could teach Rene and the other girls to surf today. You'll have more luck than I did."

Once his dad turned to go, Caleb took off running, dove into the waves and swam underwater until I could feel his hands on my bum. When he came up, he kissed me hard and pulled me close to press my body against his.

"I've missed you so much." Then he pulled back a little. "But I'm not looking to rush anything, all right?"

I smiled. "All right."

"We'll ease back in slowly if that's what you want."

"I'm sure about this, I am, but I want to take it slow."

He nodded. "We'll take it slow. God, you don't know how happy you make me." He kissed me and then picked me up and carried me back to the shore. When he put me back down on the sand he looked over my body, smiling as he took in the sight of me. "When I first saw you yesterday wearing that suit, I hoped it was a good omen."

"It's my lucky bikini."

"I'm the one who's lucky."

He smacked my ass then, giving me a head start back to the house.

And while I was pretty much grinning like a fool all day, it wasn't all that hard to pretend we were just friends around everyone else because truly, we *were* friends.

Caleb made sure to talk to all of us girls equally that day, and took each one of us out on the waves for a surf lesson. He may have been a little more handsy with me than the others when he was my surf instructor. I doubt he had his hand on anyone else's upper thigh, rubbing his thumb in slow agonizing circles as he steadied them on the board, and I'm sure he didn't tell them to keep their "perfect tits" pressed close to the board before pushing up to a stand.

Caitlin knew, of course, but I was pretty certain no one else did.

Sarah suggested we head to the same beachside café for dinner on our last night, but Caleb insisted on treating everyone to a nicer place in town. By nicer, I mean you could still wear your shorts and flip flops, but they had a selection of beers and served food on actual plates. The mood was festive and everyone had a lot of laughs, but the realization that I was flying out the next morning was hitting me hard. I just got him back and now we had to part ways again so soon? What I wouldn't give to stay here a few more days with Caleb alone.

After I was fairly certain everyone was in bed, I snuck out again and went down to the beach. He was in the same spot, patting the sand next to him as I got closer. When I plopped down, he took my hand and kissed it just like he had the night before. "Any chance you'll take a swim with me tonight?"

Lifting my shirt over my head, I said, "I'll race you in." With that, he pushed me down and jumped over me, stripped down to nothing and then ran in. I called after him trying not to raise my voice, "A little overly competitive, aren't we?"

I followed, diving under the waves and coming up within inches of him. "Should I go suit on or suit off?"

He shook his head. "I can't weigh in on this decision. I promised you I'd take it slow."

I undid the strings on my new white top and then took off the bottoms as well. I teased, "Please don't lose this suit. It's brand new. I just got it in Paris."

"Ooh la la. In that case, mon amour, I'll personally walk it in."

He looked like a Greek god, strong and powerful, with his wet skin glistening in the light of the moon. He turned to face me, naked and shameless, then slowly made his way back in until he was less than a foot away from me.

"Remember that first swim?"

I nodded. "I remember wanting to get closer to you."

"I was fighting with myself to keep a proper distance."

I closed the short distance between us now and wrapped my arms and legs around him.

He swallowed. "Hey now, you're making it hard to go slow."

"I've wanted to feel your body against mine for so long."

His look turned serious. "You know you're the most beautiful woman I've ever held in my arms, don't you? I feel like everything is going to be all right now, Rene. All the pain, all the fucking sadness... It's over."

"I'm so sorry."

"It wasn't your fault, so don't apologize. I just couldn't be happy without you. You're the first person I've ever really loved. I wasn't prepared for how bad losing you would make me feel."

"You'll never be able to get rid of me again."

He kissed me deep, cupping my bottom and pulling me in closer to him. We were a tangle of mouths and hands, exploring each other in a way that felt desperate.

This going slow thing was overrated, and I was already looking to amend the rules. I thought Caleb was on the same page when he led me out of the water and stood close behind me on the shore. I could feel all of him pressing into my lower back, and I ached for him. As I arched my body and lifted my arms to lace my hands into his hair, giving him full access, he began to put my top back on. *What???* After he had me tied in relatively well, he moved down my body, kissing a trail from the area right under my breast, down to my hips and then down the side of one thigh. He gestured for me to lift one foot at a time and then slid my bottoms back up to cover me. I turned to face him, let out a frustrated sigh and then smiled. "I know, you're taking it slow because I asked you to."

"Yes, even if it kills me."

We walked back hand in hand, and he kissed me possessively once more before I made my way back to my room. I took a speedy shower to get the sand off me and then slid between the sheets. I drifted off to sleep with a smile on my face.

Standing around the kitchen drinking coffee early the next morning, I could have sworn I saw Darcy look between me and Caleb a few times, but maybe I was imagining it. And she didn't look curious or suspicious when Caleb volunteered to take us to the airport, so it was all good.

He walked us inside, dragging most of our bags like a pack mule. Looking to me, he asked, "Rene, you only packed that one small bag?"

I did pack light as a rule, but I was missing one small carry-on. "I know I put it in the car. I'm sure of it."

"Run back out with me and we'll check the trunk. If it's not there I'll make sure Darcy takes it back with her tomorrow."

When we got back outside he handed me the bag he'd purposely stashed in a far corner of the trunk. "I'm crafty."

He pulled me close, pressing every part of his body against mine. He moaned into my mouth as he gave me one last lingering kiss. My heart was already hurting when he pulled back and cradled my face in his hands.

"We need to figure out how we want this to work for the next few months while you're still in school."

"I know." I had to look away when I said, "I have to take care of some things this week."

"Me too."

Just the idea of him being involved with someone else, of being in the position to have to break off a relationship with another person had me squeezing my eyes tight shut against the visual. I nodded when he took me gently by the shoulders, knowing I wasn't alone, knowing he was feeling the same way.

"I'll come to you, to make it easier for you with school and work."

"No, I don't want to be holed up in a hotel in Boston. If it's ok with you, I'd like to stay at your place."

"I'd love that. Call me later so I know you made it home safe."

"I love you, so much."

"I love you too, Rene."

* * *

CALEB

I came back from the airport to find some of the best surfing conditions I've ever had on the island. Was this the universe telling me that yes, Caleb, all is now officially right in the world?

I spent the next four hours out on the water. Between sets I had time to think and to relive the past two days. I kept shaking my head, reassuring myself that this was reality, that she was back in my life.

I couldn't wait to get home. I knew I probably wouldn't be seeing Rene for a little over a week, but I was itching to set things straight, to get my life in order.

When Sarah said she had a craving for the mofungo they served at *that place right on the water*, I made an executive decision to skip dinner with the fam. Tempestuous was putting it nicely—sometimes Elena was straight-up violent. I was pretty certain that a beer bottle would be hurled in my general vicinity if I went in there telling her, once again, that I couldn't see her anymore. She was engaged now, I didn't owe her anything, but I knew steering clear of that café for the rest of my natural born life would be for the best. But Cherry was a different story. She knew this was coming, but I owed her an explanation and would give her a full one. Our history was twisted and complicated, but Cherry had always been a good friend to me—a soft place to land when my life was a mess and I was hurting.

Staying at the firm was not a good idea, I knew that. Not just because leaving would make it easier on Cherry, but a nagging voice in my head kept asking that if I did intend to venture out and start something on my own, what was I waiting for?

"You see what some good surfing does for that kid? He looks as happy as can be."

I could hear my father clear as day as I rinsed off in the outdoor shower.

Sarah chimed in, "Wonder if it was just the surfing?"

Darcy asked, "What do you mean?"

"Nothing really, it's just that there were several beautiful women here this week. That alone could make someone like Caleb very happy."

"I'm gonna go gag right now."

Little sister was going to have to deal because, like it or not, this was happening.

Damn, I wanted to burst in and yell at the top of my lungs that I loved Rene, that someday I was going to marry her, and that she's made me happier than I've ever been. Not just because I was pretty much bursting with emotion at that point, but also because I really loved my family and I wanted to share the best things in my life with them. But that time would come. Maybe Rene and I would decide to tell certain people soon, but maybe we wouldn't. We'd make that decision, and all others, together.

The only exception to that rule was Luke. Just as Rene had

Caitlin to confide in, Luke knew what was really going on. He picked up on the first ring.

"What the hell happened?"

"It's all good."

He let out a breath. "I'm happy for you, Caleb."

"I'm fucking ecstatic."

"Does anyone else know?"

"No, just you and Kate. And uh, did you tell Kate everything? I mean, it's ok if you did."

"No, not everything. Kate and I were trying to get pregnant then, but even without that, I just…"

I knew what he was trying to say. "Thanks. I just want Rene's privacy protected."

"I know that."

"And thanks for everything, Luke. I don't tell you often enough, but I don't know what I'd do without you."

He laughed. "I worry about that myself sometimes."

"You can't even let me say something nice. Later, dick."

"Bye."

Chapter Seventeen

What to do, what to do?

Since the dorms were closed over the break, I was crashing with Cara just outside of Boston. My plan was to stay with her for a week, then head down to see Caleb, and then move back into the dorm.

I couldn't wait to be working full-time and living in a place of my own. I didn't like to stop and dwell on it, but for a good part of my life I've lived like a nomad. Moving from place to place, crashing with this one, subletting that one's place for a few months—it was sad and I was so tired of it.

My dilemma now, being temporarily out of the dorms, was finding a time and place to meet up with Tanner. I could not go visit him at home, couldn't stage a break-up with his family around, but I still had ten days until we were due back at school.

My inner voice was schizo. One moment I'm all: *It can wait...Best to do this in person.* Then: *Seriously? You're going to string the poor guy along for another ten days? That's just cruel.*

His name and picture popped up on my home screen at that very moment.

"Were you even going to call to tell me you're back? I was thinking maybe you flew off on a third vacation."

I laughed nervously, my face heating with the stress of lying as I blamed a delayed flight and exhaustion for my screw-up. Meanwhile, I'd already spoken to Caleb three times in the past twenty-four hours.

"And where are you? The dorms are still closed, right?"

"I'm at Cara's. It's pretty close to the restaurant."

"Can I see you tonight?"

I was so not looking forward to doing this. "I'd love to see you, but are you sure? It's like an ice storm out there. I don't like the idea of you driving in this miserable weather at night."

"You're sweet, and you're probably right." *No, I'm awful.* "But then I won't see you. I'm leaving for Vermont tomorrow."

"I forgot you were going skiing."

"Are you sure you can't come? My family would love to have you."

"Besides the fact that I cannot ski to save my life, I'm committed to two days at the station this week and I'm waitressing."

"Shit. I'm going crazy without you. I'll be back a week from this Sunday. Do *not* work that day. I need to see you, ok?"

"Sure."

As soon as I hung up with Tanner, I called Caleb and told him I wanted to come see him sooner than I'd originally planned.

"Are you all right, Rene?"

"Never better. I mean that. I just want to see you."

"I'll be at the airport, just tell me when."

"Does the day after tomorrow sound good?"

"Yes, your twenty-first birthday sounds very good." When I groaned, he asked, "Did you think I'd forget?"

"I wasn't sure. But really, I don't want to do anything crazy. I just want to talk and to be with you. Low key, do you promise?"

"I promise."

* * *

CALEB

I was sweating when I walked into the break room, and it wasn't even eight in the morning.

It was empty except for Cherry.

"Can we grab lunch later?"

She stopped stirring her coffee but kept her eyes fixed on the mug. "I know what this is. This is the letting me down easy lunch, am I right?"

I had to swallow past the damn lump in my throat. "I was wrong to pull you back into my bullshit. You were pretty clear last year that this wasn't good for you." Shaking my head, I laid the truth out, plain and simple. "I was hurting, you were good to me and I took advantage. You're a beautiful woman and you've always been a great friend to me. I just can't do this anymore."

"Is she back in your life?"

"Yeah, I hope so."

"I'm not totally innocent in this." Her eyes were shimmering when she looked back up to me. "I knew you didn't love me but I thought maybe I could change that." When I went to take her hand, she backed away shaking her head. "Don't, Caleb."

Cherry wasn't at her desk when I left for an early client meeting. One of the secretaries told me she took the day, wasn't feeling well.

I felt like a total bastard.

The next day was awkward, to say the least. We were both keeping our distance, but that was hard because we still had to talk about clients and exchange emails. I was a guilt-ridden mess. But then that next morning, when I caught sight of Rene walking though airport security with a smile bright enough to power up all of Manhattan, everything lifted. The sun was shining again.

We dropped her bags with my doorman and then sat for hours at a great little place around the corner from my apartment. We had a long lunch that morphed into dinner. We talked about school, about work, and then talk moved on to the uncomfortable things that sat between us.

Rene told me she wasn't going to speak to Tanner until they were back at school. I was disappointed at first, wanted her to do it as soon as possible, but she explained that she didn't want to talk to him over the phone and she definitely couldn't talk to him with his family around.

"I'm dreading it. It's not like this is totally coming out of left field, but he'll feel blindsided. I don't want to hurt him."

Cherry's hurt expression came to mind. "Yeah, it's not pleasant."

"That situation makes me unhappy, but then at the same time, the thought of being with you makes me feel like I'm bursting with, I don't know, joy!" She laughed. "I feel kind of nutty, like I keep finding myself smiling for no reason."

I totally got it. I was the same.

Rene asked how Kate was doing, and asked if it was difficult spending the past few months hearing about the pregnancy with the whole family getting ready for the baby's arrival. I told her there were times it gave me a passing feeling of sadness, but mostly I was excited for Luke and Kate. That was the truth, but it sounded callous and unfeeling to my own ears.

"I think about the fact that I would have given birth in October." She let out a deep breath. "I can get stuck on that sometimes, you know? Calculating how old he or she would be."

He or she.

I took a sip of wine that was more like a gulp, and sensing my torment, Rene reached across the table and took one of my hands in hers.

"You know, I went to stay at Tanner's house over Thanksgiving."

"Yeah I heard about that." I slid my wine glass away on reflex. "I went on a bender that weekend."

She cocked her head to the side and frowned, but her eyes were twinkling. "I want to feel sad about that, but there's a part of me that's so happy you cared." She squeezed my hand and smiled. "You know I only went because I had *nowhere* to go. God, I was so mad. Everyone was on me about staying in the dorms by myself, so I finally caved in and went. Anyway, he has a young cousin with a baby." Rene looked out the window for a moment as if she was lost in the memory. "She caught me staring and asked if I wanted to hold her daughter. Holding that baby felt *so* good, but my heart..."

"I'm so sorry."

She shook her head. "That's not my point. The pain wasn't regret or guilt or whatever...I mean it was to some degree, but I was hurting because I felt like such a fraud, and I felt so alone in that room full of strangers." She let out a shaky breath. "Tanner's mom has some pretty strong opinions on abortion and the women who get them. Don't get me wrong, she's a nice woman, but it was just awful."

"I want to take away everything that hurts, do you understand that? But I know I can't."

Rene nodded and shrugged. "There will always be times when it hurts. I met a doctor at the clinic when I went in for a follow-up visit. Once I put on that paper robe, I was a sobbing wreck. It was kind of embarrassing." I clutched her hand and she met my eyes with a faint smile that did nothing to mask her sadness. "Anyway, the doctor shared that she'd gotten pregnant while she was in med school. She just understood me, she understood everything. Listening to her really helped me, more than she'll ever know. There were times I let myself feel it, but most of the time I pushed you, the baby—I pushed it all out of my mind. I was on autopilot, you know? I just put my head down, worked harder than I ever had, and forced myself to move on."

"I wish I would've been there to help you through it."

She shook her head. "I don't think you could have. I think I would have come to resent you if you were around me then. I don't know."

"Whatever happens from now on, we have to make decisions together."

"I know, and I hope that's the one thing that's changed for me after going through all this. Making decisions alone, not accepting help from people who love you, and keeping secrets...It's a lonely way to live. I don't want to do that anymore."

"You'll never have to."

After I said that I realized it might sound too possessive, too final for Rene—as if I intended to have her close to me forever. But that *was* my truth and I wasn't going to waste any more time being cautious.

"I know you're only twenty-one, birthday girl. I don't want you to feel like I've mapped out your entire future for you, but I just...I really love you."

"I can't see a future with anyone but you, Caleb."

* * *

RENE

Being here with him, talking for hours—I felt like I had my friend back and I was so thankful. Caitlin listened patiently for countless hours over the past year, but talking with Caleb was entirely different. He was a part of everything and he was a part of me.

He asked if I was ready for my birthday present when we got back to his apartment. Looking nervous, he took a box out from a kitchen drawer. "I hope you like it."

My hands trembled as I untied the red satin ribbon from the small Cartier box. There was another small velvet box inside. Don't get me wrong, I did not think for a minute he was proposing. In fact, I would have thought he'd bumped his head or something if he actually dropped down to one knee. But it was a ring, one with a wide band made from of a triple strand of white gold with two ends that met in the center where they intertwined. It was a cool, contemporary design, and to me, the strands spoke of two people coming together, inextricably linked to one another.

"I love it, I absolutely love it."

"What I meant to say is that I hope you like it because it's engraved, so I can't take it back."

The word *Someday* was etched inside. I looked up at him with a question in my eyes.

"A lot of times over the past year I found myself saying that word. Maybe someday Rene will let me back in. Someday I won't miss her so badly." He shook his head when he added, "But I could never stop missing you." He lowered his head and took my hand. "And now that you've come back to me, I've let myself think that someday soon you'll be in New York again with me, all the time. That someday I'll make you my wife. Someday it will be you getting ready to be a mother, and you'll be carrying my baby." He looked back up to me, uncertain. "I'm sorry if that's too much."

When I lowered myself into his lap and wrapped my arms around him, he whispered in my ear, "Baby, I need you."

"Yes, I don't want to go slow anymore."

What followed was two hours of the most mind blowing, intimate love that both my mind and body would probably ever experience.

After lying there for a long while, both of us lost in our own thoughts, he rolled over and cupped my cheek in his hand. "Do you know how many times I dreamed of that? Then convinced myself I'd never feel it again?" He shifted me so that I was lying on top of him.

He ran his hands down my back and then rested them on my bum. "Your body feels so good, Rene. I'll always want you, this, us."

His body felt strong and hard beneath me. I wanted him again. I rested my forearms on his chest. "Hmm, I could stay like this forever." Then I sat up straddling him. "Or like this. I could stay like this."

His smile turned wicked. "Yes, stay like this. I like the view."

He put his hands on my stomach and slowly, gently ran his touch up my body, lingering on my breasts before taking my face in his hands. He sat himself up so we were face to face.

We moved together like that, our faces an inch apart. And while my instinct was too look away, Caleb kept me anchored to him, to the moment. I would never stop wanting this and couldn't imagine being this close to anyone else.

Later when I thought back to it, I was relieved I hadn't gone ahead and been impulsive with Tanner. I only wanted this with Caleb. I felt like he was my heart, my life.

Satisfied and lazy in his bed, I felt like a contented cat. He rubbed his hands over my hips. "What can I do for you now, madam? Would you like me to feed you in bed, rub your feet? Anything, tell me what I can do for you."

"You can run me a bubble bath and then get in there with me. I want to feel you behind me, want you to wash my hair and every inch of me."

"You got it, but if I'm sitting behind you and this body is against mine, I can't promise that I won't want you again."

My eyes went wide. "I might not be able to walk tomorrow!"

He gave me a playful spank. "There's something hot about that. All day while I'm at work tomorrow, I can think about you and how you'll still be able to feel me."

"I actually love the thought of that myself."

He looked at me seriously. "I can call in tomorrow if you want."

"No, it's Monday. And weren't you just out last week?"

"Yeah, I do need to go in. I can sneak out a little early, though."

"Don't. I plan to be down as often as I can, and you can't take off every time I'm here. Besides, this is my favorite city. I can totally amuse myself for the day in New York. I'm going to call Maureen and Caroline and see if we can meet for lunch after the show tomorrow."

"Good. Hey, we never really got to talk about how things went with Bennett. Darcy told me you had a great experience so I'm assuming he wasn't a total ass."

I laughed. "No, he was an ass. I mean, there were some days that were rough, but I was able to navigate around it and I handled him as best I could. It's not the kind of business where I would have garnered any respect by complaining, which is wrong and it sucks. And if it got really awful I would have, but he's not on *that* level. He's just a creepy flirt."

"I watched the show a few times this summer. Couldn't help but see him as a sleazy bastard."

"You watched the show?"

Caleb shrugged. "I knew you were there."

I wrapped my arms around his neck and kissed him again. I loved this man.

"We definitely came to an understanding by the end of the summer. Bennett actually offered me a job."

"Would you really even consider working for him?"

"You know what? If that was the only job on the table, then yes, I would use him as a stepping stone to something better. Like I said, I was able to handle him. But thankfully, I won't have to. Meredith Carey also offered me a job, so I'm hopeful that pans out."

"Wow, that's impressive."

I went on to tell him the crazy series of events that led up to that job offer, which had him laughing.

"You know, while I'm here I'd like to go see Marcel and get a trim. I'll do that Tuesday. Is that ok, if I hang out until Wednesday?"

"Please don't ever ask me a question like that again. You can move in with me today if you want." With that, he lifted me up and carried me into the bathroom. He held me in his lap as he sat on the side of the tub and ran the water. He looked down at my body appreciatively. "I could run you a bath every night. Bring you a glass of wine while you soak. Cook you dinner. Kiss you and love every inch of your body morning, noon and night. If you stay here with me, I'll be your slave."

"Umm, that sounds nice."

"It would be nice."

"But I'll be in a fourth floor walk-up again come June. Hopefully a little better than the one I had last summer. If I don't upgrade, I don't know if Caitlin will come to visit."

"I knew it wouldn't be so easy to sell you."

Soaking in the tub with Caleb was heaven. He washed my hair and then slid us both down and just held me with his arms wrapped around my chest.

"After work tomorrow I'll cook dinner for us here. I'd love to take you home to eat with my parents, but that day will come soon enough."

"I love your parents. I can't imagine what my life would have been like..."

He held me tighter. "I hate it, just knowing you had it tough. I mean, Darcy's life wasn't easy with my mother dying and all, but she had a lot of people doting on her. And I'm sure you already know this, but my parents adore you, Rene. You were one of the main topics of conversation that last day in Puerto Rico. I know they're going to be happy when they find out about us."

"I hope so. I really think Darcy will be fine with it, too. I hope I'm not wrong."

"No chance. She really only cares if I'm happy or not, and I'm *very* happy." His tone was cautious when he added, "Luke and Kate already know. Luke was the person who got me through this year."

"I understand."

"Luke knows everything, but no one else does. He didn't share that with Kate."

I squeezed his hand. "It's all right. I mean, I left you alone without anyone to help you through it. I know the whole thing wasn't just hard on me, it was hard on you, too."

* * *

CALEB

I wanted to stay in bed with her this morning. I had the feeling, I guess since everything was still so new, that if I didn't hold her close she might slip away.

Duty called, though, and coming off the elevator that Monday morning, I began to take it all in with a more critical eye.

No fake plants in the reception area, it looks ridiculous. Passing Bradley's little cubicle on the way to my office, I thought about the potential pitfalls of nepotism. And Finn with the sports section spread out before him, his morning slacker routine pointing out the obvious: *You need to cut the dead wood.*

From now on I'd be focusing on the strategies I'd adopt versus what I planned to do differently. Yup, in one year's time I'd be out on my own.

"Hey, boy."

"Morning, Cherry. You good?"

She smiled. "I will be." She paused, considering her words before she said, "I saw you yesterday, uh, with her." I must have looked confused, so she spelled it out for me. "I was in your neighborhood shopping. What can I say? I have terrible luck. But I can see that you're different with her. It's obvious that you love her."

It hurt to do it, but there was no sense in making this worse by lying to her. "I do. I love her."

She nodded, forced a smile and walked away as I let out a deep breath. I sent up a silent prayer: *Please let her meet a good man soon.*

"Classes don't start until Monday." I was pleading with her to stay. "Why do you have to fly out tomorrow?"

"I should be flying out tonight. As it is, I was supposed to do two days at the station this week and I cut it to one. Also, I'm on the schedule for Friday and Saturday at the restaurant. There will be weekends coming up that I'll want off from work, so I don't want to start pissing my manager off now. Believe me, I'd love to stay. As it is, I'm crashing with Cara until the dorms open again on Saturday, and I'm so, so tired of feeling like a homeless wanderer."

I took her to the airport early Thursday morning, hugging her close like I was holding on for dear life. "I'll miss you."

"Same here, and I just want to tell you again how much I love my birthday gift. It means more to me than you could ever imagine."

"It looks great on you. Bye, twenty-one, I love you."

"Love you right back."

"Call me if you need me," I added as she turned to go. She nodded, her smile falling.

Breaking up is hard to do.

I trusted her one hundred percent, and knew she could handle it on her own, but I still didn't like the idea of Rene having a heart to heart with that guy. I didn't want him holding her hand or kissing her, even if it was just to kiss her goodbye.

RENE

Tanner asked me a while ago not to work this Sunday, but here I was, happily taking lunch orders and refilling water glasses. I was avoiding him—avoiding the awful conversation we were about to have.

Sundays generally mean Darcy's cooking a feast at our place, and tonight was no exception. And, oh joy, my roommate extended the invite to my soon-to-be ex-boyfriend without asking me first. My shoulders slumped when I read his text telling me he'd be over soon. By the time he got there, no more than fifteen minutes later, I already had one giant glass of red wine in me.

He scooped me up right away and whispered, "I've been going crazy for the past few weeks. I want to run you upstairs and peel off everything you're wearing."

The wine felt like it was sloshing around my empty stomach. I was queasy and so damn nervous. Before I could tell him we needed to talk, Tom and Chris drew him into a conversation. He took a spot on the couch and pulled me down into his lap, wrapping an arm around my waist to keep me close.

"Rene, I need a little help."

I jumped up, so relieved to get away. Yeah, I was starting to *feel* just how much Tanner had missed me. "I'm coming."

Beth handed me a salad bowl she could have easily put out herself. "You were looking simultaneously sick and terrified back there. Is everything ok?"

I whispered, "Thanks for the save, and no, I'm not ok. I'm breaking up with Tanner. I feel terrible."

She whispered back, "Shit, but I can't say that I'm shocked. I never thought you were really into him. Just get it over with because he's *definitely* into you. The longer you drag it out, the worse it will be for both of you."

"I know it. Thanks, Beth."

After everyone ate, I helped clean up while fighting off the tight knots forming in my stomach. I think the rest of the girls could sense the impending doom, or Beth had quietly filled them in, as they all cleared out pretty quickly.

Tanner sat on the couch waiting for me. As I made my way over, he grabbed me, playfully pulling me back onto his lap as he said, "I missed you."

Coward that I am, I started off with small talk. "How was your Christmas?"

"Great. You know, lots of family, good food. Everyone asked about you." He took my hands in his. "I really did miss you, Rene."

I cleared my throat. "Listen—"

But Tanner cut me off, pushing forward. "We're graduating soon, baby, and I've been doing a lot of thinking."

No, no, no. The thought of him making plans for our future nearly had me in tears.

"Anne told me you and her talked a lot over Thanksgiving. You even told her a little bit about your father, right?"

"Yes," I answered, confused.

"Would it help if we went to go see him together, to try and mend fences between the two of you?"

I stared at him, still confused. "What makes you think I want to fix my relationship with him? He's, he's...an alcoholic among many other things, Tanner."

"My uncle is an alcoholic, and having family around helps him. It's not just about your dad, I think it would help you too. There's something, I don't know...You keep me at arm's length. I think maybe you had a rough time growing up and that's why you have such a hard time letting me in. I want us to move forward. I think you need this."

I took a deep breath, tried to quell my simmering anger. "You don't know the half of my rough time, and if you did, you wouldn't be suggesting something so idiotic. Reconcile with my father?" My laugh was bitter and mean. "Tell Anne thank you, really, but she should use her social work degree on someone who actually wants her help." A full minute passed in silence before I spoke again. "Tanner, I'm sorry. I know you care about me, but you know very little about my life, and there are things I just know I'll never be able to share with you." I steadied myself and then looked at him. "I'm just going to say this...I know in my heart we're not right for one another."

"What? Wait—"

"I'm sorry."

His grasp on me tightened as he shook his head from side to side. "No, *I'm* sorry. I'm sorry I pushed the issue. You're right, I don't know anything about your father."

It was cruel, but I had to end this. "It's not just that. What you said is true, I have kept you at arm's length and I was wrong to do that. But it really has nothing to do with you. I've only had one other real relationship besides you, and he knows. He knows everything there is to know about me."

I moved off his lap to sit beside him.

"So you trusted him, but you don't trust me? Why? Do you think there could possibly be something about you, something about your past or something you've done that would make me turn away from you? There is *nothing* you could tell me that would make me stop loving you."

As he raked his hands over his face, I said, "I wasn't leading you on, I swear. I had strong feelings for you and I thought maybe I could open up to you someday."

"You're saying everything in the past tense."

"I am."

"Holy shit, I feel like an ass. I didn't see this coming."

"I don't want to hurt you."

But I had hurt him, deeply. "Do you mind if I go?"

"Tanner—"

He stood up. "Can I just ask who this guy is?"

"He doesn't go to school here. You don't know him. He's a few years older."

"Where has he been all this time?"

"We went through something and broke up about a year ago. I pushed him away but I never got over him. I never should have started dating you, Tanner. It wasn't fair to you."

"I know you'd never aim to hurt me, Rene, but this fucking hurts."

With that, he turned and left.

I crept upstairs, face planted onto my bed and cried. Within two minutes I had Beth, Darcy, Jenna and Caitlin crammed onto my bed with me. We talked for over an hour. Correction: they talked, I just sniffled and cried. I felt so terrible.

Darcy and Jenna were more than a little disappointed. They really liked Tanner. Everyone did. I thought Darcy might be fishing when she asked, "Is there another guy?"

I didn't give her a straight answer. "It wouldn't matter if there was or if there wasn't. Did you ever feel like someone cared about you more than you cared about them? That's how I feel when I'm with Tanner. And no matter how great he is and how lucky some other girl will be to have him, I'll never feel differently."

Darcy took my hand. "I get it. With Nick, I mean that was a different situation *entirely*, but there were times he was sober and pouring his heart out to me, and I felt so dishonest. I just couldn't wait to get away from him. I'm sorry. I know you must feel terrible."

Beth added, "Better to just rip the band-aid off. It hurts, but the longer it drags on, the harder it is."

"He's a great guy, but that doesn't mean he's great for you. Someone else will be, though."

"Thanks, Jenna." I tried to smile as I wiped the tears from my face. "You know what I'd love? I'd love it if some knockout fell desperately in love with Tanner. I don't want him to waste even one minute thinking about me."

Caitlin laughed. "I hope you mean that because when word gets out that he's single, that's likely to happen."

"The thought of running into him knowing he's hurting just kills me. I'll be avoiding the social scene for a while."

Beth nodded. "Keeping a low profile would probably be a good idea for now."

Later that night I called Caleb.

"Were you asleep already? I know you have to get up early, but I just wanted to say hi and to hear your voice."

"You don't sound right. Did you talk to him tonight?"

"Yeah, and I feel pretty crappy, like I'm the worst person on the planet."

"Been there. You ok?"

"I'm fine, but I wish I was back in New York with you. I have this pressing desire to run away."

"Feel free to run away *to* me whenever you want. Really, do you want to come back down?"

"Can't. I have to do those annoying things like go to class and work. It's actually good, though. I'll busy myself with work and studying. I'm definitely not looking to go to any parties around here for a bit. I'd be rubbing salt in a wound."

"The weekend after next I'm coming up for Drew's Super Bowl party. I'll get a room Friday night in the city and we'll have the weekend together. If you can sneak down here before that, I'll be missing you, so come. Any day of the week, anytime you want to get away, just come and I'll be at the airport waiting for you."

"Thank you. Now get some sleep."

"Goodnight, sweet Rene."

The next two weeks were not the easiest. I still met the girls for lunch, but I steered clear of all parties. And now that we were in the second semester of senior year, the parties were raging in full force by

Thursday afternoon and didn't die down until late Sunday night. Some people, like Darcy's old boyfriend Nick, were running on seven days straight. But I was missing in action. I worked that entire first weekend, double shifts for the most part.

I ran into Tanner only once that week, when I was coming out of the library. He looked pained but then put on a smile for my sake. It made me feel even worse.

"How are you doing?"

"I'm good, Tanner. You?"

"I'm getting there."

"I feel the need to tell you I'm sorry every time I see you. I feel like a stupid broken record."

"Don't beat yourself up. I've had some time to just sit and stew." He looked down at his boots as he laughed. "I don't think I showered for two days after we broke up. I was literally in a funk." *Lord, strike me down.* "But I'm doing better. We never really stood a chance if someone else is still in your heart. And I don't resent you. I know you wouldn't have done anything to hurt me on purpose, ok? I know that."

He left without waiting for a response, and I was glad for it. All I could have said was, "I'm sorry," like the broken record I was.

I was still moping around until later the following week. My mood lifted at the thought of seeing Caleb. I asked the girls if they wanted to go shopping Thursday night and grab dinner, but only Caitlin took me up on it. The rest of them were uncharacteristically glum.

Coming back from break, I think I started a chain reaction of heartache after ending things with Tanner. Beth and Marcus were fighting like cats and dogs, and Darcy and Tom seemed to have hit a rough patch too. She even asked me to say she wasn't home when he knocked on the door last night, and Tom left looking beyond bummed. It wasn't like her to lie, but I figured she had her reasons. Even Jenna wasn't her usual upbeat self.

Thank goodness for Caitlin. She happily waltzed me from store to store, dropping Benjamins like they were singles.

"Is it me, or do you feel like we're living in a morgue lately? You've been a downer with the whole Tanner thing, and I feel like you're Miss Susie Sunshine compared to the rest of them."

"Yes, I've definitely noticed. Winter blues?"

"Maybe they're dreading graduation," she said absently, flicking through a rack of bikinis. "Hey, my mom is heading to Antigua in a few weeks. You game?"

"No, one free vacation from your family per year is my limit."

"It's officially the next calendar year."

"Thanks, Caitlin, but I really do feel uneasy when I accept too much. That would be too much."

"If you change your mind, let me know. Until then, help me pick out some new bathing suits."

I managed to get myself a few new things, too. I picked out an outfit for tomorrow night and some new lingerie. I wanted to look beautiful...for him.

Chapter Eighteen

CALEB

I was antsy, and it was only five minutes past the time we agreed to meet at the hotel. I was rewarded a minute later when she entered the lobby, scanning the faces and then smiling with a look of sweet happiness when her eyes landed on me.

The way she looked at me made me feel like a king.

"Two weeks is a long time to be away from you," I said, grabbing her into a bear hug.

She was laughing as I lifted her off the ground. "I could get used to this kind of welcome. You'll have to do it every time you see me."

"Not a problem. I was just going to order room service and keep you locked in the room with me all night, but you look too damn good. We're hitting the town."

But that great place on Newbury Street I was itching to introduce her to, the one with the best ribeye I've ever tasted? My mood soured the moment we walked in and ran into an old college friend of mine who just happened to be out on a date with that canker sore, Danielle. What was Marty thinking?

I squeezed Rene's hand for moral support as we approached their table, but I needn't have. She didn't need help standing her ground with anyone.

I looked between them. "Marty, it's good to see you. I'd like you to meet my girlfriend, Rene." I couldn't help the clipped tone I switched to when I added, "Danielle, how's it going?"

Marty stood, took Rene's hand and said hello, while Danielle sat there managing to look mean-spirited even though she was smiling. She acted all surprised and concerned, pouring it on heavy when she spoke to my girl. "How *are* you? Wow, it's been *such* a long time. But you two...I'm confused. Caleb, weren't you dating Lauren the last time I saw you?"

Rene narrowed her eyes and cocked her head to the side. "Is that the best you've got? Yes, Caleb and I did break up for a long while. We *both* dated other people. Now we're back together. You up to speed now, or are you still...confused?"

Rene looked to Marty and then me. "It was really nice meeting you, Marty. Can we sit now, Caleb? I'm starving."

I couldn't help but smile. There were times when I wished Rene was someone who needed me to be the man who rescued her and protected her, but I was in awe of this girl. She just knew who she was. She was polite and elegant but didn't take any crap.

"Yeah, let's sit. Good seeing you, Marty. Have fun."

I saw Marty shoot Danielle an annoyed look before he sat back down.

As we walked towards our table, I touched the small of her back and leaned in. "Sorry about that."

"She is *so* nasty. How on earth were you ever even remotely attracted to her?" I went to answer, but she raised her palm to me. "Don't. I don't want to talk about her, and I don't want to know who Lauren is."

"Wait, I need you to know that the thing with Lauren was short-lived and it was nothing. She was just someone I was using to try and get over you, same with Cherry. It didn't work. I was miserable."

"Enough," she said softly. "I've been waiting two long weeks to see you. I don't want to think about anything or anyone else, ok?"

"Agreed, but I just have to say you handled Danielle pretty well."

Rene waved me off. "She's her own worst enemy."

I let out a sigh of relief. I'd also been looking forward to this weekend and I didn't want it ruined. The fact that Danielle tried to plant that ugly seed just solidified my poor opinion of her. I couldn't figure her out. I never led that girl on, never mistreated her. We hooked up a few times during our junior year of college, went out on one or two dates—it didn't work out. Normal people moved on, but Danielle was stewing over it as if it went down yesterday.

I didn't want Rene thinking of me with anyone else, and I certainly didn't want to picture her with that guy Tanner. But thanks to Danielle, the question of whether or not they'd slept together was gnawing at me as I tried and failed to focus on the wine list. It didn't matter. It couldn't. I certainly hadn't been celibate.

"I love this place already. Mmm, this crostini is *so* good. I can't figure out the topping, though. Maybe it's a black olive tapenade?" I was half-listening and she noticed. "Hey, what are you so lost in thought about?"

"Uh...I was just thinking that your hands are beautiful. I was looking at the ring and thinking that you have really beautiful hands."

Wasn't a total lie. I did think her hands were just as beautiful as every other part of her body. She didn't need to know what was really on my mind at the moment.

She looked at her hand. "I love this ring. I catch myself looking down at it all day."

I did my best to shake it off, the memories from our past and the reminders of how I'd screwed up, but it was a struggle.

I wanted to get back to the room, to hole up with Rene and

block everyone else out, to forget. I needed to bury myself inside of her, feel the kind of peace I only knew when I was with her.

But when Rene stood before me later that night, undressing herself as I sat on the bed taking it all in, I still felt weighed down by this sadness that I couldn't define or relate to anything in particular.

She'd gone shopping for me. The beautiful new lingerie was bought for me, to please *me*, and I didn't feel deserving of the effort. I drew her in closer, rested my head against her belly when I wrapped my arms around her waist. And it's like she knew that I needed a moment, needed to collect myself and needed her comfort. She didn't make a move other than to run her fingers through my hair the way a mother would tend to her child.

I'm so fucked up. What do you see in me?

She answered my unspoken question, "You're perfect, you know that?" She gestured for me to lay back and then set about the task of undressing me too. "You're perfect for me."

I let myself believe her. Gave in at that moment, hungry for everything she gave me. I wanted to give her everything, kissing, licking and tasting every bit of her. And when she whispered to me that I made her feel so good, I wanted to keep doing it, keep pushing into her and making her feel nothing and no one but me for the rest of her life.

"Are you all right?" she asked. Her body was wrapped around mine, her head lifted off my chest where she'd been resting.

"I'm so much better than good now, baby." I ran my finger along her hairline, damp with sweat. "Didn't realize how much I needed you."

She laid her head back down on my chest, pressing her body in closer. "I need you too. I wish I could fast forward through the next few months. I want to see you every day. I want to sleep next to you at night. I feel like we were apart for so long, and now I just miss you so badly when we're not together."

Sleep next to me at night, wake up next to me every morning. I wanted that.

"Are you saying you'll live with me next year?"

"Nope!" She slapped my chest playfully. "I'll live in my crappy apartment and stay with you whenever I so desire."

I pinched her backside. "You'll stay every night because I'll command it."

"Ouch! All right, but you'll have to cook for me, do my laundry, service me whenever I'm needy..."

The night went by like this, talking and playing around with each other in bed. The best place on earth was next to her.

It was odd being in Boston and not popping in on Darcy. I could tell something was off when Rene suggested that I go see Darcy before I head to Drew's.

"She could use a visit from you."

I eyed her suspiciously. "Why, what's up with her? Is Tom treating her right?"

She thought for a moment. "Tom is definitely a good person. You don't have anything to worry about there. They're just all in a funk...Darcy, Jenna *and* Beth. Darcy and Tom just seem like they've hit a bump in the road, that's all. But you know what? This is what's not right about me living with Darcy and seeing you at the same time. I really shouldn't be telling you stuff about her private life unless she's in trouble, and she's not."

That didn't exactly make me rest easy, but I knew from experience that Rene wouldn't leave me in the dark if there was anything serious going on.

"Parting is such sweet sorrow, Romeo," Rene teased as she packed her bag.

"Gotta make that cheddar, right?"

I held back from asking her to change her plans. I used to do that in an absentminded way, but had come to see that it weighed on her. She needed to work. She was responsible and I had to respect that. But damn, our time together was always so limited and it physically hurt to leave her.

"I don't even know who's playing in tonight's game," she said, laughing as she put her coat on. "I hope the restaurant isn't totally dead."

"Maybe it'll be a bunch of ladies out while their husbands are watching the game?"

"A lot of women like football, Caleb. My friends all have bets in and they'll be dressed in jerseys later on. I'm just a freak." She put her hand up, eyes wide but laughing as I stalked towards her. "Use of the word freak is *not* an invitation to maul me!" But when I pressed her up against the wall, her giggles soon turned to murmurs and then moans. "You're lucky I'm wearing a skirt, aren't you?" she purred as she wriggled her hips and led my hand up and along the creamy skin of her thigh.

And that quick but memorable fuck had me smiling from ear to ear as I drove to Drew and Chloe's.

Pulling onto their street, I told myself it was no big deal that Rene was working, but I was wrong. This Super Bowl party turned out to be a total couples' affair.

Chloe seemed genuinely disappointed when I told her Rene had to bail, but then smirked when she added, "That's mostly because I really like your girlfriend, but partly because Marty will be bringing Danielle and I get off on seeing her consumed with jealousy."

"Aw fuck." I felt a tension headache coming on at the mere mention of her name. "I wish you would have told me Danielle was gonna be here. I would've bailed."

As I turned and went to grab a beer from the fridge, Danielle and Melody approached. Danielle jabbed me on the shoulder with one of her talon-like fingernails. "You would have *bailed* if you knew I was coming? Nice, Caleb."

Guess she had big ears to go along with that big mouth of hers.

"What was your deal the other night? Why did you say that shit to Rene? It's like you've aged at warp speed into some sour old witch."

Melody's eyes went wide but Danielle didn't miss a beat. "You're just mad that I let your little friend know how you really are. Hope explaining who Lauren is ruined your night."

"Sorry to disappoint, but it didn't."

I noticed Marty standing off to the side then, listening and taking in the entire scene. He was an ass if he was looking to get with this. Walking away, I shook my head and shrugged. If he was mad at me, so be it. I was not apologizing to his girl.

Not five minutes later, I practically downed my full beer when I saw Lauren walk through the door. *What the hell?* Chloe was on me in a second, she knew I was pissed. After Danielle, I had no energy to deal with another disgruntled female.

"I didn't invite her, I swear. She tagged along with—"

"Stop, it's not your fault. Probably better if I just head back to the hotel, though."

"No, I'll run interference for you. Go over by the guys. You're *not* leaving. Drew will be really disappointed."

I'd already checked out of the hotel, had a few beers in my system, and I was planning on crashing at Drew's tonight. Even if I wanted to leave, I was kind of stuck.

I snuck up to the guest room at some point during the half-time show—first time I didn't watch a Super Bowl game in its entirety in my life. The game was a blow-out, so it's not like anyone was paying attention to it anyway, but when the drinking games started up, I made a conscious decision to bolt. And I was content as my head hit the pillow, knew I wasn't missing a thing. I didn't need the scene anymore, didn't need parties or girls. I just needed one girl, and I had her.

She was mine.

Chapter Nineteen

RENE

Darcy was dashing around her room, throwing clothes, books and other random objects into a duffel bag. When I asked her where she was going, she pulled me into the room, closed the door and told me Kate was in labor and that she was catching the next flight to New York.

I didn't feel the crush of misery, the loss. No, I was happy, but also confused as to why she was being so quiet about the whole thing. "That's so exciting, but why are we whispering?"

"I'm, well...I think Jenna's lying down. But I'm so excited! I just want to get there!"

"Can I take you to the airport? Beth won't mind if I borrow the car."

"Thanks, but Tom's taking me." I couldn't help but smile and she noticed. "Yes, I'm happy about it too."

"I just love you two together, Darcy."

I felt relief wash over me as we hugged each other tight.

The weeks leading up to that moment had been rough for Tom

and Darcy. I was torn over how much I should, or needed to share with Caleb. There were rumors Tom was cheating, but I never believed them given the source, a truly mean-spirited girl who'd always had a thing for Tom that seemed borderline obsessive.

Now things had finally started to return to normal for them and I was glad. They were meant to be. He loved her and she loved him. You couldn't be in their presence and not feel it.

I reached out to Caleb right after she left. I wanted him to know I was good, more than good, and that he didn't have to walk on eggshells around me.

At two in the morning I got a text:

Didn't want to wake you, sweet Rene. Mom and baby are doing great. Rebecca Rose Donovan. She's tiny and really cute. I love you.

I didn't reply until the morning, even though I was wide awake when I got the message. The sadness wasn't totally unexpected, but when it hit, it hit hard. It was like being tossed around in rough surf, and I knew I had to ride it out, just be in it and let it wash over me.

I went out for an early run, and although it was bitter cold, the sun was shining. That's how life is, I thought, bitterly cold and painful at times but joyful at others. So I made the decision to focus on the warmth and happiness that Caleb's love wrapped me in, and when I got in I replied:

Your mother's name, how beautiful. I'm so happy for them. Call me when you can. I love you.

My phone rang less than a minute later. "Morning, my love."

His voice always made me smile. "I thought you'd still be asleep."

"No, I left the hospital last night right after I sent you that text. I've been up for a while. Already took a run."

"Me too. I just got back."

"I'm impressed, Rene. It's cold out there. Ah, just think, soon we'll be able to run together. Sunday mornings along Hudson River

Park, me peeling your clothes off before we shower together, leisurely brunch afterwards...I have it all figured out."

"That does sound dreamy, but I don't think I'll be able to keep up with you. Darcy basically kicks my ass whenever I tag along with her."

"It'll be me running behind you so I can gaze at that sweet ass of yours the entire time."

"Oh lordy." He was impossible and I loved it. "Hey, no pictures yet? I've been waiting to get a look at Miss Rebecca Rose."

"I'll snap a pic as soon as I get to the hospital. I think visiting hours start at two-thirty. Hey," he paused, "I know I tell you all the time, but I love you, so much."

His words warmed me like the summer sun. "You can never tell me that too many times. I love you too, Caleb."

It was an odd Saturday morning in that I didn't have to be at the restaurant and I was ahead on my schoolwork. An entire day with no plans or obligations. I hardly knew what to do with myself.

I decided to go shopping and pick out a gift for the baby. Luke and Kate knew about us so it wouldn't be weird if Caleb gave them a gift from me. And I was glad I had an urge to shop for the baby instead of feeling sad or wistful over what might have been. This baby wasn't mine, and I was happy for Luke and Kate. I knew they'd been down a long, painful road, and now they must be overjoyed holding their precious little girl.

Caitlin came along, and the two of us really got into sifting through all those sweet little pink things. I settled on a cozy blanket and two adorable outfits that were delicate, pretty and looked super soft and comfortable. I was with Caitlin, so of course I was steered into Neiman Marcus. But the way the sales clerk wrapped the boxes made the extra expense worth it. I wanted it to be special.

On our way back to campus, Caitlin and I simultaneously got word from Darcy about the baby.

Caitlin laughed. "I'm so tempted to write back: Honey, your brother told us this *hours* ago."

* * *

CALEB

I didn't have a clue.

All this time, I'd put the events of last year into a drawer, something filed away under: *Uncomfortable Stuff I'd Rather Not Think About.*

But holding my niece, holding this warm and soft little bundle, looking into her blinking eyes and watching in awe as her mouth stretched in a lazy yawn, it hit me like a freight train.

It was the first time I truly acknowledged there was a baby involved, a life. Was it a boy or a girl? My son or my daughter? I'll never know.

Back then, I was consumed with losing Rene and that's all. I was such an ass, thinking I could just breeze in, come to the rescue and get her to move past it. To carry on with me like we could still be the same two people in love.

Choked up as I handed the baby back over to Luke, I spoke to Rene, spoke my vow in silence: *Someday it will be us...Someday.*

Normally I don't make a daily habit of checking in on Darcy, but as we sat eating dinner together after visiting hours the other night, Rene's comment from a few weeks back came to mind. Darcy was so damn skinny and she looked tired. She assured me all was good, that Tom was a good person and all that, but I wasn't totally convinced.

Darcy answered on the first ring then told me to hang on. She said, "See you later, Tanner" before turning her attention back to me.

"Where are you, Darcy?"

"At my place."

He was at their place? What the fuck?

I decided to play dumb. "Who's Tanner?"

"Rene's boyfriend. Well, he's not her boyfriend right now...Or anymore...I don't know. He's a great guy. I don't know what she's thinking."

The pencil I was holding snapped in two. "Don't go playing matchmaker."

"I know, I know. So what's up? I love hearing from you, but I just saw you yesterday. Everything ok?"

"Just checking in. You had me worried there."

She let out a frustrated groan. "I am *fine*. Tom is *great*. I promise, Caleb."

"Good."

We spent the next few minutes talking about the baby, about her classes, about nonsense, but the entire time I was thinking about that guy.

I had a countdown going, and now we were down to three months. *Rene will be graduating, she'll be moving back to New York, we'll be starting our life together. Just need to wait it out for three more months.* That's the pep talk I'd give to myself whenever I was missing her or feeling impatient.

Three months wasn't an eternity, wasn't a big deal, but now that I knew he was spending time at her place? I mean, this guy had access to her every day, and I could only manage to see her, what, twice a month?

I dialed Rene the second I hung up with Darcy, and tried my best not to sound like a jealous prick. "I just spoke to my sister. Your *boyfriend* is over at your place, you know."

"No, I'm speaking with my *boyfriend* at this very moment. Wow, you're jealous? I kinda like it," she teased, laughing.

I laughed then too. "I'm crazy jealous."

"Well, you're just going to have to stew for a few more days. And don't be ridiculous. You know you're it for me."

"When are you going to be here?"

"Saturday morning. I'll take an early shuttle."

"Come Friday night."

"Your sister and my other roommates are starting to get suspicious that I disappear for days on end, you know? And I have to work Friday night because I'm taking off the rest of the weekend."

"Come on, I need you."

"Wow, jealous and possessive. You're turning me on. How am I going to sit in class for the next two hours?"

"You're a tease."

"See you Saturday morning, early."

I knew I'd have to settle for that.

* * *

RENE

I know I shouldn't desperately crave the reassurance, but every time Caleb said those words, *I need you*, I breathed a sigh of relief.

I was smiling throughout my shift Friday night, so excited to get on that plane the next morning. I planned to sneak out before everyone else got up, but Jenna was in the kitchen when I came downstairs.

"Off to see the mystery man again, Rene? Why can't we meet him?" She smiled and teased, "We won't embarrass you...Not on purpose, anyway."

"I'm totally aware that I'm being ridiculous about the whole thing, and I promise I'll introduce him soon. It's just weird because he doesn't go here. He's older. And I'd just about die if I ran into Tanner with him."

"I know, that poor thing. He's still walking around like a wounded puppy, but that's not on you. It happens. After my tenth-grade homecoming date dumped me for a close friend of mine, my mother told me that if it doesn't end badly then it doesn't end." Her smile faded. "Someone has to get hurt."

I let out a sad sigh. "I feel like an awful person. Has he met anyone, hooked up, anything?"

She sipped her tea then shook her head. "Don't think so. He's still holding onto hope where you're concerned."

I felt the weight of his sadness as I made my way to the airport, and it was hard to shake those negative vibes until I caught sight of Caleb waiting for me.

"Hey, beautiful."

I dropped my bags and sank into his embrace as he squeezed me tight. "I've missed you."

"Come on, let's go. I feel like I have you on borrowed time. Are you heading back tomorrow night?"

I cringed. "I have to. I have an exam Monday."

He let out a sigh. "Just a few more months. Hey, what's all this?"

"Oh, just a gift for Rebecca. I figured you can drop it off the next time you visit."

His face lit up. "No, we'll go over there today and you can give it to them yourself."

"Are you sure?"

He took both of my hands. "Keeping this, keeping *us* from my family has been killing me. Luke and Kate are in the loop anyway, so I want this, please." He stopped then and looked at me, his expression pained. "Wait, I mean, will you be ok with it, with being around the baby? I'm sorry, I just didn't think—"

I squeezed his hands, nodding. "I promise you, I'm fine."

Caleb let out a relieved breath and smiled as he dug his phone from his pocket. He sounded like an excited kid when he called Luke and asked if we could head over to see Rebecca. We went straight there.

I let out a surprised laugh when we pulled up onto their tree-lined street in the West Village. I'd been on this block before, admiring the stately, well-kept rows of brownstones. In the summer, the street was cloistered by the shade of linden trees and every home's window boxes overflowed with colorful flowers. It was an area of New York City that felt like a true community, with mothers pushing strollers and young couples sitting out on their stoops talking with neighbors.

"When I was living in my fleabag of an apartment this summer, I walked all over lower Manhattan, daydreaming about where I would live one day when I was a famous network executive. I've been on this block, like, a dozen times."

"That's wild, right? And who knows, maybe you will live here someday." He winked and added, "I like the West Village, too."

Caleb grabbed the gift bags from the back and led me across the street. "You should have seen what this place looked like before they got a hold of it. It was an absolute dump. Kate and Luke are really good at what they do."

He wasn't kidding, their home was beautiful. If a potential client came in and saw this place, there would be no doubt about hiring them as your team. Besides that, they were just wonderful. They radiated happiness and you could understand why. Rebecca was a sweet little angel, just beautiful.

Kate put her right into my arms so that she could open my gift. Rebecca was so small, so soft, and my heart swelled when I leaned in and got a whiff of that oh so good baby scent. When I felt Caleb come up behind me, gently put his hands on my shoulders and press a kiss to my cheek, I had to hold back the urge to cry. I wasn't sad at all, just overwhelmed with the feeling of love...from Caleb, for Caleb, from his family and for this sweet baby.

"These outfits are adorable. And the blanket is gorgeous. Thank you."

"I'm so glad you like them."

Luke chimed in, "Thanks, Rene. Hey, Caleb said you'll be moving back to the city after graduation?"

"That's the plan, and luckily I already have a job lined up. I just heard yesterday that it's all confirmed. Ohmigod, Caleb, I totally forgot to tell you!"

"Really? With Carey right, not Bennett?"

I laughed. "Yes, with Meredith Carey."

Kate and Luke congratulated me, and Caleb took Rebecca from my arms and handed her to Luke so that he could pick me up and spin me around. "Best news ever."

"I know, I'm so excited. And it sounds terrible to say this out loud, but I just can't wait for school to be over."

Caleb added, "*You* can't wait? I'm counting down the days until you graduate."

As we were leaving and saying our goodbyes, Luke held me for an extra beat and spoke so that only I could hear. "You make Caleb so happy." That warmed me from the inside out.

"Should I just tell Darcy now?" I asked as we made our way back to Caleb's place. "I feel dishonest spending time with your family and then living with her while she's in the dark, you know?"

He nodded. "I'm fine with that. I'll leave it to you. Just let me know what you decide so I'm ready."

It just seemed like the right thing to do, but twenty-four hours later I didn't give a damn about right or wrong. I just wanted to wring Darcy's neck.

I could smell garlic bread as I approached the door, and I could hear voices, people laughing.

Darcy was cooking a big dinner and a bunch of people were over

—typical Sunday night, no biggie. The first floor was packed. Some people were sitting around the table, some with plates on their laps on the couch, some eating at the kitchen counter. All of my roommates were there, of course. So were Tom, Chris, Mac, Ben, Dan, a few other stragglers and…Tanner. What the hell?

I skulked in like a coward with my overnight bag. So much for not pouring salt in Tanner's wounds.

Chris bellowed, "Look who's back!" He could be so freaking loud sometimes. "Where you been, Rene?"

"Nowhere."

"You missed a good party last night."

"Some of us have to work, Chris."

Caitlin came over and handed me a beer. "The party was here, Rene."

"Oh."

I threw my bag in the corner and tried to act normal. I was a little pissed at Darcy because I had the feeling Tanner was here at her invitation. I was also mad they had a party while I was away. I knew that was ridiculous on my part. I was the one leaving all the time, but still.

I smiled at Tanner when our eyes met, but I didn't make my way over to him. What for, so I could say sorry again? I stayed on the couch next to Chris and tried to focus on the conversations going on around me. Chris and Tom were talking about the spring rugby season—which teams were going to be their toughest competition and blah, blah, blah. Caleb's name came up when Tom was telling everyone about some tournament they'd played in together last fall. Darcy chimed in about another tournament Caleb was planning on playing in San Diego this summer, and how she and Tom were going to head out there if they could swing it. Now I was mad at Caleb. San Diego? I was hearing about his plans second-hand through Darcy? And she was just getting started. She plopped down, wedging herself in between me and Jenna.

"I forgot to tell you," she said to Jenna, "my mother said Caleb brought a girl over to Luke and Kate's yesterday to see the baby."

"That's good, right?"

"Yeah, I'm totally happy he's seeing someone and it's serious, but I swear, if this girl hurts him like the last one did, I'll hunt her down and kill her."

I felt like snapping back: *Maybe Saint Caleb had something to do with that last disaster, did you ever consider that?* but of course I kept my mouth shut.

Caitlin was taking it all in, her twinkling eyes and smile proof that she found the entire scene amusing. I wasn't amused, not one bit. I was nothing but aggravated.

Tanner tapped my arm as I was making my way towards the stairs. Screw dinner, I was too angry to eat. "Rene, are you all right?"

"I'm fine, just tired. How have you been?"

He nodded to reassure me. "I'm good. Is it ok that I'm here?"

"Of course it is. I just figured I'm the last person you'd want to see."

He laughed and looked down, shifting on his feet as he shoved his hands into his pockets. "Actually, it's the opposite." I shook my head, so close to breaking down. "Rene, I'm good, really." He lifted my chin. "I'm ok, but I do miss you. If it doesn't work out with this other guy, you know how I feel."

Now I really wanted to kill Darcy. "Tanner, you're too good for words. I don't know what to say."

He nodded, resigned.

I went upstairs, fell onto my bed and texted Caleb:

I'm home safe. Decided I'm not going to tell Darcy.

Beth flopped down next to me a few minutes later. "What's up, girl?"

"Why is Tanner here?"

"He left."

"I know, he left after I was put in the shitty position of having to turn him down again. Why was he here in the first place?"

"I don't know."

"Did Darcy go out of her way to invite him?"

"I think she might have. I'm not sure though, Rene."

"Why would she do that? I've been staying away from him for weeks."

With that, Darcy walked in. "Hey."

"What possessed you to invite him over? Can't you see how you're hurting him? And what about me? Do you think I'm incapable of making my own decisions, and what, you have to play matchmaker?"

She put her hands up defensively. "Whoa! You weren't even here. And I *am* friends with him." She took a spot on the corner of my bed. "And maybe I do want to push you two back together. Is that so terrible? He's in love with you."

"Do *not* do that again." I couldn't help but cry. "You've made it worse. You're making him feel like there's a chance we'll get back together and there's *no* chance of that. Do you understand?"

"I'm sorry!"

"I know you want something good for me. I know that's why you did this, but I can make my own decisions. And I'm happy. I'm *finally* happy. The only sadness I have in my life right now is feeling bad about hurting Tanner. If you want to do something positive, use your matchmaking skills to find him a new girlfriend."

And now she was crying too. "I really am sorry, Rene."

I sent them back downstairs and then drifted off to sleep feeling defeated. Just a few more months until graduation. The truth would have to wait.

Keeping this from my family has been killing me. Resting back on Caleb's couch, his words troubled me, but I decided that with only ten weeks left to go, I'd made the right decision. I was better off not rocking the boat.

Darcy bought my favorite orange scones *twice* in the week following the Tanner debacle, and I found myself having to choke down her peace offering. *Please don't be nice to me, Darcy, I'm boning your brother.* I couldn't imagine dropping that bombshell now or any time soon.

When Caleb asked what made me change my mind about telling Darcy, I told him about her futile attempt to reunite me with Tanner.

"Little sister means well, but she can go overboard sometimes. If she does it again, and believe me, Rene, she can be stubborn, just tell her about us. That way she'll stop."

"She won't do it again. I made myself clear, and besides, she likes Tanner, she doesn't want him getting hurt any more than he already is. I told her to use her skills on finding him a nice, insanely hot new girlfriend."

"I almost feel bad for the poor bastard."

"I feel awful. He's a nice guy. And when we broke up I was kind of harsh. I didn't mean for it to go down like that, but he set me off. I apologized, but I wish I hadn't lashed out at him."

When he looked confused, I told him about Tanner's wish to reunite me with my neglectful, dear old dad.

"I knew we never had that strong of a connection, but when Tanner suggested mending fences with my father, it made everything crystal clear. He doesn't know me. How could he think a reunion with that man would be a good thing? God, I was fourteen the last time I saw him. The night I ran out of that house I told myself I'd never step foot in there again. Never."

* * *

CALEB

I didn't want to ask, didn't want to know, but this wasn't about what I wanted.

Sitting on the couch across from me, with her knees pressed up into her chest and her eyes focused on nothing, she looked so far away.

I moved to sit behind her and pulled her into me. "What happened the night you ran?"

She kept her gaze fixed out the window and didn't say anything for a minute or two. My discomfort grew with each passing second. When she finally did speak, her voice was low and she wouldn't look my way.

"The night before, my father came staggering in at around eight o'clock with some loser in tow. He always came home alone, so it was weird. The guy was skinny, and I remember his hands were black around the fingertips. He wasn't clean. And as soon as he spotted me, he flashed his stained teeth, leering at me like a fucking pig."

Never heard Rene curse before, so I figured this was bad. I took a deep breath and braced myself for what was coming.

"God, I was fourteen. I had just...I mean, I wasn't really even fully developed. I felt so exposed, like dirty, the way this guy looked at me. No one had ever looked at me like that before." She shook her head. "I went to my room and closed the door and the guy left before long. The next night, though, I was afraid...Just had a bad feeling. Sure enough, he comes home with the same guy again, but this time my father is legless. I'm sure the guy plied him with extra drinks so that my dad was in no shape to get between him and what he wanted."

I didn't want to hear anymore, didn't want to know how this horror story played out, but I fought back the urge, kept my hold on her so she knew she was safe here with me.

"He dropped my father on the couch, and when I told him that I could take it from there, he just smiled at me and said something like, 'That's all right, honey, I'll keep you company.' He sat next to me on the couch, too close, and I stayed there, frozen. He started asking me questions about school, asked if I had a boyfriend…You know, trying to make it seem like he was my pal or something. When he moved in closer and started twirling a piece of my hair, I stood up and asked him to leave. I was trying to say it in a nice way, to placate him, you know? But he turned on a dime. He got angry and started accusing me of being a tease, that I was teasing him the way I looked at him the night before. I managed to escape to the bathroom, but of course in that unkempt dump the lock was practically busted. It felt like he was going to break my legs the way he was charging at the door with my feet braced against it."

I tightened my hold on her. "Did he get in?"

Her hands went up to cover her face roughly, like she was trying to erase the image from her mind. "Yeah, he did. God, he was all over me. His hands were pawing at me, he was trying to kiss me, he was tearing at my clothes. I just kept trying to land a hit to anywhere—his nose, clawing at his eyes, kicking for his groin. I felt like I couldn't breathe. He was getting the best of me and I felt helpless, like I was losing the fight. He just kept pushing his face up against mine, forcing his tongue into my mouth with that boozy, stale cigarette breath. He was grabbing at me, hurting me. I knew he was going to —" She shook her head again forcefully before going on. "I got hold of a bottle of after shave and brought it down hard on his face. I nicked him right above the eye and he spouted blood. He'd also been drinking, so that split second he stumbled back to hold his face was all I needed to break away. I had nowhere to run, so I went underneath the house into a crawl space. I had no socks on, my pajama top was torn—"

"Did he find you?"

She shook her head slowly. "No. I could hear him cursing, calling me a little bitch and words much worse than that. He gave up pretty quickly I think, but I didn't move for over two hours. I was afraid he was still there, waiting on me. Thank God it was only November, but it was still so cold out there. When I thought it was finally safe, I went back in and grabbed my books and some clothes and then I called my uncle."

"You lived with them after that?"

"Off and on. When my uncle brought me back to their house that night, his wife was annoyed. Can you believe that? She never made me feel like I was welcome there. I still don't know why."

"What a bitch."

Rene finally turned her head to look at me and then laughed a little. "Yes, she's an absolute bitch." She took a deep breath. "And since that night, I've lived here, there and everywhere." She shook her head. "It's not like my father was totally responsible for that night, but it was the last straw, you know? He'd never really taken care of me. It's like I was born to a mother and a father, but I had no parents."

I pulled her in even closer. "Rene." I had no other words and I don't think she needed more. She just needed to know I was there with her.

"I hope you're ok with hearing all that."

"You hope *I'm* ok? I just want to make it better for you."

"You do make it better. I just know it's probably difficult hearing that story. I've never told anyone before. It makes me feel ashamed to say it out loud."

"Don't you dare feel ashamed. God, I want to beat that loser to death for what he did to you."

She smiled up at me through her tears. "I wish you were my neighbor growing up or something. I think you would have looked out for me, even as a kid."

"You *know* I would have. I'm here to take care of you now, Rene. I won't ever let you go."

She told me she loved me and then let out a big yawn, which made us both laugh.

"I'm taking you up to bed, my love."

Opening up like that took everything out of her, so she was asleep within minutes. I, on the other hand, couldn't settle down. That old familiar sensation was taking over—rage and adrenaline coursing through my veins. In the old days I'd find someone or something to hit. Now I just had to talk myself down, let it pass.

I held her close, felt her breaths moving in and out, felt her heart beating against my hand. I had so much to lose.

I couldn't lose Rene.

* * *

RENE

I woke up alone, with a light heart, at peace and relieved. For better or worse, Caleb knew everything there was to know about me. My secrets were safe with him. I was safe here.

I walked downstairs to find him standing in front of the window, both hands fisted in his hair.

"Hearing all of that stressed you out, huh?"

His first instinct was to reassure me. "No." But then walking towards me, he shook his head. "It did, but I can't help it. I just want to set out and kill anyone who's hurt you. Just hate thinking about what you've been through."

"And here I am feeling so relaxed and free. I dumped my stress onto you."

"I need to know you'll lean on me like that. I mean it, Rene. You don't know how grateful I am that you trusted me with all that last night." And yes, even though he was obviously a mass of tangled emotions right now, he was still Caleb—his eyes were fixed on my breasts. "God, look at you," he said as he rested his head against my chest and his hands settled on my hips. "My Rene."

"You're exhausted. Come back up to bed."

We lay down together with his head resting on my belly and his arms wrapped firm around my lower back. I rubbed his head until he was breathing heavily and sound asleep against me. This big, strong man was weary with concern over me.

I made myself believe over the years that I needed nothing, I needed no one. Expect nothing and you won't be disappointed. But things were changing. I wanted this. I wanted Caleb to love me, protect me and take care of me, and I wanted to do the same for him.

Caleb loved me from head to toe as the sun rose and streamed through his windows early that Monday morning. His body was all rippling muscles, so powerful, but he loved me gently, holding back. Don't get me wrong, it was sweet, slow pleasure, but I knew what was up.

"I won't break, you know. What happened to me happened a long time ago. I'm ok."

"Listen, love, give me time. I want it slow and sweet now." He smiled. "I'll ravage you again someday soon, I promise."

As he was getting ready to go to work, it took everything in me not to grab his tie and drag him back to bed. I needed more and I was surprised by the feeling. I wanted him and I wanted it a little rough. And with Caleb I *could* want that because I trusted him completely. I knew that no matter what we did—what he did to me, what I did to him—that I was safe.

I wanted to make him late for work but settled for admiring the view.

"What are you smiling about?"

"I can't believe someone who looks like you is actually mine."

With that, he swooped down and wrestled the sheet I had tucked around my breasts away from me. I laughed as he laid his fully clothed body on top of my naked body. He teased, "Really? Did you think you'd end up with some troll with no teeth and a hairy mole on his face?" As he ran a hand over my breast, down the curve of my hip and then around to cup my bum, he growled, "You are so gorgeous, woman. I could lock us in here and fuck you all day long. I'll never get enough of you."

"Caleb," I whined like the needy girl I was, "how can you say something like that and then leave?"

He looked over at the clock. "I really *am* sorry. I'm late already and I have a client coming in. You think you're hot and bothered? I'll have blue balls all day thinking about you."

Unpacking that night, I found the gift box Caleb had tucked into my bag. It was a beautiful, baby blue pashmina, but the words he wrote in the card were the real gift.

Rene,
No one has ever made me happier and no one ever will. I'll love you forever-C
P.S. I hope you like the scarf. I like this color on you.

* * *

CALEB

Leaving her this morning was torture, and coming home to an empty apartment after work was—well, it just sucked.

I asked Mick, Sean, Finn and Ed to come over to watch whatever game was on tonight. I just wanted a distraction. I didn't even notice the envelope on the coffee table when I got in. Mick saw it first.

"Here, I got you a belated Valentine."

"You're such a dick. Gimme that."

As they all cracked open their first beers and were bullshitting in my living room, I went into the kitchen. I smiled just holding the envelope. Anything that had to do with her made me happy.

Caleb,
I haven't even left your place yet and I miss you like crazy.
-Your Rene

What I wouldn't give to have her here with me right now. It's been what, twelve hours since I last saw her? Just the thought of being separated from her caused an actual physical ache in my chest.

My phone pinged with a new text:

I love my gift.

I wrote right back:

I'm glad. Just read your note. Another two long weeks until I see u again...Gonna go insane.

"Are you done reading and rereading your card, lover boy? Order the fucking wings. I'm starving!"

Leave it to Mick to jolt me back to reality.

Chapter Twenty

RENE

It *was* two very long weeks before I decided to head down to New York again instead of having Caleb come up here. I just liked staying with him so much better than holing up in a hotel, and I was anxious to pick up where we'd left off. I decided to make a long weekend out of it, meeting him at a bar close to his office on Friday night.

I made an appointment to see Marcel Friday afternoon and went there straight from the airport. He kissed me on both cheeks and spoke to me in French the entire time he cut my hair. Twice I had to ask him to slow down, and he corrected my word usage once or twice, but Marcel assured me my French was "sans défaut." I think flawless was a kind-hearted exaggeration, but I was pleased with how easily I could fall back into the language. And it was so good to see Marcel again. In reality, he was a new acquaintance, but he felt more like a dear old friend.

Marcel gave me yet another new look: a chic, chin-length bob. I loved it. It was perfectly professional, yet flirty and sexy.

I went back to Caleb's to change before going to meet him. I took a quick shower, taking care not to wet my hair. I slathered lotion on every inch of my body and then put on the beautiful, lacy lavender set I'd picked out for today. I'd taken to lingerie shopping when I was missing Caleb during those long stretches of time away from him.

Taking extra care with my makeup, I put on more than I normally did, which was hardly any. I liked this more mature, sophisticated version of myself smiling back at me in the mirror.

* * *

CALEB

Damn, she was hot.

My first instinct was to head right over to Rene, but I took my place at the other end of the crowded bar, fascinated and oddly turned on as I watched some guy attempt to pick her up. He must have offered to buy her a drink because she gestured down to her full wine glass, smiled and then said something that made him nod and smile back before turning away. Two other men stood nearby, gesturing towards her appreciatively, desiring her while she was none the wiser.

Rene was wearing make-up. Red stained lips, smoky eyes, sweet blush. Her hair looked glossy and chic. The grey satin sleeveless top and black pencil skirt hugged her curves. I'm sure she had the attention of every straight man in the place.

When the bartender, who was far too busy to be lingering, returned to talk to her a second time, I snapped out of it and went to claim what was mine. Swooping in, I whispered in her ear, "How many men have hit on you since you got here?"

She let out a relieved breath. "I dunno, three? I'm glad you're here. I'm not good at playing that game."

"I hate the idea of another man even looking at you, but I can't say that I blame them. You look like every guy's dream tonight."

She leaned in, gave me that smile that was reserved just for me. "I just want to be *your* dream. Do you dream about me at night?"

I'd wager at this moment my sweet Rene was feeling more sinful than sweet. The bar was packed, so I was able to slide my hand up her leg and under the hem of her skirt unnoticed. I lowered my mouth to whisper in her ear. "I dream about you, Rene. I dream about your naked body pressed up against mine in the warm ocean, about laying you down in the sand and pushing deep inside of you. I dream about your hands braced against the tiles in my shower as I take you from behind. I dream about you in my bed, with you on top, grinding against me. I always dream about you."

"Take me home, Caleb."

Cab drivers are oblivious in New York—seen it all before. I pulled Rene into my lap in the back seat and she hiked up her skirt so she could straddle me. My hands moved to her hips and we kissed like two desperate people. On the elevator ride up to my place, I had to stop myself from taking her right then and there. Once I successfully fumbled with the key and we were in my apartment, I broke away and took a breath.

"I also dream about sitting back and watching you undress."

I fell back onto the couch and loosened my tie as Rene stood before me. Her eyes were lust-filled and heavy. She smiled and then turned around to look at me over her shoulder. She took her sweet time as she undid the buttons on her blouse and lowered the zipper down the back of her skirt. The way she looked as the fabric slid down to reveal the sweetest hips and ass known to man, barely covered in lace...

She turned to me and said, "Tonight you're not going to be gentle with me."

She was aching with the same need I was, grinding against me, looking lost as she dug her nails into my shoulders. I fucked her up against the wall, bent over the couch, in the shower, and the last of the night was wrapped around her, worshipping her body in my bed.

"Are you ok, love?"

"I'm more than ok."

And I was so much more than ok now. She was here with me.

* * *

RENE

Waking up wrapped up in his arms, I breathed him in. Caleb smelled masculine and woodsy. And he smelled like sex. Last night, I thought as I smiled, we broke a record. I hit my new personal best in the big-O department.

"Morning, big guy."

He snuggled in closer into me. "You are the most beautiful girl in the world, you know that?"

"I think your beautiful girl needs a shower."

"No, stay right here with me. You smell like vanilla mixed with a night of raunchy sex. Best scent ever."

"It's already twelve. I don't think I've slept this late in my entire life. I need a shower and coffee."

"You have me totally relaxed and happy. I could stay here in bed with you all weekend."

"You're not getting off that easy. I need to be wined and dined. A bacon and egg sandwich from the corner deli would do me just fine, though."

He bolted upright. "Oh shit! I got us tickets to the Rangers game today. Let me check the tickets. It might be at one. We'll have to hustle." He returned a minute later with a satisfied grin and jumped back into bed. "Three o'clock. We have all the time in the world."

I tried to get up but he overpowered me. "No. I need at least a few lazy kisses before you can leave me."

God, I was in so deep with him.

And my first experience at The Garden was like everything else that involved Caleb lately: intense in a very good way.

Caleb's seats were right up close. I flinched whenever those mammoth dudes slammed into the plexiglass or a puck came flying full speed in our general direction. Caleb held me close, leaning in to explain the game whenever something happened, but I was only half listening. I spent most of the game daydreaming about a future with Caleb.

This is how good it will be, I told myself on weekends like this one. We'll work hard during the week, spend weekends exploring the city, and our nights will be filled with sex more decadent than the best chocolate.

After another lazy morning naked in Caleb's bed, we met up with Mick and his newest flame for a late lunch. When she got up to use the ladies' room, Caleb asked, "Was she named after Farrah Fawcett?"

Mick cocked a brow. "I'm perplexed. Who's Farrah Fawcett?"

"She was before our time, but you never saw any Charlie's Angels reruns? Farrah...Even to this day, the *best* poster of a girl in a bathing suit ever. Look it up."

"I don't know who she's named after. I don't even know her last name. By the way, Rene, how's Caitlin?"

"She's great. Do you remember her last name?"

"As a matter of fact, Beaumont, I do. Richards, correct?"

"Yes. I'm impressed."

"I always remember the names of the ones who don't like me. That girl was the polar opposite of clingy. She pretty much shot me down cold when I asked if she wanted my number."

"No, she likes you. She's just not looking for the love of her life right now, you know?"

He laughed. "Yeah, that's why I'm still kinda obsessed with her."

Farrah came back and Mick ordered us another round. When the waitress came back, Caleb said, "Hey, I almost forgot. We have to toast Rene on her job offer. Rene's going to be working with Meredith Carey on her morning news program."

Mick clinked glasses with me. "Wow, that's great." Then he clinked glasses with Caleb. "And it's great for my boy here that you'll be back in New York."

Farrah said, "Congratulations! Who's Meredith Carey?"

"She's the morning news anchor on the A.M. America show."

Caleb was rubbing my hand under the table, lulling me into a dreamy state. I had to shake myself out of it when he asked, "What's she like, Rene?"

"I've only met her a few times, but it's just a feeling...Have you ever felt like you're meant to cross paths with someone? And you're certain you're going to know that person for a long time?"

"Yes, I know exactly how that feels."

I smiled right back at him, overcome with a rush of emotion.

Mick cleared his throat. "Ok, love birds. You know you just stopped mid-conversation to gaze into each other's eyes?"

Caleb laughed before asking, "So you think Meredith Carey is like some kind of kindred spirit?"

"Yes! And also like she's going to be my mentor, someone who supports and guides me. I hope I'm right."

"She's lucky to have you on her team. And I'm so glad that prick isn't going to be your boss anymore."

I silently agreed. "Oh, and I don't want to get ahead of myself, but the last time we spoke she mentioned the upcoming Winter Olympics, and how, since I spoke French, there might be an opportunity for me to go. Wouldn't that be amazing?"

Caleb's face scrunched up. "You speak French?"

"Oui!"

"How did I not know that? I just assumed your parents were of French descent."

"No, they were both born and raised there. French was the only language we spoke at home when I was little."

"What else don't I know about you, Rene?"

"Let's see…I have a terrible throwing arm."

"Knew that."

"But I'm freakishly good at beer pong."

"Good to know. Any other hidden talents?"

"Plenty, but you'll have to discover them as you go along."

Mick chimed in, "Hey, if you do go over maybe you could hook us up. I've only been to the Olympics once, in Sydney. That was a great trip."

"Like I said, I'm getting way ahead of myself. I haven't even started working yet. But if I do get the assignment, I'm sure I'd be able to score some perks for my friends."

Caleb was now drawing circles on my thigh with his index finger. Gah. "Maybe you should pop over to the studio tomorrow before you leave."

"I contacted her personal assistant already. I'm going to catch the broadcast at seven, so I have to leave a little earlier than you tomorrow."

"Then we're heading out now."

As Caleb tossed money onto the table, he said, "Good to meet you, Farrah. Mick, tomorrow?"

"Yep, see you at four."

Mick got up and gave me a kiss and a crushing hug. "It's really good to see you again, Rene."

"You too, Mick." And just so he could hear, I added, "I'm so glad I ran into you this summer."

Walking into the station's lobby was like coming home in a way. The massive space, with every surface gleaming and pictures of the journalists I've admired for years adorning the walls—I had to hold back my strong urge to fist pump and call out: *I'm back people, and I'm here to stay!*

"Is that you, Rene? Hello!"

And my favorite security guard remembered me by name, bless his heart.

"Pat, how are you? I feel like I've been gone for so long, I'm glad you remembered me."

"How could I forget the girl who went out of her way to get me coffee when I looked extra tired? I hope you're back for good now."

"Just visiting today but I'll be back right after graduation."

He waved me through security. "That's good news. You head right on up."

Meredith's assistant was walking through the foyer as I came off the elevator. "Rene, Meredith is very glad you're here. Come, I'm going to show you around and then you can watch the rest of the show. We'll meet Meredith in her dressing room after."

And it couldn't have gone better. Meredith and I caught up, and she was so informative when I asked her questions about the production. We wound up having lunch with the executive producer, Chris Quivers, who turned out to be Matt's uncle. Small world. Good thing I don't make a habit out of burning bridges.

It was getting closer, it was real. My start date was June first. I was on the phone with Caleb afterward, relaying basically everything that was said over lunch, what I'd observed during the broadcast, my need to go clothes shopping—I was rambling.

He broke in, "I'm so proud of you. This is huge and you sound so happy."

"I am. I'm so happy that I'm scared."

"What do you mean?"

Shaking my head in the backseat of the cab, I wasn't exactly sure. "Everything is great...the job, my life, and especially you. I'm afraid that it's all *too* good. I don't want anything to change."

"I know what you mean, angel, but everything *should* be good for you. Get used to it."

* * *

CALEB

Hiking out west, winery bike tour through France—I was tapping through travel sites during that mostly one-sided phone call. *Ready or not, Rene, I'm whisking you away the day after graduation.* A big giant no to the sporty active trips. What she needed was rest and relaxation before starting her new gig. As the low gal on the totem pole, I imagined they'd be working her to the bone for at least the first year.

The Maldives. We had ten days so we could take a longer trip, and the last time I was there I remember feeling so totally blissed out. I wanted her to experience it with me, our own perfect little paradise.

I paused before finalizing the details. Anyone else would be crazy happy to have the trip of a lifetime sprung on them, but with her? Yeah, I didn't know.

"Can I take you away after graduation?"

"As my graduation present?"

"Yes, your graduation present."

"I'd love that!"

Sweet relief.

"Do I have to fill you in on where we're going, or can I just tell you to bring your passport?"

"You want me to just jump on a plane without knowing where I'm heading?"

"Woman, be spontaneous and just say yes. I was thinking of surprising you on your graduation day, but you kinda scare me. Like maybe you'd haul off and kick me in the nuts instead of hug me."

She cracked up at that. "You know me well, Caleb. All right, just tell me city, country or beach. It's killing me, but I'll leave the rest up to you."

"Really?"

"Yes! And hurry up before I change my mind!"

"Beach."

"Ok, I'm in."

I finalized the trip details, awesome multi-tasker that I am, noticing a few moments later that she was quiet on her end. "You still there?"

"I'm here. Hey, I feel weird asking you this, but I, uh, found a roommate. A friend from Bennett's show, Maureen, is going to have a spot for me when her roommate gets married this summer, but I can't move in until August first. Can I stay with you until then?"

"You're kidding me, right? It's now looking like June and July are going to be my best months ever."

"Thank you. You're so good to me, Caleb."

I was selfish, is what I was. All sorts of crazy thoughts were running through my head. Shit that was foreign to me. Like I wanted to ask Kate to go shopping with me to help pick out some work outfits for Rene as a gift. I wanted to stock up on that nasty strawberry kefir crap she liked to drink before bed. I wanted to clear out a part of the closet in my bedroom so that she'd have room for her things.

I wanted my home to be hers.

I wanted her to stay.

I knew it was temporary. No way she'd agree to live with me right away. But I was just happy with anything I could get where she was concerned.

Chapter Twenty-One

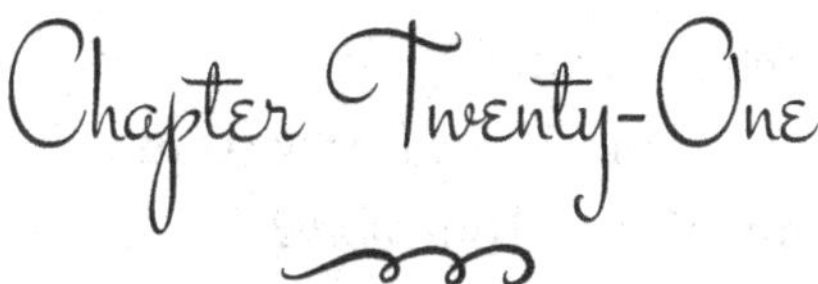

RENE

Everyone else was in the moment, but I was half-in at best. It was Senior Week, which meant days on end of parties, reminiscing and goodbyes, but I was already looking past Graduation Day. I was walking around in a dream state, excited about traveling with my hot boyfriend and starting my super-glamorous, fantastic job in broadcasting.

It just couldn't get any better.

But I fought with that voice in the back of my head—the one that kept telling me to prepare for the inevitable apocalypse.

It can't last, Rene.

It's too good to be true, Rene.

Don't get too used to this, Rene.

It was my default mode. All those years of living a hardscrabble life left me with a deep-rooted belief that when things were going well, I needed to brace for impact. But with Caleb, I so wanted to believe it would last.

Please God, let me have this.

Shaking off the dark cloud hovering over me, I walked back into my place to see Jenna, Caitlin and Beth sitting in the living room, all looking shell-shocked. Dan was there with them.

"What's happening? You all look like someone died."

Beth said, "No, but you'd better sit down for this one."

"Tell me. You're scaring me!"

Caitlin broke the silence. "It's Darcy. Tom—"

I was getting impatient. "Tom *what*?"

"Tom has a baby. He just found out. He's three months old."

I sank into the couch. "Holy mother. Where is Darcy?"

Dan piped up as he pulled Jenna onto his lap. "She's with Tom in Connecticut. They took the baby there. Tom's parents are in Europe."

"Wait, where's the mother? *Who* is the mother?"

"Some random hook-up from last year." Dan corrected himself. "I guess I shouldn't say that. A girl I vaguely remember. We were in Newport. She actually died in a car accident last month. The great-grandmother was caring for James but she can't handle it. Tom said she's sick. Anyway, she reached out to Tom and now he sounds like a fucking lost zombie."

I didn't even realize I'd spoken out loud when I said, "James is three months old? Same age as Rebecca."

Dan asked, "Rebecca who?"

Jenna answered, "Darcy's niece."

He looked sad and far off. "Oh, weird."

I looked to Jenna. "Have you spoken to her?"

"Just before you walked in. She's ok. She actually sounds kind of happy, like totally infatuated with the baby. And I think she's doing most of the caretaking. Sounds like Tom's kind of out of it."

"I can imagine. Wow, I can't believe this."

Ugh. I dreaded the call I had to make to Caleb, so I reached out to Darcy first.

U ok?

She wrote right back:

Yup :) I know it's crazy but I am. Tom is freaking me out a little but we're ok.

Hmm, the smiley face seemed a little off, but better that than despair, right?

LMK if u need anything.

-Seriously, I'm good.

Do ur parents know?

-Yes.

Yikes.

-Lol. Yeah, I'll tell you about that convo some other time. Tell girls I'm fine.

Ok. Love u.

Now for the hard part.

"Hey, sweetness."

"I'm back, smooth flight." *Why do I have to be the bearer of crappy news? I don't want to do this, I don't want to do this.* "So, what are you doing right now?"

"Are you, like, initiating phone sex? Believe me, I'm down, just a little surprised. Ask me what I'm wearing, 'cause I'm stripping down right now as we speak."

"You are such a perv."

"Right back atcha. Glad you made it home safe, baby."

"Listen, I've got something to tell you but promise you won't freak?"

He paused. "I'll try."

"It's about Tom and Darcy."

"What happened?"

I broke out the calmest tone I could muster. "She's ok and your parents already know. Tom apparently just found out he has a baby."

"*What?* What the *fuck?*"

"She's ok. She's in Connecticut with Tom and the baby. Can I ask you not to call her right now, though?"

"When? How did this happen?"

"I don't know all the details. Apparently a fling he had before he started dating Darcy."

"What a fucking asshole."

"Caleb."

"He's an asshole."

I had to let him vent. It wouldn't do any good to defend Tom right now.

"Jesus, Rene, she's so young."

"Darcy's my age. She's actually a year older."

He was silent for a moment, then calmer when he asked, "Have you spoken to her?"

"We've texted. She's good. She's staying there for a few days until Tom's parents get home."

"Should I head up?"

"No! I mean, touch base with your parents, but she cannot know that I told you."

"Ok. Listen, thanks for letting me know. I gotta go right now."

"Call me later."

"Yeah, I will."

I hated spilling Darcy's business. I was telling her about us on Graduation Day no matter what. I couldn't do this anymore.

When he called me back later that night, he sounded more like my Caleb. "Hey, sweetness."

"Are you all right? I feel like I dropped a bomb on you."

"Are *you* ok? I shouldn't have hung up before without first checking on you. I'm sorry."

"I'm fine, really. Did you discuss it with your parents?"

"Uh, no. I stopped by there tonight after work. It was obvious there was something up, but they didn't tell me so I played dumb. They asked me to come over for dinner Friday night. Your graduation is Saturday, so I'm guessing they want to tell me, Kate and Luke together before we head up."

"If this interferes with the trip and all, I'll understand if you can't get away right now."

"No way. However this plays out, I doubt I'm being tapped for diaper changing duty. My parents will be here for Darcy to lean on. And no matter what happens, I want to tell my family about us before we take off. Is that ok with you?"

"Yes. I'm thinking I can't do this, I can't keep secrets anymore."

"Me neither. It doesn't suit me."

I couldn't help but smile. "Doesn't suit me anymore either."

The next few days were filled with parties. Some were organized school events, but the best parties were the informal ones in the Village. I ran into Tanner too many times. It was inevitable. We had a nice conversation one night, and I was happy to hear he had a date for the Commencement Dance. I would have felt awful if he wasn't going. He told me about his plans for the summer and beyond, and I told him about mine. I could tell he was still hurting, but he didn't lay that at my feet. I hoped the girl who eventually landed Tanner knew how truly lucky she was.

It was a bittersweet week. I was going to miss my girls once we parted ways. I knew I'd see Caitlin. She was going right onto grad school in Chicago but the girl could travel at will. She could easily be in New York twice a month. And I knew I'd be seeing Darcy, although she had no idea just how much of me she'd be seeing. Jenna and Beth, I hoped, would not drift away with the distance between us.

Darcy's situation wasn't so great at the moment. She came back to campus nothing short of crestfallen. The Commencement Dance was the next day, and when she practically stumbled in the door, looking exhausted after driving back and forth in one evening to Tom's house, you knew things were heading downhill. Tom had all but cut her out. She flat-out sobbed as we sat crammed onto her bed, and there was nothing anyone could say to comfort her. Darcy looked like she was in the kind of twisted pain that I knew all too well.

Caleb had been checking in with me every day for an update. Not being able to comfort his sister was hard, but he knew she was in good hands. I reassured him that Darcy would be out with me, Chris, Cara and a few others who weren't going to the dance tomorrow night.

"Rene, I feel like a shit."

"Don't. There's nothing you can do for her right now."

"No, that's not it. Here I am asking all about Darcy, and you're missing out on the dance because of me, because we're not out in the open. I'm so sorry you're not going. You should be there."

"When I tell you that I'm not disappointed at all, I mean it. Really, Caleb, I've been feeling like the luckiest, most fortunate girl on the planet lately. Do you understand?"

He let out a resigned sigh. "Yeah, babe. I just don't want you missing out on anything because of me."

"Stop. Don't want to hear another word about it, ok?"

"Ok."

I groaned, already thinking about the hangover I'd be battling the day after. "I'm probably going to wind up getting pretty tipsy tomorrow night while Darcy drowns her sorrows."

"Be careful, angel."

"Don't worry, we'll have our bodyguard Chris with us. Six-two, two-twenty...No one messes with him."

"Good, I trust that guy."

And Darcy woke up the next morning ready to do battle. She came into my room sporting a sunny expression that nearly masked the red rimmed eyes and dark circles.

"Ok, Rene, we're a team today. I want to help the girls get ready before you and I go out on the town. I give you full permission to force feed me a pre-game shot if I start looking teary eyed at any point today, ok?"

"You got it. But since I'm a total lightweight, I suggest we leave the shots until later on or else I won't make it out of here with you at all." I sat up on the bed and hugged her. "I feel just awful for you. You're a strong girl, though. You'll get through the next few days."

"It just feels so bad."

"How could it not?"

She got through the day like a champ, but gave me the signal to leave a few minutes early. I knew she had to get out of there before all the happy couples started milling around.

Beth was pressuring Darcy to accept one of the last-minute date offers that came her way that afternoon, but I knew she'd never spend tonight with anyone else. I'd feel the same.

Chris and his friend Denny had the cab waiting when we got to his place. Cara and another girl rounded out our group. We went to a bar that had live music and a great crowd. Hands down, Denny and I were the happiest duo in the group. I was more than fine with skipping the dance, and Denny's girlfriend went to school in California, so they just couldn't make it work. But Chris was nursing a wound, and obviously so was Darcy. Chris was stewing over Caitlin going to the dance with her latest flavor of the month, while Cara, of course, had been waiting in vain for Chris to ask her. Darcy was putting on a brave face but she was miserable.

Denny was grabbing all of us girls up to dance, and as the drinks started flowing, so did the laughs. When I came back from the bathroom I caught the tail end of Darcy telling Chris about her situation. The three of us subsequently did a shot and had a good laugh about the absurdity of it all. Sometimes when things were this bad there was nothing to do but laugh.

When Denny dragged Darcy back onto the dance floor, Chris smiled at me, shaking his head. "Tom's having quite the year, right? I love that dipshit, but I know him pretty well. He's gonna totally screw up the good thing he's got going with her." He fixed his eyes on me after taking a healthy swig. "So missy, where's the older, sophisticated mystery man tonight? I have to say, you don't seem bummed at all about missing the dance."

"I'm the opposite of bummed. My life is crazy good right now."

He reached across the table and took my hands. "I'm glad. Is he going to be here for graduation?"

"Yes. I don't know if I can introduce you that day, though."

He looked skeptical. "All right, but why? I *am* one of your closer friends."

I looked around. He *was* a close friend and I suddenly had an overwhelming need to let someone in on my secret, to share my happy news. "Will you put this in the vault?"

"Of course, you know I don't blab."

"I can't let anyone know until I tell Darcy myself."

He cocked his head to the side. "Come again?"

"It's Darcy's brother, Caleb Donovan. He's my older, sophisticated mystery man. I was going to tell her a while ago but she was hell bent on reuniting me with Tanner. Ugh, and now there's this mess with Tom. It just never feels like the right time."

Chris squeezed my hand. "I've met him and I can tell he's a good person."

"I've never been this happy in my life, Chris."

With that, Darcy slid back into the booth laughing after Denny dipped her dramatically on the dance floor. An absolutely inappropriate dance move given it was an alternative rock band, not an orchestra playing a waltz. But whatever, I was just so glad she wasn't a puddle of mope tonight.

She took both of our hands as a moment of clarity overtook her, albeit a tipsy one. "Whatever happens, guys, I'm going to be all right. I love him and this sucks, but I'm going to be all right."

Chapter Twenty-Two

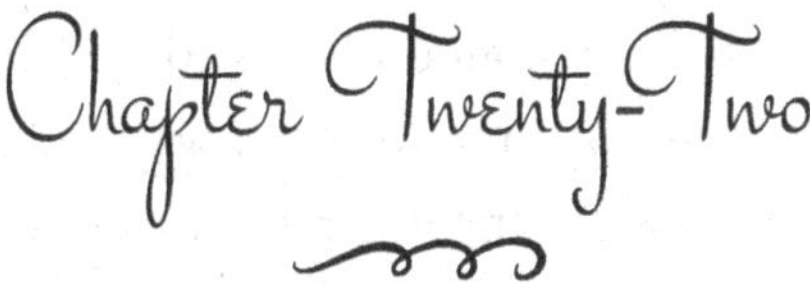

RENE

Everyone's Graduation Day should be as bright and sunny.

One by one, my girls came into my room and hugged me extra tight. I wasn't imagining it. They felt bad thinking that while their families were here to stand beside them, I was all alone. But I wasn't alone. I had someone who was proud of me and someone to holler when I walked across that stage today.

I had Caleb.

Are u packed for tomorrow?

Excited?

I can't wait to see u.

The day I'd been waiting for had finally arrived.

He caught up to me, Caitlin and Darcy as we were about to enter the stadium. He told us we all looked beautiful, but as he said the words, he never took his eyes off me. I no longer cared about appearances. Soon enough everyone would know.

Caleb pulled Darcy off to the side, and seeing the way he interacted with her made me feel, if possible, an even deeper love for him.

He was a loving, nurturing brother. I knew he would be good at every role he played in life, husband and father included. Yes, it was an emotional day.

I drank in every word from the keynote speakers and the valedictorian. This was a big day for all of us, but I recognized that for me, it was a day I'd arrived at against all odds. I said a silent prayer for Miss Parsons, hoping she was with me in some way today. I also thought of my parents. There was no anger, no resentment. They were what they were. I wished they were better, different, but at the end of the day, people make choices in their lives—good ones, bad ones, ones they regret. I knew that as well as anyone else. I wouldn't say I'd entirely forgiven my mother and father, but maybe I'd moved past any ill will.

I was good. I was better than good.

When I crossed the stage I was hoping to hear Caleb, but the sounds of all my girls, along with Chris, Mac and Dan, drowned out anyone else. I know they planned the extra loud holler to make up for my lack of family.

As several hundred caps were thrown in the air, I looked around me, taking it all in. Friends hugged tearful goodbyes, families crowded around their own, I saw Tom knocking over chairs trying to get to Darcy, and I saw Dan grab Jenna in the most loving embrace.

Two arms wrapped around me from behind and pulled me in close. "I'm so proud of you."

I turned in his arms to face him. I could feel tears pooling in my eyes, but I was smiling. It hit me all at once, the sadness of not having a family mixed with the relief of having him.

"I'm so glad you're here for me, Caleb. You can't imagine."

He lifted my chin and landed a tender kiss on my lips. His eyes were damp as well. It's like he knew exactly what was going through my mind when he said, "I'm your family, Rene. It's you and me."

I'd made plans to dine out with Caitlin's family after the ceremony, but Caleb was not having it.

"No way, Beaumont. Today's the day. I'm not looking to make a big announcement at lunch or anything, but later on I'm telling my parents and you can tell Darcy. I want you with us, with the family."

"You don't have to ask me twice."

And I don't know how anyone could have been sitting at that table and not figured it out. Caleb held my hand under the table and barely took his eyes off me the entire time. But since Darcy's situation was so dire, the focus was not on us.

The Donovans dropped me and Darcy off at our place afterward. Everyone was coming back for one last night of parties, and then we would all be heading our separate ways the next morning. Darcy's family was staying at a hotel in town tonight, and Caleb informed me we were meeting up for brunch before setting off for the airport. Knowing that it would all be out in the open tomorrow made me feel some messed up combination of relieved and anxious.

As soon as Darcy and I grabbed a beer at the party, she cornered me. "So, are you going to tell me or what?"

She knew.

"Are you mad?"

"Why would I be? I love my brother and you obviously make him ridiculously happy."

"I haven't been honest with you, though. I was going to tell you one night a few months ago, but that was the night I came back home and Tanner was there. It just never seemed like the right time."

She laughed, spitting out a little beer when she said, "Now I feel really bad about trying to push you two back together! How long has this been going on?"

I looked at her and braced for the worst. "Off and on? I started seeing him during your year abroad."

Once the initial shock wore off, Darcy looked sad. "So when he was having a rough time last year, did that have something to do with you?"

I nodded. "We went through a lot and broke up for a long time. We just started up again—"

She broke in, "In Rincon. I knew it! I couldn't figure out why he came down. The waves were crap."

"I'm sorry I kept it from you. A lot happened. It was complicated. I hope you understand, but I just couldn't—"

"It's ok. Weird but ok." She hugged me tight. "I understand how things can be complicated, Rene, just—"

"What?"

"Take care of him. I know he seems like a big, strong, got-it-all together guy, but he's...I just hate the idea of him hurting. And I'd never want Caleb to hurt you either."

"I have no intention of ever hurting him, Darcy. I love him completely. And he loves me. I've never met anyone like him. I've never opened up to anyone the way I do with him. He just...He makes me feel safe."

Darcy looked heartbroken, and how could she not? I hugged her, wanting to comfort her, but also because I was happy in the knowledge that I had another wonderful person in my life.

"Give him time, Darcy. Tom's probably still in shock. He'll come to his senses, but it just might take some time."

With that, Jenna, Dan and Caitlin practically crashed into us. Darcy nodded and then smiled. "Come on. Let's go have one last great night here together."

* * *

CALEB

Mom looked teary eyed while my dad cleared his throat. I couldn't believe they were getting all choked up over this. Then he let out a little laugh. "I was wondering what was going on during lunch."

My mom squeezed my hand. "She's warm, beautiful and just lovely. You seem happy, and that makes us very happy."

"I'm crazy about her. I've never felt this way about any girl."

Dad asked, "Does Darcy know?"

"By now she probably does. I think she'll be ok with everything."

Mom waved it off. "She only cares about your happiness, Caleb. I just hope our little Darcy is ok. What an awful situation for them both. I feel so bad for Tom. He looked awful at the ceremony."

With that, Darcy and Rene came walking into the restaurant. Darcy made her way straight to me and threw her arms around my neck, squeezing tight.

"I love you, Caleb. And this is just great in my opinion. I couldn't hope for a better match for you than Rene."

Mom and Dad were hugging Rene, and then Luke and Kate went in for the kill. She lowered her head into my chest when I finally got the chance to hug her. The Donovans were a bunch of mushes, but I knew Rene, and this was probably an overwhelming show of emotion for her.

She whispered against my neck. "I'm so happy."

I looked around the table as we ate, laughed, and also talked about some pretty heavy stuff, given Darcy's situation. I gave silent thanks for the hand that I'd been dealt in life. No one's life was perfect, including mine, but I had so much to be grateful for.

Chapter Twenty-Three

CALEB

"Are you going to tell me before we get to the airport?"

"Nope."

"Jeez, I hope I packed appropriately."

"You literally need a bikini, that's all."

"Check. Got that."

"I hope you packed my favorite one."

"It's a few seasons old now. I haven't worn it much, but this is probably its last trip."

"No way. I want you to wear that thing until I can no longer stomach the sight of you in a bikini...Like sixty years from now."

"Yeah, right."

It was a long trip but well worth it when we finally arrived. I arranged for a speedboat to take us from Malé to our resort, where we had a private villa that was set on pilings over the water. I went all out on this trip for Rene. The last time I was here, it was a laid back surfing trip with Mick, Conner and a few other guys. I loved it, but it was not a luxury experience. And while this trip with Rene was laid back, it was definitely five-star. She was speechless when the steward handed her champagne as she boarded the boat transfer.

She looked to me, eyes wide. "I've never seen water this color."

"It's paradise, right?"

We spent the next six days in the closest state to nirvana that I've ever experienced. We lazed in our giant, luxurious bed as long as we liked. A chef came in to cook for us, serving on our deck that jutted into the Indian Ocean. We jumped into the water off our private dock morning, noon and night, and there was definitely some naughty night swimming. I forced Rene to get pampered in the spa, and on the last day she came along to spectate when we trekked to my favorite local surf spot.

Paradise.

And unlike the past few months, when we'd been limited to a few weekends here and there, this was the first time we had an uninterrupted stretch of time to just be together and talk.

"I know if you did this every day it could get old, but really, wouldn't it be heaven to just stay here, eat food like this, swim in the ocean and have sex all day?"

When she said things like that I couldn't help but rip the sheets from her body and have at it. And it was heaven, drowsy and sated with her in my arms afterwards.

"Tomorrow we head back, can't get too used to this. Once we get home it's going to be long hours for you and crazy long days for me."

She already knew Mick and I were striking out on our own, but it was imminent now. I was leaving my job after the end-of-year bonuses were distributed. Come January, Mick and I would be in a development phase, then renting office space and launching by March. It was going to be a lot of work. I was ready and excited for it, but I needed her to know what it entailed. It was going to take years to build the business.

"Just let me know what I can do to help you, Caleb. Let me know when you need time without me, let me know when you're so stressed out that you need a neck rub." She laughed when she added, "Let me know when you're in need of a home-cooked meal and I'll find someone to cook one for you."

"Seriously, Beaumont, you're French. You're probably a master chef and you don't even realize it."

"I do like to watch cooking shows, but right now my repertoire is limited to spaghetti with butter."

"Butter?"

"I like sauce, you dope. It's just that there was usually a shortage of groceries in my house growing up. I worked with what I had."

"Sorry, I shouldn't have teased."

She smiled and grabbed my face in her hands. "Stop, I'm fine. And don't worry about me being lonely when you're out entertaining clients and all. I'm going to be really busy, too. I'm going to have to put my time in if I want to make it."

"Let's just promise each other something. Plans and goals are important, but life gets in the way sometimes. Everything doesn't have to be planned out and etched in stone. We can adapt to whatever comes our way and we'll deal with things together."

Her eyes watered because she knew exactly what I was saying. She nodded and curled into me. We stayed like that for a while, lost in our own thoughts. When she shifted her body and nudged me to lay with my hips resting between her legs, I knew she needed to feel close, to feel connected to me. That's what I needed too. I'd always need it.

* * *

RENE

My mind was racing.

It would be Friday when we got home, and Monday morning I was reporting to the studio at 5:30 a.m. I was no stranger to early mornings, but I was going to have to stick to an early bedtime on work nights. I needed to unpack some things at Caleb's, shop for some work clothes and shoes, and just get settled and ready for my big day on Monday.

As I went through my bag looking for a pen and my notepad, where I was forever writing to-do lists, I came across a flash drive. I'd nearly forgotten about the woman on the beach who handed it to me as I sat watching Caleb catch those last few waves of the day.

She told me she was a photographer taking candids of the surfers. She took a few pictures of me and Caleb as we were sitting on the beach, hoped we didn't mind, and thought I would want them. She was this exotic looking woman, mid-sixties I'd guessed, with piercing blue eyes and long grey hair braided down her back. She was one of those effortlessly stylish women who looked totally chic wearing nothing but a bohemian tunic.

I was restless, so while Caleb slept on the plane I used his laptop to view the pictures. Each one had a signature on it, like a watermark...Beatrix Drew. Her face wasn't familiar but her name was. She'd photographed most of the pop icons of her time. And the pictures she snapped of us were...Well, they rendered me speechless. She captured us in the most intimate way. In one, Caleb had just laid me back into the sand and covered me with his body. He was moving a piece of stray hair from my face as he smiled down at me. Another had me sitting astride him with our faces inches apart. We were looking at one another as if we shared some kind of secret. In another he stood behind me with his arms wrapped around me and his chin resting on the top of my head. We both looked out towards the surf lost in good thoughts. There were a dozen in all, each one a beautiful gift.

I was going to wake Caleb to show him but then thought better of it. I missed his birthday last year and this time around I wanted to give him something really special, something from my heart. Any one of these pictures framed would be perfect.

We were so tired when we got "home" to Caleb's place that we both fell into bed and slept the afternoon away. That night we were both still wiped out and fell back into bed early. I felt so cosmopolitan at the thought of having jet lag.

The next morning I woke up with the sun, feeling refreshed. I had a lot to do and wanted to get an early jump on the day. Since the stores wouldn't be open for a few hours, I started unpacking. When I went to go find a nook in the closet to hang some clothes, I saw that Caleb had cleared out an entire half of his large walk-in closet. Hanging on "my" side were nearly a dozen really great shift dresses, a few skirts, tops, pants, sweaters and a light topper coat—all with the tags on. There were several shoeboxes on the floor, all from upscale women's designers. Did he buy me an entirely new wardrobe?

The old Rene would have been indignant, as if such a gesture was an insult to my ability to take care of myself. But now I was grateful and recognized the love that was behind an act like this. Caleb knew I wasn't rolling in dough, he knew it was important for me to look good at work, and he didn't want me stressing about shopping on the two days I had left to enjoy with him.

I crawled back into bed and kissed him. He kept his eyes closed as he whispered, "Good morning, my love."

"You have good taste in clothes, Caleb. I just found my new wardrobe. Thank you."

He opened one eye and smiled. "I didn't want you running around like a nut shopping this weekend. I'm selfish. I want you to myself for a few more days."

"You've got me."

"And for the record, I don't enjoy shopping. Kate helped. Actually, she picked all of that out."

"So now that you have me for the weekend, what are you going to do with me?"

He pulled me in close, my back pressed against his front. "What do you think?"

I could feel him and wiggled in even closer. "Is this how you say good morning every day?"

"Yup, get used to it."

Lying in bed later on as Caleb went downstairs to make us coffee, I thought maybe I was being silly about not moving in with him. I mean, I could get used to falling into a nice routine with him and waking up like this every day. But my rational side said it was too soon. I was too young. I needed to prove that I could be on my own, supporting myself. Moving in with Maureen was the right thing to do. I knew that.

We spent the rest of the weekend enjoying the great weather outdoors in the city. Caleb showed me his favorite running routes, the best place to grab coffee on my way to work, and the best local dinner spots.

We had lunch with his parents on Sunday. And while I still felt a little awkward when we first got there, that dissipated within a few minutes. The Donovans always made me feel completely at ease and at home.

When we were alone I told Sarah about the pictures.

"Are you serious? I'm a little star struck right now. In my world, she's a total rock star. I can't wait to see them."

Sarah gave me the name of a good framer. I planned to head there one night this week after work so the pictures would be ready by his birthday.

Monday came quickly, and then the next several weeks flew by in a blur. There was no easing in period at work and I was glad. I wanted to shoulder responsibilities from day one and Meredith definitely expected that from me. After handling production issues during the broadcast, I spent my days researching, planning the logistics for upcoming guests, and reaching out to snag guests for future broadcasts.

About one month in, Meredith asked me to lunch. She asked for my feedback and I asked her for a performance review of my work so far. She was constructive and generous with her praise. She also gave me guidance and pointers on how to handle some of the other duties she was going to have assigned to me in the coming months.

She switched to French about halfway through lunch, and I wanted to high-five myself for working daily to improve my fluency since returning from Paris last year. She asked if I still remembered our conversation about Chamonix, and then told me she'd just received her tentative schedule, which included two weeks broadcasting live from the winter Olympics. I couldn't hide my excitement when she told me I would need to clear a month on my schedule, as she'd need me over there two weeks early to prep. When I thanked her again for the opportunity, she laughed and said I might be cursing her by the end of the assignment. Meredith told me that assignments like these were around-the-clock work, and anything but glamorous, but I didn't care. I was thrilled to be invited—to be a part of it. I knew I could make myself indispensable there, as a translator in the very least, and that was my plan.

Who am I? I thought to myself as I woke Caleb up on his birthday by crawling underneath the covers and taking him in my mouth. I couldn't tell if he was fully awake yet, but I knew from the way he fisted my hair and his contented moans that he was enjoying this. Before his release, he lazily dragged me up over him and entered me as he kissed me slowly, with purpose. The first few months we were together we never went without a condom, even though I was on birth control. Both of us were gun-shy about taking even the slightest chance. But now there was nothing between us, and the warm surge of him when he came deep inside of me was pure bliss. He didn't move for a few minutes and I didn't want him to. I didn't want to break the connection between us.

"Best birthday present ever, Beaumont."

"Wait, I'll be right back."

I went into the bathroom to clean up and then came back out wearing only a pair of lacy underwear. I knew Caleb loved to look at me topless, so I let him get his fill as I went to go get his present from the closet.

"Get back in here so I can get my hands on those."

"Patience, Caleb."

I plopped back on the bed, laughing as I watched him stare at my bouncing breasts with lust in his eyes. But when I handed him the gift, I had to look away. I couldn't watch as he read the note.

I wasn't one for saying much in terms of my feelings, but I tended to lay it all out there when I put pen to the page. His eyes were wet when he raised my face to his and laid one gentle kiss on my lips. When he unwrapped the first frame, he stared at the picture for over a minute before he looked back up to me with wonder in his eyes. "How did you do this?"

I told him the story about Beatrix Drew and then grabbed the rest of the pictures. The one I had framed was the black and white where we were sitting close, face to face. The framer steered me towards a driftwood-like frame that was perfect. This was a smaller picture, for his desk. I also framed a larger, different print for his apartment. It was the one where he was standing behind me, holding on as we both looked out at the ocean. I think I liked that one best because no matter how much I fought against it, there was a part of me that loved the idea of this strong, capable man standing behind me, holding onto me and keeping me safe.

* * *

CALEB

By far, it was my best birthday ever.

Just having Rene in my life was the best gift I could hope for. But having her here, living with me for at least a few weeks, being able to hold her in my arms all through the night—it was just so good.

After a lazy morning, we took off for the beach where my entire family was already set up. Darcy had Rebecca in her arms most of the day. I think she took Darcy's mind off her troubles. Luke and Kate, my parents, me and Rene all spent the day in and out of the water and then had a barbecue at the house. Not the usual drink-ups of my previous birthdays but so much better.

I spied Rene holding Rebecca a few times during the day and wondered when that desire would strike. Knowing her well, I didn't think it was a question of *if* she wanted children but when. She probably wasn't in any particular rush and that was fine by me. Besides making it official by asking her to be my wife, I wanted time as a couple, time to travel, time to goof off and just be us. And I figured Rene wanted to achieve a certain level in her career before we took that step.

And as the summer transitioned to fall, Mick and I were busy setting the groundwork for our venture. I was killing it at work, hoping for a giant bonus as a send-off when I went out on my own. I really didn't fear the financial repercussions of not having a paycheck, as I had a trust from my mother's estate to fall back on. It was just my competitive nature. I always wanted to beat my personal best. Last year's bonus was a huge number to top and I was making it my mission to do just that.

Chapter Twenty-Four

RENE

It was a sad day when I moved into Maureen's. I know Caleb would have preferred I stayed put, and to be honest I would have preferred it too. Living with him was like playing house, playing the role of Mrs. Donovan, and I liked it. I actually cooked for him a few times with passable results, and curling up next to him at night was familiar and comforting.

I pretty much stayed at Caleb's every weekend and spent at least one night during the week with him. He was working long hours lately, so on those nights it made more sense to stay at my place, closer to the studio. And I couldn't have asked for a better roommate than Maureen. We commuted together, usually went to the gym after work, and Thursday nights we always went out with our work friends. They were a great group of people—it almost felt like an extension of college.

As I'd hoped, Caitlin was averaging at least one trip to New York per month, and I managed to make it out to Chicago twice—once on my own and once with Caleb. Caitlin was busy with grad school, traveling, shopping and boys. She combined her talents with her love of retail therapy by starting an online store that specialized in upscale, but lesser known up-and-coming designers. I had no doubt she would grow the business into a success. For someone who came off as totally carefree, Caitlin had razor sharp instincts and wasn't afraid of hard work.

Whenever Caitlin came into town, we would try to get Jenna down and the four of us girls would make a weekend out of it. Sometimes Darcy's high school friend Kasia joined us and she was a great addition to our group. Caitlin and Kasia immediately hit it off, as they were both into fashion and merchandising, and I also found Kasia easy and fun to be with. She started coming to spin class with me and Maureen, and just like that, another kindred spirit drifted into my life.

Everyone was in a good place. Darcy and Jenna were teaching, both of them made to work with kids. Darcy's life had become pretty hectic, as she was teaching and taking care of James with Tom. Yes, Tom had come to his senses after a few months, realizing that being apart was achieving nothing except making them both miserable. Darcy was cautious at first but now she was all in. It was a lot of responsibility but she seemed truly happy. She loved being a mother.

I couldn't see myself as a mother yet, but one day I wanted children. I knew Caleb would make a great father. I wasn't nearly there yet, though. I was loving work, having fun living in the city, and was just enjoying being part of a couple. Caleb was as attentive as he could be between spending long hours at work and plotting out the logistics for the new business with Mick. We spent most of our nights off together at his place or out with friends.

To be with Caleb in New York was to be on his home turf. On occasion, it was unnerving. After the rugby matches, when we were out at clubs, when we ran into his old high school friends—it didn't happen often, but occasionally an old flame would approach and overtly flirt. He always shut the girl down right away but it got to me.

"What's wrong, Rene?"

I always kept it bottled up. I wouldn't allow myself to be the whiny, jealous girlfriend, but one night after a few drinks I let it fly.

"I wish, just once, you knew what it felt like. I wish you had to put up with one of my old fuck buddies sidling up to me looking for a hook-up for old time's sake."

His lips formed a surprised O and then he *laughed* at me. When he saw I was not amused, he got defensive.

"First off, I was never the manwhore you're making me out to be." He shook his head, disgusted. "That's just unfair. And, what, you think I don't know what it's like to feel jealousy where you're concerned?"

I gave him my most bored, petulant look. "No, I don't."

He nodded sarcastically. "Right, Rene. Finn practically eye fucks you every time I take you to a work function. I'd like you to stay home after the rugby games because I want to slap guys senseless when I see the way they look at you. Come on, I don't get mad because I trust you. Am I encouraging any of those women?"

"No."

"I will never hurt you like that, Rene, so let it go."

I'll never hurt you.

I remembered those words after leaving Caleb's office Christmas party one Friday night in early December.

Caleb asked me to go but I knew I wouldn't be able to make it. Meredith was taking just a few members of her team out for a holiday dinner, and attendance wasn't optional for a newbie looking to stay on her boss's good side.

This was Caleb's last holiday party at the firm and he was looking forward to it. Ed was the only one who knew he was leaving after the New Year.

When our group broke after the late dinner, Dana, one of my friends from the show, came with me downtown last minute to meet up with Caleb.

Coming in from the cold, Ed was the first person I saw and he was well on his way. He greeted me loudly, grabbed me into a big hug and spun me around. I really liked Ed and knew that Caleb was looking to poach him away from the firm after he was established. While Ed went to grab drinks for me and Dana, we took in the scene. Dana was commenting on how gorgeous all of these finance guys were when my eyes landed on Finn. I went to smile but his eyes went wide, panicked, and then he looked in the direction of the dance floor. My eyes followed. Caleb was dancing with a redhead. I knew this had to be Cherry.

I don't know how long I stood there staring. It was probably no more than thirty seconds, but it was enough time to take it all in. Caleb's arms were around her waist, hands resting no more than a few inches above her ass, and her arms were around his neck. Their bodies were close. They were talking, smiling at one another and swaying to the beat of the slow song.

My hand instinctively reached out and grabbed Dana's wrist. I practically barked, "We have to go."

Dana started to protest, but when her gaze followed mine she snatched our coats and followed me out of the trendy Meatpacking District spot and back out onto the street.

"What the fuck was that, Rene?"

"Am I overreacting? Would you consider that being way too cozy with an ex?"

"That was an ex? She looked like a Playboy centerfold."

"Thanks."

"Sorry."

"So?"

"Um, yeah, that would have totally upset me if I were in your shoes."

My phone pinged with a text:

Where r u?

Please, he knew exactly where I was.

Don't worry about it. Keep dancing.

Before I could even hit send, I got:

Come back inside.

I responded to that with:

Fuck no. I mean, fuck u.

"You up for a late one, Dana?"

She plastered a smile on her worried face. "Yep, lead the way."

We hit a bar close by that was packed with good looking twenty-somethings. I was filled with anger that was born out of hurt and embarrassment. Not only did I feel like he was a dishonest shit, I felt ashamed. The way Finn looked at me, as if he also thought Caleb had been caught in the act, just burned. I never thought of myself as a stupid girl who believed in fairy tales, but I *had* believed in Caleb.

Now I felt like I'd been conned.

I drank shots, danced like a stripper, and flirted right back when guys hit on me. I wanted to hurt him. Go home with one of these guys. Make love? No, I wanted to straight-up fuck.

I was lying to myself. I didn't want that, but did I want him to feel my pain. I wanted him to know what it felt like to be deceived by the one person you cherished most in this world.

Yeah, so thank God *that* didn't happen, but I did drink twice as much as I normally would have. Dana was a good friend. She stayed out with me, rallied when she was tired, and kept her wits about her. She watched out for me, knowing that I could get myself into serious trouble that night.

It was probably four by the time we made it back to her apartment in Chelsea. I woke up the next morning on her couch with my head throbbing and a mouth that felt like it was caked in sand. I dragged myself to the kitchen and drank nearly a liter of water, then grabbed my phone off the floor and turned it back on.

There were about twenty missed calls from Caleb. *Screw him.* And multiple texts. The font was too small for my eyes to focus on in my current condition, and I was in no mood to read his sorry ass excuses anyway.

I shot a quick text to Maureen, and my phone rang a moment later.

"Where are you? Caleb practically busted the door down last night. What the hell happened?"

Her voice reverberated like a jackhammer. "I'm at Dana's. I can't get into it now or I'll be sick. I'll tell you later but I'm going back to sleep now."

"Please text him. He looked like he was going to lose it when you weren't home by three."

"I can't. Can you just text him that I'm at Dana's. And don't tell him you know where she lives, ok? I just need a break. I'll be home later."

I woke several hours later to Dana gently tapping me. "Hey, stay and crash as long as you like. I'm going out with my sister in a little while. I wanted to make sure you were ok."

"I'm so sorry. I feel like I dragged you into my downward spiral last night."

She waved me off. "You'd do the same for me."

I felt the tears well up again when I asked, "Dana, be straight with me. Do you think Caleb was cheating on me?"

She let out a pained sigh. "Rene, I don't know. I would have felt the same way you did. It didn't look so innocent. I mean, her tits were practically right up under his nostrils! But last night you told me Caleb was leaving the firm after several years. You think maybe that was just a goodbye between two people who shared a past?"

"The way they were dancing, holding each other? When I picture it...God, it hurts so much."

"I know, sweetie. Promise me no drinks for you tonight, ok? I think we both may have permanently damaged our livers last night."

* * *

CALEB

I thought Finn was looking to cut in. I was annoyed he was interrupting us and shot him a look over my shoulder that said, "Are you kidding me?"

I didn't have any lingering feelings for Cherry, but we were still friends. She'd heard the gossip that I might be leaving so we got to talking. And then I asked her to dance—no harm in that. It was no more than a proper goodbye. Cherry was in the middle of telling me that even though she was disappointed things didn't work out between us, she was happy for me.

"Caleb?"

"Can it wait, Finn?"

He shrugged. "Yeah, it can wait. Just thought you'd want to know that Rene was here and she left. Ok, carry on. Don't want to interrupt whatever *this* is, asshole."

I'd been talking all night, joking, laughing—the belle of the fucking ball—but suddenly I had nothing to say. My mouth clamped shut as a sense of cold dread clawed its way up and gripped me by the throat.

I wasn't doing anything wrong, technically, but looking down at Cherry's body, I saw it pressed up close enough to mine to make this look messed up. My arms dropped to my sides. "I gotta go."

"Do you want me to call her to explain?"

Grabbing my suit jacket, I shook my head, annoyed. "No, Cherry, I don't think that would go over big."

"Finn, did she say where she was going?"

Suddenly he was disinterested, acted like I was bothering him. "Nope."

"You don't have to be a total dick about it. I wasn't doing anything."

He rolled his eyes, nodding sarcastically. "Yeah, that was nothing.

If you were any closer you would have been fucking Cherry on the dance floor. I'm sure Rene will be very understanding."

"Can't say I'm going to miss you, Finn."

I didn't wait for him to shoot off a snotty retort. I bolted. On my way downstairs I texted her and got a reply that did nothing to ease my fears. I didn't see her on the street outside. My calls went straight to voicemail and she didn't respond to any more of my texts. I called Maureen just after midnight—not a word from Rene.

I started walking, poking my head into clubs and bars. There were half a dozen places on each block in this neighborhood. It was like looking for a needle in a haystack. Midnight turned to one, then two. I made my way uptown to her apartment. When Maureen woke up to the sound of me pounding on the door and said she still hadn't heard from Rene, I practically lost it. Where the hell was she? Who was she with? At three I left, thinking maybe she'd gone to my place to confront me.

Empty.

I was furious, proof being the fist-sized hole in my living room wall. I was mad at myself and scared knowing that Rene was probably drinking and could be putting herself in danger.

Running on next to no sleep, I woke with a start when my phone vibrated on my chest. *Damn.* It was only Maureen.

Didn't want u to worry. R stayed at Dana's last night.

When I texted back asking if she was home now, I got:

No. Bye.

Bye. It's like Maureen was saying: Don't ask me anything, don't attempt to explain yourself, and that's all the help you're getting from me, douchebag.

I knew the drill. Rene would shut me out now. No communication. She would keep it up, too. I wouldn't get the opportunity to tell my side of the story—and I wasn't exactly sure what that was—until I tracked her down and cornered her.

* * *

RENE

It was getting dark outside when I finally dragged my sorry ass into the shower, threw on some of Dana's workout clothes with a pair of her flip flops and went home. It was December but I didn't even feel the cold.

I wanted to tell the cab driver to keep going when I saw him sitting on the stoop. Instead, I got out of the cab. I wanted to kick him, slap his face, claw at his eyes—I wanted to inflict physical pain.

"I hope you're not here to tell me that I didn't see what I saw."

"It isn't what you think."

"You're a walking cliché."

"We were saying goodbye. I shouldn't have danced with her like that. I realize what it must have looked like to you."

"And how's that?"

"Like there was more to it than there was."

"You mean like her tits were pressed up against you, you looked like you were enjoying her body, and you were looking at her with the same look I thought was reserved only for me? Just leave me alone, Caleb."

I went to push past him and had my hand on the doorknob when he grabbed my shoulders.

"Rene, please stop. I know what I did was wrong. I mean, if I thought you were in the room then I wouldn't have been having that moment with her, so I know it went too far. But don't ever think for a minute that I feel close to anyone, love anyone but you. That girl, I needed to apologize to her. She was there when I was at my worst and I used her. I knew she cared about me but I never felt the same. Honestly, what you saw last night was us telling each other goodbye again and me telling her that I was sorry."

"You made me look like a fool."

"You're no one's fool."

I was choking back a sob, fighting with myself not to cry. "Don't patronize me. The way you held her...You wanted her. If I didn't show up I think things may have gone further between you two. You're going to deny that but I know what I saw. You were looking at her and she was looking at you with desire."

He tightened his grip on me. "You're wrong!"

"I don't want to be hurt or jealous. I hate this feeling. I feel stupid, like you see me as naïve. Sweet Rene, never been around the block, your little virgin. How would you feel if you walked in and found me in the same position, looking at some other guy like that?"

"I'd feel like I was punched in the gut. I know I fucked up, Rene."

"That was more than fucking up. You gave me a reason not to trust you. I just can't get the image out of my mind. You two looked...intimate. You looked so...so...into her." I tried to twist out of his hold. "I've gotta go."

But he didn't let go. With two big paws planted on my shoulders and his voice cracking, he said, "No, you're not going. I'm not going to let you go in there, then ignore my calls, shut me out and send me away. You can't do that anymore. It fucking hurts too much. You've got to face things with me, no matter what. I *know* what I did was wrong. I also know there is *nothing* between me and her, and there is no way anything would have happened last night. *No. Way.* I love you with everything I have."

My shoulders slumped and I cried, too tired to fight. He held me close and kissed the top of my head. We stood there for a long while in the same position. At one point he whispered, "Please tell me we're ok."

"We're not ok."

"Will you come back home with me?"

"No. I feel drained. I just want to take another shower and fall into bed. And I don't want to be with you...I can't even be near you."

He hung his head. "Please don't shut me out. Can I please come pick you up tomorrow?"

"I don't know."

He choked out the words. "You're not doing this. I'll be here at twelve."

Maureen was waiting for me when I got in. After I spilled all the gory details, she didn't say anything at first, just sat there looking pensive.

"This isn't grounds for ending anything, Rene. Shit like this happens. I would be hurt too, but I believe what he said."

"Deep down, I do believe him. I just have this strong urge to hurt him back. To cut him off, ignore him."

"Passive aggressive, are we?"

"Totally. I'm working on it, though. I did speak to him, which is totally out of character for me. The old Rene would have blocked his number by now and forgotten his name."

"Are you going to see him tonight?"

"No, I'm too angry. He wants to pick me up tomorrow for lunch, but...I don't know."

"You'll get through this. He's crazy about you." Maureen shook her head, pained. "Every woman hopes to have a man look at her the way he looks at you. And last night when Caleb came over, it was more than just fearing he'd messed up. He was afraid for you, worried you might not be safe. It's not a stretch to say he was frantic with worry. You mean the world to him."

I wasn't convinced. "I was pissed last night thinking I just spent half a month's salary buying that prick his Christmas present. I swear, I have such a strong urge to punch him."

"What did you get him?"

"A plane ticket to Paris. He's leaving his job around the same time I'm heading over for the Olympics assignment, so I figured we could spend a long weekend together in Paris before I head off to

Chamonix. I don't really feel like strolling hand in hand along the banks of the Seine with him anymore, though."

She laughed and waved me off. "You're just in for a few crappy days and then I predict things will be back to normal. Really, this is a small bump in a very long road."

Can't say I agreed with her.

I fell back into bed after another long shower. My phone had a missed call and a text from Caleb:

Sorry sounds like a lame and empty word, but I'm so sorry. I love you.

My instinct was to turn off my phone, shut him out and make him sweat it out. In an effort to be better, though, I wrote back.

See u tomorrow.

I made a concerted effort not to replay images from last night in my head before I drifted off to sleep, but it was too hard. I'd love to say I felt a little better in the morning, but I didn't. I was heartbroken.

* * *

CALEB

Only a stupid, motherfucking dumbass does something like that. I prayed I hadn't totally jacked things up, but after the two rocky years we'd been through, I should have known better than to do even the slightest thing to chance what I had with Rene.

Regret and anger coursed through me. I took a long, punishing run and then went straight to the gym. I couldn't sit still, and I deserved to feel some physical pain in exchange for what I'd put her through. I was bone tired by the time I got home, falling into bed after a shower.

When I woke up, reality greeted me like a slap in the face on a cold day. I was wary of what the day would bring, but desperate to see her at the same time.

When I picked her up she gave Bosco a warmer greeting than she gave me. That was ok—I didn't expect things to be back to normal. I took her hand and thanked her for letting me take her out. She gently pulled her hand back and placed it in her lap as I pulled away from the curb. The ride to the beach was quick, thankfully, because the conversation was not flowing. Rene basically stared out the passenger side window the entire time.

She took the dog and headed straight for the shore. I followed her down after I went into the house to turn the thermostat higher. When I got to the top of the beach, I stopped. It was fairly warm for December, so she was wearing only a knit sweater and jeans. She was throwing a tennis ball to the dog and smiling as he raced after it, but even from a distance you could see that the smile didn't reach her eyes.

What have I done?

When I came up behind Rene and wrapped my arms around her, I felt her body stiffen. I didn't know what to say so I kept quiet. My heart physically ached when I noticed her reaching up to wipe away tears.

"Do you still care about her?"

"No," I croaked, feeling desperate. "You are the only girl I care about. The only girl I've ever loved."

"Don't ever do that to me again, Caleb."

I squeezed her tighter and kissed her head. "I won't. I promise you that."

She didn't look at me but turned and buried her head into my chest and hugged me back. I was so grateful for her forgiveness. I knew Rene, knew she was fighting her instinct to cut and run.

Heading back into the city, I wanted to ask if she'd stay at my place, but I didn't push it. It was raw between us, and I knew it was going to be a while before things felt normal again.

So I was alone in my big empty apartment, and being on my own had never felt this lonely before. I called Rene. She answered and we spoke for a few minutes, but it was strained. I hated this distance I'd created, and the idea of not having her full trust fucking burned. I imagined, as she'd asked, what it would feel like to walk in on her, to watch as she looked up into someone's eyes the way she looked at me. The image of that, and the thought of her pressed up against another man sickened me. And I couldn't help but replay something Rene said to me on the beach. She told me that in the moment, hurt and devastated, she wanted to sleep with someone, with anyone else. She wanted to hurt me back. God help me if she'd gone through with it. Just picturing it led to a matching hole in the sheetrock, this one in my bedroom.

Cherry approached me Monday morning, asking if everything was all right. I could feel eyes on us. I gave her a curt response—not rude, but one that made it crystal clear I wouldn't be discussing my love life with her.

Finn, who was all smug and condescending the other night, looked downright contrite when he came to me to apologize. He really didn't do anything wrong, and I told him as much—waved him the fuck off like the nuisance he was.

I'd lost my love for that guy a long time ago. I knew he got off on watching others fail, so that spectacle the other night? That was more satisfying to him than watching the last few seconds of overtime in a playoff game.

I didn't want to leave with any bad blood, but Finn and I wouldn't be hanging out again or meeting up for drinks—ever.

Chapter Twenty-Five

RENE

You better watch out.

Christmas was only a few days away, and for the first time in my life I was in the spirit. I had a place to live that was my very own, decorated with a tree, mistletoe, and an obnoxious talking Santa figure that made crude jokes and passed gas—an early gift from Caleb. I smiled every time I put my key in the lock, admiring the candy cane striped wreath that adorned our door. But I was truly looking forward to Christmas this year because, for once, I had family to spend it with.

I only remembered bits and pieces from the very early years, but I can't imagine that my parents ever hung a stocking by the chimney with care. I vaguely remember eating special chocolates on Christmas morning while watching the parade on television, but there were no wrapped presents, no tree decorated with lights and ornaments. This year would be a first for me in many ways.

Darcy and I went shopping for Tom and Caleb together. She was itching to take that next step, to marry Tom, and while she poured her heart out to me over lunch, I kept my trap shut about our latest drama. Darcy and I were now close like sisters, but she would always be Caleb's sister, so some topics were off limits.

A few weeks had passed, the pain had lessened to some degree. It's not that it didn't hurt anymore, it did, but I knew he loved me. Best to say I was not completely over it but I was getting there.

Just as I imagined, Christmas at the Donovan's was something out of a storybook. Every square foot of the house was decorated, it was like a two-week long open house for friends and family, and the place just radiated holiday cheer.

On Christmas Eve it was just the immediate family. Caleb was smiling from ear to ear as we walked up the front stairs of the brownstone, our arms laden with packages.

"What are you smiling about?"

He kissed my hand. "Last year I told my father, without naming you, that I hoped you'd be here with me next Christmas Eve, and you *are* here."

There were moments that night when I felt overwhelmed with emotion. Looking around the room at people laughing, picking up the babies, couples sitting and holding hands—*So this is what it was always supposed to be like?* I wasn't feeling sorry for myself. I was just in awe, and grateful that this family was now a part of my life.

After dinner, everyone got one present from Mr. and Mrs. Donovan. My eyes welled up when I realized they'd included me, as if I was one of their own. The Donovans gave me a camera so that I could capture my first trip to the Olympics. I managed to choke out a thank you, but my emotions were getting the better of me.

All of the Donovan kids spent Christmas Eve together, but then headed off to their significant others' families for Christmas Day. Darcy and Tom were driving back up to Connecticut later that night with James, and Luke and Kate would be with her family in upstate New York.

While we gathered the dishes, I joked with Sarah that she was stuck with us again tomorrow. Everyone knew I had no family to speak of. She laughed and hugged me tight. "We are so happy to be stuck with you!"

Sarah went on to share that she didn't have much family growing up either. She was raised by her grandmother, who passed when Sarah was in college. She believed that was part of the reason she was so drawn to this family. She told me how Caleb's mother was so wonderful to her, sensing that Sarah needed them. Sarah joked there were times when Rebecca asked her to babysit but then never even left the house. Rebecca would insist Sarah stay for dinner, stay for a movie—just let her hang around.

"When Rebecca died so suddenly, it was awful. I just wanted to do anything I could to make the children happy again. I never question whether or not Rebecca would have approved. It's almost as if I could always feel her blessing." She smiled wistfully and then said, "You know, I've never seen Caleb this happy before."

"I feel like he was made for me."

"That's true love."

Caleb woke me on Christmas morning with a cup of coffee and a small, beautifully wrapped box attached to a slightly larger box underneath.

"Merry Christmas, sweet Rene."

"I'll be back in one second."

After a quick trip to the bathroom to rid myself of sleep breath, I jumped back on the bed. I was as excited as a five-year-old.

"Okay, I'm ready."

I opened the small box. It held an old, battered key. I was baffled.

"You have to open the other one for that to make sense."

The other box had a picture of a house. I stared at it for a minute because it looked familiar, but I couldn't place it. Then it hit me. "You bought the house across from your parents' place at the beach?"

"Merry Christmas!"

"You got us a house? What? Caleb, when did you do this?"

"That day we were on the beach a couple of weeks ago." He paused for the briefest moment, pain clouding his expression at the memory of what had brought us to the beach that day, but then he shook it off. "As we were leaving you mentioned how much you loved it there, and how lucky I was to have spent my summers there as a kid. The next day my dad calls and tells me Mr. Baum died. He's the old man who owned the bungalow, but no one has seen him in years. Turns out he's spent like the last twenty years in Boca. I hate to admit what a dirt bag I am at heart, but I wasn't really feeling much in the way of sympathy and condolences. Right off, I was asking for contact information for his son so I could get my hands on it for us."

His hands on it for us.

For us.

I choked up a little but then laughed. "You call that a bungalow? In my world, that's a house!"

He noticed my initial reaction and I think he mistook it for something else. He tilted my chin up towards him. "Hey, I hope this doesn't freak you out. It's not like I'm getting this house so you're trapped with me." He laughed. "Well, maybe I am. But I want this house for us, for us to spend summers in and someday our family."

"You're a big *someday* guy. And no, you didn't freak me out. I like it when you refer to me and you as us."

I crawled into his lap and hugged him. "Thank you. That's going to be hard to top, Donovan. I hope you're not disappointed when you open your gift. I only got you a yacht."

"Don't thank me yet. You might not be so thrilled when you see the inside of the place. Mr. Baum had a thing for dark, jewel-toned velvet wallpaper."

I jumped up and got my gifts for Caleb. I got him new running sneakers, a cashmere sweater, and then there were the last two boxes, which held his real gift. The first was a black beret.

"I like it. I might look a little fruity in it, but I like it."

"Open the other one, you goof."

He looked a little misty eyed when he saw the plane ticket to Paris. "A trip to the most romantic city in the world with the love of my life? Thank you, Beaumont, I can't wait."

"I figured we can spend a few days together before I'm swamped with work."

"It's going to be great. And like I said, I don't want to be there during the Olympics. You need to be focused on what you're doing, and I don't want to be a distraction. It's better for you if I'm home."

"I know. I think I'm going to be working eighteen-hour days. I'd feel terrible if you were there and I couldn't spend any time with you."

"What day do you officially start?"

"Well, you head back home on the twenty-first, the same day Meredith flies in. She said we're doing two days of pre, pre-production, but someone told me that means she really just wants to shop. And then we head to the Olympics site on the twenty-third."

"You're going to learn so much. It's going to be a great experience."

"I know it is. I hate the idea of being away from you for a month, but you're going to be really busy anyway."

"Mick found a space he thinks will be perfect. I have to go check it out next week. Yeah, the month of February is going to be kind of crazy." He shook his head and then smiled. "The next year or two is going to be crazy."

"Can we head down to the beach tomorrow? I'm excited to check out the house."

"Done. I already have my parents watching Rebecca so Luke and Kate can take a look at it with us. I mean, brace yourself. It's kind of nasty inside."

"I like a challenge."

And Caleb was right, it was in need of some serious TLC, but when Luke and Kate were done with their walk-through, they were drawing up a total re-hab, gutting it to the studs and adding a second floor. Caleb looked to me and then back to them.

"Not sure what Rene wants, but—"

"But I think we should keep it simple for now."

Caleb wrapped an arm around my shoulders and nodded. "Yeah, I was thinking new kitchen, bathrooms and paint. The floors are in great condition, right?"

Luke laughed. "We can't help ourselves. The place does have good bones, and you don't have any structural concerns. You don't really need to do anything beyond cosmetic stuff."

Caleb looked to me and smiled.

Home.

Chapter Twenty-Six

CALEB

I've always loved Paris, but being here with Rene made it so much more special.

Here was this beauty, leading me around the city like it was her own, taking charge. Listening to her flit back and forth between English with me and French with everyone else was hot. And I couldn't help but laugh, watching as the waiters fell all over her, taking pleasure in engaging her in prolonged conversations in front of her uncultured, American boyfriend.

Rene was in her element. She took me to a little bistro off a side street that was a favorite during her last trip here. When she walked in, the owner acted as if they were long lost pals. Rene explained she'd been here on her last trip with one of his oldest and most loyal customers. When Rene told him she wished she could cook the love of her life a roast chicken that tasted half as good as the one he'd made us, he demanded she spend an afternoon with him and do just that, have a free cooking lesson.

As we walked through the streets of Paris on our way back to the hotel that night, I asked, "Another kindred spirit in Bernard?"

"Right? That's what I was thinking. Do you mind, Caleb, if I spend tomorrow afternoon there?"

"Not if you can cook for me when we get home. Believe me, I can occupy myself for a few hours in Paris."

I did not like shopping, but I did like spoiling Rene. After parting ways the next day, I walked aimlessly down Rue de Rennes, texting Darcy for some suggestions. She texted back a few spots to hit, along with a recommendation for a good place to get *what you really want her to wear*. I don't know what my sister was thinking sending me in there, but that store was an experience. Every sales-person was some glamazon model-type, and mine offered to *try things on* to help me decide if I wanted to purchase. I declined. In the back of my mind I was thinking that if I was stupid enough to sit there and let one of these beauties put on an R-rated fashion show for me, Rene was likely to jump out from behind a curtain and scream, "Gotcha!" I wasn't taking any chances in that department ever again.

By the time she got back with some really delicious to-go containers of trout meuniere amandine with some kind of potato and leek gratin, I had the bed covered with my day's work.

"Caleb, you're a maniac!"

"I'm eating first, but then you're trying on every single one of these outfits for me."

"Are there any actual clothes or just lingerie?"

I came up behind her and pulled her close. "Yeah, I got you a scarf."

She swatted at me. "You're lucky I love you."

She led me to the couch in the suite and handed me one of two tins. "Bon appetit!"

"Rene, this is unreal."

"Right? Butter and wine make everything taste wonderful."

"Can you actually cook this on your own?"

"Yes! I taped it on my phone. He also showed me the roast chicken preparation. I can cook you two things. We'll leave it at that for now."

"I'm satisfied with that."

It was my last night with Rene in Paris, and neither one of us felt like a crazy night out dancing or clubbing. After a leisurely bubble bath, Rene tried on her new outfits, and ooh-la-fucking-la, I done good. After a world-class romp we went down to the hotel bar and had dessert and champagne. Came right back upstairs for another round.

One of the best nights ever.

I was sorry to head to the airport the next day, but I could see Rene's wheels were already spinning with ideas she wanted to run by Meredith. I was also feeling the need to get back and dig in. Mick had secured the new office space and I was flying out to San Francisco in two days to meet with some potential clients.

She held me tight at the gate. "I'm going to miss you."

"You're not allowed to wear those lacy things until you get home, you know."

"Oh no!" Rene deadpanned, "I have that black thong on now. You're going to have to spank me."

"You're putting me on a plane like that? Thanks!"

"Tell me you love me, Caleb."

"I love you, more than anything."

Lord I missed her, but I was so busy the next three weeks that it made being apart easier. While working with Mick on the design for the new office space and outreaching to new business contacts, I had Luke and Kate supervising our mini-remodel on the bungalow.

Rene and Kate had poured over home design magazines together before she left, so Kate knew what direction to head in. And my girl had good taste. She chose simple Nantucket-style siding and a clean coastal design for the kitchen and bathrooms. I couldn't wait for her to come home so I could surprise her with it.

Our home.

It was time to make an honest woman out of Rene.

Chapter Twenty-Seven

RENE

The moment everything changed, we were prepping for Meredith's interview with the U.S. women's figure skating team as they geared up for a run at a team gold in the next day's final events.

I was close enough to get knocked off my feet by the explosion.

Close enough to hear the screams.

Close enough to choke on the acrid smoke.

Charlie, one of the cameramen, instinctively covered my body with his. We were completely still for a full minute before he asked, "You good?"

"I'm fine. What the hell just happened?"

He rolled me over to inspect me and I saw he was covered in ash and debris. "Are you ok, Charlie?"

"I'm fine. Stay down, another one may go off."

It was eerily quiet. After a few minutes passed, Charlie and I slowly got up and started walking around, surveying the scene and trying to help victims. It was gruesome. Thankfully, medical teams were on site within minutes caring for the injured. I prayed there were no causalities, but couldn't see how that was possible. The damage, as far as I could see, was extensive.

As we were pushed back by the first responders, Charlie tugged on my sleeve with one hand as he was reaching for equipment with the other. "If I can get this up, let's tape. We'll have the first images of the scene."

I was still shaken and utterly confused. "How?"

"Get ready for your close-up."

I frantically tried to text Caleb and then tried to get a call off to Meredith. No signal.

Charlie was able to get a link going to the studio. The producers instructed him to get any footage he could and to get me on camera to report. I guess they figured they could just use the scene footage if I was no good.

Charlie nodded reassuringly as he handed me the microphone. "You got this, Rene."

* * *

CALEB

I was on with a client when my phone pinged with an incoming text, then another, then another. It was either Sean, who left text messages that were more like novels, or I was suddenly very popular for some reason.

I spent another few minutes wrapping up, and heard a few more messages come through before I finally checked the phone.

Have you heard from Rene?

The same message from Caitlin, my father, Kate, Maureen, Kasia, Darcy, Chris and Tom.

My stomach dropped into my shoes.

I called my father. "What's going on?"

"Turn on the television. There's been some sort of terrorist

290

attack. I'm sure she's all right, so don't worry. I was just curious if you'd heard from her. Caleb?"

My mind immediately conjured up the worst case scenario.

"I'm here. How long ago did it happen?"

"Seems like it was less than an hour ago. The only news I'm seeing is coming out of London right now."

"Dad, I'm going to get off the phone in case she calls."

"Let me know when you hear from her."

"I will."

Next I called Maureen. She said she was staying at the station to get any available information and would call me. I jumped in a cab and headed up to the station myself. I couldn't just sit here. I was either going to put my hand through a wall or tear the hair out of my head.

If anything happened to her—if she was gone—there'd be nothing left. It would be the end of me.

I felt numb by the time I made it uptown to the station. The security guard recognized me and waved me through, and walking off the elevator was like entering a crazy beehive on steroids. There were people everywhere with headsets on, lots of pointing and shouting. I walked through it all like a dazed zombie.

Caroline called out to me over the noise, "Caleb, over here." When I looked up she was smiling and waving. "Hurry up!"

"Did you hear from her?"

"We're all about to hear from her! My boss just got word from Meredith. She's going to be broadcasting from the location studio and Rene is going to be doing live coverage from the site. I think Rene and Charlie were there when it happened and have the only live feed right now."

I fell into the chair behind me as my head sank into my hands. She wrapped her arms around me and gave me a quick squeeze.

"Come, Caleb, I don't want to miss this."

I managed to send off a quick text to my dad:

Think she's ok. Tell everyone for me. Turn on her channel. Might be on camera.

A few minutes later, Meredith came onto the big screen reporting the story of a suicide bomber who'd wreaked havoc on the Olympic Village. I tried to listen, but my heart was in my throat until I heard her say, "I'm cutting to Rene Beaumont right now, live at the scene of the attack. Rene, what can you tell us about the explosion?"

I let out a shaky half-laugh-half-cry when I saw her face. She looked battle weary but beautiful—and alive.

"The explosion rocked us, knocking us off our feet as we were setting up about one hundred yards away. It's a tragic scene here now, with multiple injured and we're hearing estimates of as many as sixty casualties. Rescue crews were here within minutes, but the sound of the explosion and the cries of the injured are not something I'll soon forget."

Footage was aired that looked as though it was taken seconds after the blast—smoke rose off piles of debris, victims cried out in agony, ambulance sirens blared. Rene was *right* there, *right* in the middle of this apocalypse. The realization of how close I'd actually come to losing her shook me.

Meredith's voice broke in again. "Rene Beaumont now has one of the chief security officials with her. Rene, what can you tell us?"

"I'm here with the head of the French security detail for the Olympic Village site, Mr. Daniel Bonet."

Rene then bounced between French and English as she asked the man questions and then translated his responses. Then a security tape was played with an image of a man thought to be the bomber.

A guy I didn't know yelled out, "Holy shit, talk about a scoop!"

He high-fived Caroline and the girl next to her. The mood in the studio was celebratory. It was beyond bizarre given the tragedy, but I could understand the excitement of being the first to get a concrete story out of the disaster.

The picture went back to Meredith as Caroline shook me. "She killed it, Caleb. Holy crap, she killed it!"

I tried to laugh. "I'm glad you're excited. I'm just going to collapse from stress now if you don't mind."

Caroline punched some buttons into her phone, stopping to fist-bump everyone who passed her desk. "Hey, we just saw our girl...She nailed it! When you're talking to Meredith tell her Rene's boyfriend is here in the studio with me. I don't want her to be worried. He knows she's ok." She was still talking to the other person on the line when she laughed and smiled over at me. "Yeah, good point. The entire world now knows she's ok."

My phone was blowing up again, now with messages like:

So glad she's ok

She did great

So relieved

You have a hot newscaster girlfriend

...that one was from Mick.

I stood on shaky legs. I'd been trying and failing to push the thought of her hurt or gone out of my head for the past hour. Now the sense of relief I felt was overwhelming.

I went straight to my parents' place and had two short glasses of whiskey with my dad to settle my shaking hands and rattled nerves. Since Rene's was the only station that had early, live on-site coverage, her report and the interview with the security official were replayed numerous times on several news outlets. As I watched the same footage over and over again, I was overwhelmed with pride. Only someone close to her would see beyond the confident, capable façade and notice how she was struggling to keep her composure.

My dad and I sat there glued to the television for an hour before I made my way back home and fell asleep with my phone on my chest, hoping for a call or a message from her.

* * *

RENE

The line crackled but his voice was clear enough. "Are you all right?"

"I'm fine, Caleb, but it's so awful here. I tried to call you right away but I couldn't. I hope you weren't worried."

"I'm just thankful you're safe. I was out of my mind until I saw you on TV."

Then the tears came. I was exhausted, and the images, sounds and smells of the day were crowding my head.

"It's all right, Rene. Let it out."

"It's just...It was so bad. And I'm ...I'm just so tired. I'm sure I'll be better once I get a few hours sleep."

"I know, babe. I wish I was there with you."

"I do, too," I cried. "I'm sorry I'm blubbering."

"Don't be sorry. I know it's got to be tough. I just want you to know I'm so damn proud of you. I couldn't believe it when I saw you on television. Do you realize how great you did?"

"You mean I didn't look as petrified as I felt?"

"Not at all. You looked calm and authoritative, like you were born to do it. I mean it, you were amazing."

"Meredith is covering the national memorial service tomorrow. I'm glad I'll be back on the other side of the camera again."

"I like it when you're on camera. I like being able to see you."

The driver was waving me back towards the van.

"I'm sorry, I have to go. They're waiting for me. I'll call again as soon as I can. I love you."

The next week went by in a blur of constant activity, and I was bone tired. Thank goodness for Meredith. It was invaluable to see how a seasoned pro handled all this craziness. I knew she was battling fatigue also, but you'd never know it once the camera was rolling. And she was so generous with me; she was always lending support and pointing out details or story angles that I never would have noticed or examined on my own.

Meredith coaxed me into doing two more brief on-air spots when we were on location. She agreed with Caleb, told me I was a natural. Although it was scary at first, I'll admit, I came to like the rush of being on camera and reporting live.

The location team came to feel like family, as we were together just about twenty-four-seven. We were so close that Charlie, Sal and I could pretty much finish each other's sentences. Sal was an older tech support guy who'd been working with the network for over twenty-five years. He was the father figure while Charlie and I were like the kids. Charlie was a kind and easy-going guy. And he'd always have a place on my good side after throwing his body over mine when the blast went off.

There were regular bursts of extreme activity, but there was also a lot of down time, time to sit and do nothing but talk. I learned that Sal was born in Italy and moved to New York as a child. He spoke fluent Italian, and listening to his stories always made me smile, whether he was telling us about New York back in the day, his big, crazy Italian family, or the three grown sons back home he was insanely proud of. Charlie grew up in Seattle, and after finishing college and backpacking through Europe for a year, he landed in New York with one his friends and never left. They both filled the long stretches of time with stories that made me keel over laughing at times, and at others, feel the shared sense of loss and sadness at the low points in life we all have. The stories were a welcome diversion. I needed something to take my mind off the fact that I was growing more homesick with each passing day.

Charlie and I had formed a tight bond, maybe because we were closer in age. I don't know if I found it easy to share things with Charlie because of the type of person he was, or if Caleb had just made me into a more open person who wasn't ashamed of my past or hell bent on keeping my life one hundred percent private. As the weeks passed, I shared more and more with Charlie: the basics about my parents, my nomadic life, and I talked about Caleb, even sharing that I hoped he would ask me to marry him soon. That's why I was surprised, after a night out with the entire crew having drinks and letting off steam, when Charlie cornered me on the walk back to our hotel and kissed me. I'd tripped over a crack in the sidewalk—might have had something to do with the two or three drinks I'd consumed—and he caught me around the waist with both hands. When I was back on solid footing, he didn't move his hands away, but instead eased me back against the wall of a building as moved his knee right between my thighs and lowered his lips to mine. His hands were sliding up my torso when I turned my head away and pressed on his chest to create some space between us.

"What are you doing?"

"Please don't stop me. Let me kiss you, just this once. I need you, need to feel you."

Need to feel you? Ok, this boy was drunk and horny.

"Charlie, stop. Stop right now."

He backed off a little, but still had me caged in with his palms pressed against the brick behind me. He looked flushed. And when I lowered my eyes to avoid his penetrating gaze, I could see his massive erection pressing against the seam of his pants.

"I want you. I've never met anyone I want as much as I want you." He tipped my chin up. "Can you honestly tell me that you feel nothing for me?"

I was struggling to catch my breath. What did I feel? The feeling of his body against mine was scary and good at the same time. But I knew that was purely physical—I was feeling the loss of Caleb. I liked Charlie, I cared for Charlie, but I didn't *want* Charlie.

"I don't feel that way about you. I'm sorry."

He shook his head and let out a frustrated breath. "You reacted to me just now. I didn't imagine that."

Did I want it? Just the thought of Caleb could have my knees buckling underneath me. But I wanted Caleb, no one else.

"I'm going to say goodnight now."

With that, I ducked out from under his arm and went inside the hotel. As the shower rained hot water over me, I cried tears of frustration and loneliness.

Some days when the alarm goes off, it's hard not to bury your head underneath the blankets and hide. I was dreading our morning call time. And after a few minutes even Sal was on edge, sensing the obvious tension between me and Charlie.

When Sal left to grab a coffee, I made an attempt to clear the air. "Do you want to talk about last night?"

There was sadness mixed with anger in his expression. "I'm sorry I did that, but I meant what I said. I was being honest when I said I have feelings for you." He looked up at me. "And I was being honest when I said I think you have feelings for me too."

"Charlie, I do feel something for you. I mean, you threw yourself over me without any regard for your own safety that day, and since then we've practically spent every waking moment together."

"So what's holding you back."

Was he serious?

"I told you how I feel about Caleb. I love him. He's it for me. There's no one else." I couldn't be any clearer. "Did I do or say anything to give you a different impression?"

He took a deep breath. "No." Then he looked up and shook his head. "Rene, it's on me. I'm all right. I was just hoping...You know what I was hoping."

I put my hand on his shoulder. "I hope we can be friends. I'd miss your friendship."

"Yeah, we're good."

But we weren't, and I had a sinking feeling that our remaining time stuck together on location was going to be all sorts of awkward.

When we broke for the day, I went back to my room to call

Caleb. I just needed to hear his voice. I didn't tell him about Charlie. There was no need because nothing really happened. Caleb could sense that something was wrong, but I played it off as a combination of fatigue and missing him that had me this way.

"What date do you return?"

That question set off a torrent of pent up tears and frustration. "They keep extending it. Meredith is gone, but now they want me here for another two weeks. That's going to make it seven weeks all together and I'm not sure they won't try to extend it again. I feel like I can't say no because being put on air with my level of experience is unheard of. I know Meredith is handing me my career on a silver platter, but I can't fucking stand it here any longer."

"Hey, don't cry." He laughed a little before he went on. "I know when you curse it's *really* bad. How about if I sneak over for a few days? I can get away the day after tomorrow."

"I can't ask you to come running whenever I act like a baby and cry."

"First of all, you pretty much *never* ask for help, ever. You're not acting like a baby, and I wouldn't offer if I couldn't do it. Anyway, with all that's going on with this terrorism case, I wouldn't be surprised if they asked you to stay a few extra weeks either."

"I don't want you to come if it's going to interfere with work, but if you could make it here for a few days—"

Damn, I started crying again. I was a puddle.

"I'm coming."

My man was a sight for sore eyes. He grabbed me in the hotel lobby and didn't let go for the longest time. He backed off then, taking me in with concern. "You're too skinny. Do you feel all right?"

"I'm fine, Caleb. I've just been working long days and sometimes I don't even realize that I've skipped lunch or dinner. Once I'm home I'll be back to normal myself."

With that, Sal came over. "Is this your fella, Rene?"

I happily introduced Sal, and we chatted for a few minutes before he asked if we wanted to grab a drink with everyone at the hotel bar. I was wary but didn't want to explain why. Caleb seemed into it, so we followed Sal and joined around ten of the crew guys who were watching soccer in the sports lounge. The crowd of them called out my name, raising their glasses like it was me who'd just scored a goal —they were all happily in the cups. But Charlie wore a tight expression, looking down into his beer glass after eyeing Caleb for a beat too long.

Caleb whispered so that only I could hear, "You work with *all* guys?"

"Pretty much, now that Meredith and the hair and makeup team are gone."

One by one I introduced them to Caleb. It was a great group and Caleb fell right in with everyone, as usual. After a few minutes, Charlie came over and stuck out his hand. "So we finally get to meet the famous Caleb." After they shook hands, Charlie put his hands on my shoulders and added, "Our girl talks about you nonstop."

It was obvious he'd had too much to drink. And Caleb was irked by the sight of Charlie's hands on me.

Caleb stood to his full height and gently put his arm around my waist as he drew me in close. "I understand that you were the one who kept Rene safe that day. I owe you big, Charlie. Thank you."

He tousled my hair and then slurred when he said, "Yep, that's me, always taking care of my Rene."

Poor choice of words on Charlie's part. I needed to bail before this turned into a giant pissing contest.

"Ready, Caleb? I'm beat, let's go upstairs."

From the corner of my eye I saw Sal grab Charlie's arm and pull him back when he called after us, "Yeah, you two go upstairs."

I let out the breath I'd been holding once the elevator doors closed.

"What was that?"

"Yeah, I know." I looked away. "That was a little ridiculous."

"Has he been acting that way towards you this entire time?"

"No, he was always a perfect gentleman. But the other night he was drunk and...Ugh, he told me he has feelings for me. It's been so awkward working alongside him since. That's why I called you so miserable the other night. I'm just so ready to go home."

Caleb looked up at the elevator ceiling and let out a deep breath. "Has he tried anything with you?"

I lied. "Nothing really, and I can handle it."

He fixed his eyes on mine. "I have no doubt you can handle it, but what does *nothing really* mean, exactly?"

"It means nothing."

We walked the length of the hallway in silence before I let us into my room.

"Talk to me."

"It means I don't want to waste our time together talking about this nonsense. I've been desperate to see you for so long. I don't want to ruin this."

"Hey, things are always better when we're straight with one another. Do you think I'm so immature that I'm going to spend the few precious hours I have with you fighting that prick? I don't feel threatened by him. But I do need to know what's going on."

"He tried to kiss me, I pushed him off. End of story. But we still have to work together every day, and like I said, it's really awkward."

"Was he forceful?"

"No. Really, he's not a Neanderthal. He's harmless and I'm fine. He's just acting like a jerk today because he's drunk."

Caleb raked his hands through his hair and took a few quiet, deep breaths. "Come here." He sat on the bed and moved me to stand between his legs as he rested his hands on my hips. "I can't stand the thought of anyone putting their hands on you. You're mine. No one touches you but me."

I couldn't help but smile. I liked it when he got all cavemen possessive on me.

"I don't want anyone to touch me but you. I've been aching for you to touch me." Stroking him, I added, "And I've been dreaming about touching you." I pushed him back onto the bed and climbed up over his lap. I hiked up my skirt and pressed into him as I lifted my shirt over my head. I knew he'd like the bra I chose for today. It was a demi-cut that pushed my breasts way up like a treat. "Do you want me?"

He reached up to lift my breasts out of the lacy cups and stroked my nipples into hardened peaks. His eyes were heavy with want. "Do I want you? I'm going to fuck you so hard and so deep, Rene, you'll think I'm never coming out."

He rolled me off him and then stood above me to pull my skirt down and off. He let out a low growl when he stood gazing at me. Gesturing to the little that still covered me, he told me to take them off in a commanding voice. He undressed then, never taking his eyes off me as I lay there naked on the bed. I was literally aching for him. I moved one hand to my breast and moved the other between my legs, wanting him so badly.

"When I'm alone and thinking of you," I arched my head back when it started to feel good, "I do this, but it's no good."

He was rock hard and massive. "It's no good?"

"No. I need *you*. I need you inside me."

"You're mine, only mine."

He knelt down and pulled my hips forward. He went at me, making me cry out with just a few flicks of his tongue and his fingers expertly working me over. Then he rolled me and lifted my hips so I was on my hands and knees on the bed. He came up behind me and I could feel him, hard, pressing into my bottom. He leaned over me and cupped my breasts as he let out a satisfied groan. "Only I touch you."

He guided himself in, and the position let him in deep, so deep. I couldn't hold back the moans of pleasure. I'd gone without, needing this for so long, needing him. Every thrust reminded me of how much I'd missed this, us.

Caleb lowered my body down to the bed after and curled me onto my side, still never coming out of me. We stayed like that for a few minutes before he brushed the hair away from my face and leaned into me. "Jesus, you don't know how much I've missed you. Not just being with you like this, but just...seeing your face."

He was only staying two days. That was a terribly long trip to take for such a short stay, and I more than appreciated it. I felt better, healthier and stronger now that I had him here with me.

I never wanted to leave that bed, but duty did occasionally call. While Caleb was in town I wasn't as involved with work as I normally was, and everyone was good about it, pitching in to make up for my occasional absence. I didn't cross paths with Charlie once that weekend, which was a good thing. Avoiding a confrontation between Charlie and Caleb was my goal.

Knowing it was Caleb's last night made me wistful, but his visit had done wonders for my morale. We walked back from dinner and went straight back up to the room. Hugging me tight, he breathed in the scent of my skin. "I wish you were coming home with me tomorrow. I'm taking you away with me as soon as you get back."

"No, I'm not taking any trips. The only place you're taking me is to your apartment. I want to be locked in there with you for a week straight. I just want to be home with you."

He sat on the sofa and pulled me to stand between his legs. "I want you home with me all the time, Rene."

I closed my eyes dreaming about it. "I want to be there too."

"All the time?"

"All the time."

"Do you mean that?"

What was he asking me, to move in with him? *Please, please don't go there.* A crushing sense of disappointment lodged in my chest. It didn't take much to make me cry lately, but Caleb thinking that moving in together was the sort of commitment I wanted from him? That just might have reduced me to full-on sobs.

Unable to face him, I closed my eyes and whispered, "You know I want to be with you, Caleb."

"Do you want to be with me forever?"

"You know I do."

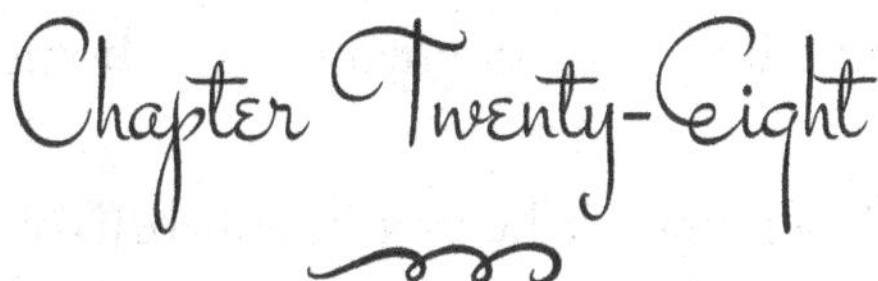

Chapter Twenty-Eight

CALEB

I wanted to whisk Rene off to Puerto Rico and propose to her on the beach, but with all that had happened in the past month, I decided before I left for this trip that I couldn't wait any longer.

I bought the ring during our last trip to Paris. I took one of her rings before she left for her cooking lesson and went straight to Cartier. It was a two carat diamond in an antique setting on a platinum band. Nothing over the top because my girl wasn't flashy or pretentious.

I prayed this was going to go my way.

I moved her back a step and got down on one knee before her, taking the velvet box out of my jacket pocket. As soon as she opened her eyes, I said the words I'd been rehearsing for the past two months.

"I started to care about you from the day I met you. And once we became friends, I was in love, and that's never happened to me before. I never wanted to commit to anyone, take care of anyone, or plan out my future with anyone until I met you. Please marry me, Rene."

She closed her eyes again and then started laughing as tears streamed down her face. "Yes, yes, I'll marry you!"

My hands were shaking as I slipped the ring onto her finger.

"It's so beautiful."

"I'm sorry this isn't the most romantic, well-staged proposal. I wanted to do something special when you got home, but I just can't wait anymore."

"Do you think I'd rather be in a hot air balloon or something?" She started laughing. "I was bracing for crushing disappointment a minute ago. I thought you were going to ask me to move in with you."

"Well, you're doing that too, and right away, understand?"

She teased, "I'll think about it."

* * *

RENE

We spent that last night together talking about our marriage, our life together and the future. He was so thoughtful. It hadn't crossed my mind before, but the whole big wedding thing? Family, dear old dad walking you down the aisle and giving you away—that was so not me.

Caleb suggested something non-traditional. He said he wanted a weekend-long wedding on the beach in Puerto Rico with just our closest friends. I knew he was doing that for my benefit, and I loved him all the more for it. We stayed up late looking at marriage license requirements and other technical details. The excitement took over and we decided on a mid-to-late April date, just weeks away. I had no doubts, no misgivings—even after he told me about Elena and her being the reason we couldn't have the rehearsal dinner at the beach-side bar close to their house that I liked so much.

I was floating on air by the time he was heading back to the airport. "Do you think we're crazy getting married so quickly?"

"No, Beaumont, I don't. Remember, we're telling only Caitlin and my family so the date works for them. Everyone else can be surprised when they get their evite."

My eyes widened. "We're inviting people by email?"

"Absolument, mon chere amour. They have really nice ones now."

I giggled in response to his dismal French, and then shrugged and nodded. I was more than all right with the simple invitations. "Ok."

"Low maintenance, I love it." His look turned serious then. "I'm leaving tomorrow. Sure you can handle this Charlie business? I had a quick word with him, so—"

I cut in, wincing, "Oh no, please tell me you didn't."

"I was nice. I didn't hit him or anything. Really, this is your job and I was mindful of that. I think we understand one another. But I don't want you to be alone with him, especially if he's had drinks, all right?"

It was sound advice. "I won't."

I hated goodbyes, but Caleb's visit had totally reenergized me, and thinking about becoming his wife filled me with pure joy.

* * *

CALEB

We were definitely not a traditional engaged couple, as I'd pretty much taken over coordinating the wedding.

The day I got back from France I went straight to my parents' place and let them know what we were set on doing. My parents, Luke, Darcy and I came up with three dates to choose from. Based on Rene's job and Caitlin's schedule, we settled on April twenty-eighth. I contacted Father Jim, a priest who also doubled as one of my coaches in high school. He was one of the several amazing people in my life who helped to shape the angry, hurt kid I was into a more aware and responsible man. Once Father Jim was on board, I handed the details over to Kate's sister, Audrey, who ran an event planning business. She was amazing. Within a few days she designed the perfect evite with a laid back, tropical vibe, she had a concierge service set up with the airline so that the guests could arrange their pre-paid flights hassle-free, and she hired a caterer to come in from San Juan.

It's a good thing I could run on less sleep than most normal people because Mick and I were fully engaged in the business at that point as well. I felt really good about it. Mick worked as hard as I did, and the boy was a mathematics, statistics and computer genius. My specialty was bringing in the clients, and I had definitely delivered. We were off to a good start.

Our group was small, with just Mick, myself, two junior associates and Margie, our all-in-one secretary, office manager and den mother. I lured her away from my old firm, and knew my boss probably hated me for that more than anything. Yes, poaching Margie probably burned his toast more than forking over the biggest year-end bonus in the firm's history to me before I jumped ship. I didn't feel guilty about Margie or the bonus. I deserved every penny they paid me, and Margie was totally undervalued there. With us, her salary finally reflected her worth.

And then my girl made it back state-side by the last week in March.

I must be a sap at heart because as she was making her way towards me after passing through customs, I couldn't help but imagine how she'd look walking up the aisle in her wedding dress.

I scooped her up in my arms, then I noticed the rest of the crew members following behind. A moment later I was shaking Charlie's hand when he approached to say hello. I figured he was the stand-up guy Rene believed him to be, and had just gotten caught up in caring for a girl that was, admittedly, impossible to resist. We were good, but that didn't mean he was invited to the wedding. Not happening.

The guest list was pretty tight with just my family, Drew and Chloe, Mick, Ed, Connor, Sean and Maggie, Rene's college roommates, her friend Chris, Kasia, Maureen, Dana, Caroline, her hairdresser friend Marcel and Meredith. With dates and spouses, we were confirmed for just under thirty guests. Only Meredith declined, as her niece's wedding was that same weekend.

We weren't doing the giant wedding party thing either, just Luke standing by my side and Caitlin by hers. I wondered why so many people stressed over planning their weddings. I mean, we left the details to Audrey, but both Rene and I were pretty relaxed about the whole thing.

Two weeks before we were set to fly down, Rene asked me what I was wearing for the ceremony. I seriously hadn't given it any thought.

"Really? I hope you don't think since our wedding is on the beach that you're wearing a bathing suit!"

Rene had a few dresses in mind, but wasn't sure which would be too casual or too formal for the setting. She wouldn't let me see them so I took James for a few hours while Darcy came over and helped her decide.

James was a little over a year now. He was a cutie but a handful. Once he started walking, it's like he no longer wanted to be confined to his stroller and was hell-bent on running everywhere. Rebecca, by comparison, was a piece of cake to babysit. I think I sprouted a few gray hairs by the time I got him back to my place.

Darcy got a kick out of my flustered expression. "Big brother, was James too hard on you?"

"If he'd sit in the stroller he'd make life a lot easier." I added proudly, "But I do think we have an athlete on our hands. The boy is fast."

She laughed looking on at James with pure love. "That's what Tom says."

After a seriously rocky period, it was good to see Tom and Darcy so solid. The three of them had formed a nice little family, and I had no doubt that Tom would make things official before long. He was a good person and good to my sister. I knew she would be loved and well provided for, and I couldn't hope for more.

Rene took over with James while Darcy, Luke and I headed uptown to pick out suits for the wedding. With Rene's input, Darcy picked out white linen shirts and a casual linen suit that was close to the color of sand—no ties, thank heaven. I liked the look, but knew that even though the fabric was light, Luke and I were probably going to be sweating bullets wearing them on the beach in Puerto Rico in late April.

For Rene, I would suffer.

I would pretty much do anything that girl asked of me.

Chapter Twenty-Nine

RENE

"How many bags did you bring, Caitlin?"

"It's not all mine! Most of it's for you, silly. If that rumor about you turns out to be true, you're going to need a *ton* of clothes. These are samples the designers provide for my site."

"Don't jinx me. I feel like it's bad luck to even talk about it."

She rolled her eyes. "Please. You have been making your own luck your whole life. Luck has *nothing* to do with it."

I smiled at her confidence in me.

A rumor had been swirling at the station that when Mike Turner retired at the end of June, network executives were looking at me to replace him. It was the lead-in contributing reporter position, meaning that I would do a brief spot at the opening of Meredith's show and then lead off the second half-hour reporting the day's top national and international events. Nothing was official and I'd kept mum about it, except for telling Caleb and Caitlin. I didn't want to get my hopes up, but Meredith had been priming me, while Chris Quivers let it slip that the response to my on-air Olympic spots was overwhelming and positive. His exact words were: *The network has big plans for you*. I was preparing myself by studying maps, nailing down the pronunciation for the most far flung locales, and making sure I was up to date on politics and world events just in case the rumor turned out to be true. I guess I *was* the confident, badass woman Caleb made me out to be, because my inner voice kept telling me something along the lines of: *YOU CAN DO THIS!*

Getting married in the midst of all this, with me working long, crazy hours and Caleb getting a new business off the ground was probably insane, but I could hardly wait another day to become his wife.

Caitlin and I were flying down to Puerto Rico Thursday night after work. Caleb was coming Friday morning with most of the guests. The plan was a casual dinner Friday night, a sunset wedding on the beach Saturday, and a lazy Sunday before people made their way back to the airport on Monday morning.

We were missing only two days of work for our wedding. Caleb promised that next year he'd jet me off to someplace great, but honestly I didn't care. I just wanted to be married to him, and to know I had a life ahead of me with him in it.

* * *

CALEB

Before the plane even touched back down in New York, I had Margie send a giant floral arrangement to Kate's sister, Audrey. Every moment of our weekend was perfect—great weather, the people who meant the most to us in life, and Rene walking down the sandy "aisle" to me barefoot in her wedding dress. The most beautiful sight I'll ever see.

Holding her hands in mine as we exchanged vows, I was overwhelmed with emotion. We'd been through a lot, but through it all there was not one moment when I wasn't deeply in love with her. Rene told me later on that she was overcome at one point during the ceremony, realizing that it was Luke and Caitlin standing beside us, the only other people in the world who knew everything and had been with us and supported us through it all. That wasn't lost on me either. I knew how blessed we were to have friends and family like ours.

With the combination of the Puerto Rican Jack Johnson impersonator and the DJ not shutting the music down until after five in the morning, the night got crazy in a good way. At one point nearly all of us were in the pool, with Mick entirely bare-assed. Like I said, not a traditional wedding.

I didn't manage to get Rene for a night swim until Sunday and it wasn't the same, as Mick and Caitlin were mauling each other in the sand when we got down there. So even though we swam one beach over, we settled for suits-on.

I know Rene was hoping there was a romance in the making with those two, but I didn't think Caitlin had more than a passing interest in Mick. When she started dropping hints that she might relocate to New York after grad school, I thought I might be wrong, but whatever, either way they were having fun.

Once we were back in New York, I felt like our life together was truly beginning. It felt like a done deal the day that Maureen, Tom and Darcy helped us move the rest of Rene's stuff to my place.

She joked that she could have done the move herself with one shopping cart. It was a nod to her nomadic past, where picking up and moving every couple of months was her version of normal. Rene still traveled light and didn't accumulate a lot, but that was about to change. She was with me now, she was home and she wasn't going anywhere.

Chapter Thirty

Five years later...

RENE

Some things never change.

When Caleb surprised me with a trip to Paris for our fifth anniversary, my initial reaction was something along the lines of: *That's so nice, but I'd rather just stay at home with you guys.* I didn't say it out loud because he would have been disappointed, but I was totally content to be home, in *our* house, with *my* men.

Leaving the boys for five days will be hard, but I'm looking forward to having some time alone, just me and Caleb, with nothing to do but be together and love one another. Sleeping in, yeah, that's going to be pretty sweet too.

Some days, I literally feel the need to pinch myself.

On this sunny Sunday morning, I'm sitting on my beautiful, albeit tiny, garden patio drinking coffee as the boys take their morning nap. They typically wake up at around five-thirty, so they're ready for a cat nap by nine and so am I. Daniel and Matthew are eighteen months old now and the loves of our lives. They were the best, most unexpected miracle.

Life changed dramatically once we found out we were expecting. Caleb was over the moon and subsequently on a mission. The bachelor pad was exchanged for a brownstone across the street from Luke and Kate, and our convertible was traded in for an SUV with the highest safety rating. Taking care of newborn twins is no joke, so Caleb had one of the downstairs rooms converted into a fully outfitted office. He works from home one or two days a week now, depending on my schedule. I kept my position working alongside Meredith as a correspondent on the A.M. America show until I was seven months pregnant, but since giving birth I've scaled back big time. Now I fill in for special assignments and cover occasional weekend anchor shifts, but for the most part I'm home taking care of the twins and loving it. I still have my foot in the door at the network, but I'm fortunate in that I can take care of my babies nearly every day.

I never thought this would be my life. I saw myself as a full-time career girl with a nanny *if* children ever came into the picture, but I've chosen a different road.

Maybe it's because I lost out that doting parent experience myself. Maybe that's why I was hell-bent, from the first day I held those two in my arms, to be committed to them entirely.

The boys will grow up so differently. They're never left alone and they'll always be surrounded by family. And not only do they have one another as constant companions who can already finish the other's sentences, but they have James, Charles and John to roughhouse with, not to mention the little ladies.

Darcy and Tom's boys are now six, four and two. When we babysit and they're all together, it's crazy mayhem and I love it. Luke and Kate's girls across the street are tame in comparison, although I'd say Rebecca can wrestle with the best of them. But their little Lucy is all frill, flowers and sweetness, and wants nothing to do with the savages once they get rowdy.

I'm so happy to be a part of this family. It's the best kind of chaos. We split our time between the city and the beach, the kids growing up alongside their cousins, my boys' childhood much like their father's.

Our beach house is still the two-bedroom bungalow we started out with, but Caleb has been talking to Luke about an expansion. When I protested one morning that I loved our little house just as it is, he came up behind me, rested his chin on my shoulder, placed both hands on my belly and whispered that he wanted more. And yes, I still melt every time he touches me. Every time he whispers in my ear I'm achy for him and he knows it. As my body eased back into him, he kept at it, pressing against me suggestively.

"I want more, baby. I want some little Renes and some more little guys running around here. Please say yes."

I shrugged. "Are you going to love me fat and lumpy if we get pregnant with twins again?"

I was playing him, and fishing for a compliment I guess. I've bounced back nicely since giving birth. I mean, it's part of my job to keep myself camera-ready, but nursing the boys whipped my body back into shape quicker than any killer workout routine ever could have. And while my body has certainly changed, the changes I see are the ones that come with motherhood, and I'm more than good with those.

That day at the beach was another one of those "pinch myself" days. With the sounds of the waves crashing and the seagulls squawking in the background, my husband turned me to face him and spoke words that I won't ever let myself forget. We've been through so much already, and I know there will be more bumps in the road for us to face together. So I'll keep his words tucked away but close to my heart, and call them to mind whenever I need reassurance or comfort. I'll think back to that exact moment, picture his face and the ways his eyes express what's in his heart. Then I'll hear his voice.

"I'm living my someday right now, every day here with you. Everything that's good in my life is because of you, Rene, and I'll love you forever."

* * *

CALEB

Ah, silence.

I toe off my sneakers, knowing better than to make even the slightest sound for fear of waking up Matt and Daniel. I creep through the kitchen and gulp down some water standing by the sink. That's when I spot her, lazy on a lounger in the backyard. Her robe is sliding off one shoulder, revealing the thin strap of a tank top that I imagine is hugging her breasts and barely covering a lacy pair of undies. Yeah, I still daydream about this woman nonstop.

I watch as she sips her coffee, and smile when I see that dreamy face she makes when she's lost in good thoughts. I make my way out to her, but I'm reluctant to disturb my beautiful, blissed-out goddess.

"Jeez, you're like a cat sneaking up on me!"

I laugh without making a sound. "No, it's just that I have to tiptoe and whisper in my own home so that I don't wake the terrors. And I do like to watch you sometimes. You look happy."

When I take a seat, facing her so that our hips are touching, she leans over to kiss me. "You're sweaty. Mmm, I like you sweaty. How was your run?"

"Forget the run. Next week, mon amour, you can have me sweaty all over Paris when I ask you, 'Voulez vous coucher avec moi?'"

She chokes on a sip of coffee and then laughs. "Just so you know, I've been teaching the boys French and you are banned from participating. Do you know anything besides cheesy pick-up lines?"

"I know the important ones, mon petit morceau doux de cul."

"Did you just attempt to call me a sweet little piece of ass?"

"Yup, I type dirty things into translating apps on my down time."

"Oh my Lord."

I move in and spread both palms across her belly, slide them up her torso and cup both of her beautiful breasts. "Mine, all mine."

She arches up and lays the hottest kiss on me as her hands slide south and take hold of me. No sooner does she have me rock hard and groaning when a fierce, assertive voice demands, "MAMA!"

It's Daniel, the spokesperson for the duo. I pull away with a frustrated groan. "I cannot wait to get you on that plane next week."

She pouts her lips, slaying me all over again. "Don't you say that. I'm going to miss my little loves so much."

"I know, I know...I will too." When she goes to stand I can't help but tease her, sliding my hand up underneath the silky robe. "But I want my mon petit morceau doux de cul."

She lets out a sexy whimper, but then swats my hand away and goes inside once Daniel barks, "MAMA!" a second time.

A minute later she's back with both of them, one in each arm, planting kisses on one and then the other, back and forth. They're giggling like this is some new fantastic thing she's doing, and looking at her like she's the absolute best thing to wake up to. I'm thinking that one, she's strong as hell—those two are heavy, and two, she's a fantastic mother to our children. She is patient, loving and meets their every need.

Sometimes my heart aches picturing Rene as a sweet little girl with no one to care for her. But I have to give her credit, she doesn't wallow in self-pity, never did. She just makes it better by being the parent to our children that she never had.

As she sets them down to toddle around the yard, she eases herself between my legs on the lounger and I wrap my arms around her. My whole world is wrapped up in my arms.

Breaking into my thoughts, she asks, "When you thought of your *someday*, is this what you envisioned?"

I squeeze her tight and breathe her scent in deep. "Beaumont, my life, because of you, is so much better than I ever could have imagined."

She turns to me and says, "Je t'aime, mon mari."

It started out as a joke when we were first married, calling me her husband in French, knowing it made me hot for her. But now, whatever language she uses, those simple, pure words have come to mean so much more.

Her love is everything.

The End, for now…

* * *

Thank you for reading *Let Me Love You*. Rene and Caleb broke my heart while I was writing, so if you shed a few tears, know that I was right there with you.

The Let Me series continues with *Let Me Go*, Dylan and Kasia's story. Their families, their upbringing and their values lie on polar ends of the spectrum. Moms shouldn't pick favorites, but Dylan might just be my favorite character in the series. Love him or love to hate him—you decide.

Two powerful men, both used to getting what they want. What happens when they both want the same thing?

Kasia has always walked a fine line between her two worlds, but navigating life as a scholarship student amid the fortunate sons and daughters of the ultra-rich isn't as easy as it looks.

When she takes a chance on someone from the other side of the tracks—the type of man Kasia has always avoided—he lures her into his world. It's a whirlwind of intoxicating decadence, of pleasure and pain, and taking it all in at warp speed leaves Kasia questioning who she is and who she wants to become.

Forced to make a choice between two men who love her deeply, which life will she choose? Will she stand beside the man who promises her the moon and the stars, or will she find her heart's desire at home?

All of the titles in the Let Me series are intended for the 18 and older crowd due to mature content, but Dylan's story is darker and steamier

Visit the website to learn more:

www.LilyFoster.com